Crush

Also by Michele Grant

Sweet Little Lies
Heard It All Before

Also by Lutishia Lovely

All Up In My Business
Heaven Forbid
Reverend Feelgood
Heaven Right Here
A Preacher's Passion
Love Like Hallelujah
Sex in the Sanctuary

Crush

MICHELE GRANT
LUTISHIA LOVELY
CYDNEY RAX

KENSINGTON PUBLISHING CORP.
http://www.kensingtonbooks.com

CONTENTS

White Mocha

Michele Grant

1

It All Starts with a Sip

"You need to do something," my assistant, Kim, said from the doorway of my office, propping a hand up on her hip.

I glanced up from the report I wasn't really reading. "What do you mean?"

"Girl, you are dragging."

"It's eight o'clock at night." I tried to justify my sluggishness.

She pursed her lips. "Um-hmm, but you looked like this at eight o'clock this morning."

I reached back and lifted my hair off my neck, kneading the knotted muscles there. I sighed, knowing she was right. I'd been lethargic, restless, and listless for days. I hadn't been sleeping well either. "I don't know what's wrong with me; maybe I need some vitamins, a protein injection, some caffeine or something."

She laughed. "Oh, you need a protein injection, all right. How long since you and Say-It-Ain't-So Joe broke up?" The lovely nickname she had for my ex, Joseph.

"Nine months."

"And since then?"

I sighed again. "No one."

"No one." She shook her head in disgust. "Not a peck on

the cheek or a hand grazing your hind parts. Jayla, get some already!"

I laughed. "Kim, there's more to life than sex."

"How would you know? You have no sex nor life to speak of."

"That's harsh. I'm career focused, I am woman, hear me roar."

"Ya lonely and cranky. Fix it."

"So you want me to just jump on the next guy I see?"

She turned to leave on her crocodile stilettos and smiled at me over her shoulder. "There's an idea!"

"Yeah, right—that is SO me. . . ."

"Seriously," she called out as she strode toward the elevator. "A little spontaneity wouldn't kill you."

"That's what people say to excuse rash behavior."

"Nothing wrong with cutting loose every once in a while. You don't have to make it a lifestyle choice. And don't stay here all night—you cannot snuggle up to income projections when you're old!" Her final words caused a few of the other late-night stragglers to stick their heads out of their cubes and offices to see whom she was addressing.

"Good NIGHT, Kim."

" 'Night, boss."

The thing of it was, she was right. Since Joseph and I had split (okay, since I had kicked his lying, cheating, wallet-"borrowing" ass out) I had funneled all of my energy into my career and little else. I stopped into the coffee shop every morning (specialty mocha and zucchini muffin), I visited my grandmother once a week, I went out with friends once a month. Everything else was work related.

I had been working at a nonstop pace for months. And I was well on my way to being the youngest chief financial officer this company had ever seen. Granted, BeniCareCo was a small, independent health insurance company, but I was making my mark. As the Assistant Vice President of Financial Operations, I was two steps away from my goal. But I was tired. Maybe the listless, restless thing was my body's way of telling me to slow it down.

Slow down for whom and for what? What was I in a rush to get home to? Most of my friends were either married or on the same crazy cutthroat corporate merry-go-round I was. I was too restless to curl up with a book. Maybe I'd watch a movie, soak in a long bath. Irritated with myself, I closed the folder that was in front of me and turned away.

As I swiveled my chair toward the window, I looked out on the late summer night. Chicago was on the tail end of a heat wave. Downtown Chicago was full of people enjoying the balmy, breezy weather. Across the street, I saw a couple coming out of the new coffee shop on the corner. The couple looked happy and carefree, clutching each other with one hand and their coffee with the other. The sign reading JAY'S COFFEE CAFÉ bathed them in an electric blue and green light.

Suddenly I wanted what they had—their togetherness, their apparent happiness, a shared jovial moment. I sighed. You have to give to get. You have to look to find. And I hadn't been doing much of either lately. Maybe I couldn't get that "happy couple" vibe right away but for now I'd settle for their coffee.

By the time I packed up my desk, got downstairs, crossed the street, and entered the coffee shop, there were no other customers. Actually, looking around, there didn't appear to be any workers there either.

"Hello?" I called out.

"We're closing up," a deep voice called out from the back.

I was inexplicably disappointed. As if the promise of that light-hearted moment could truly be found in a cup of coffee. "Story of my life," I said to no one in particular and pivoted back toward the door.

"Excuse me?" The voice sounded closer.

I swiveled back around and stopped dead in my tracks. A flash of pure heat passed through me, awakening nerve endings and receptors that had been long dormant. In front of me stood a specimen of maleness that could only be described one way: "hotness." The kind of hotness that burned right through common sense and rational thought.

In the times I had visited this coffee shop, I had never seen him. And believe me, I would have remembered. He was gorgeous in an "Oh-My-GOD, where-did-you-come-from" kind of way. The kind that takes your breath away and leaves you just slightly off-balance. He was a beautiful, exotic blend of European and African-American ancestry and had a Derek Jeter kind of vibe without all the unnecessary polish. Raw, earthy, and did I say brutally hot? Light green eyes framed with thick lashes, wavy brown hair closely cropped to his head, full lips set into a square jawline currently softened with a smile. He was a solid block of a man, at just six feet tall with the muscles of a gym regular. Flat front khakis and a navy polo with the shop's logo imprinted stretched easily across his frame. He had the look of what I'd call a man's man, even while wearing a bright pink apron and clutching a purple mug decorated with green hearts.

The longer I studied him, the more he studied me. I knew what he saw: a curvy woman, busty with hips that could politely be called "generous"—a true hourglass figure no matter how hard I fought against it. I was taller than average, with caramel-colored skin and thick wavy hair of the same color curling past my shoulders. A rounded face often referred to as "cute" with wide, light brown eyes and a pouty mouth with no gloss left on it from this morning. And there we both stood, somewhat intrigued by instant chemistry, that undeniable energy—after thirty-three years of living it was happening to me. That primal spark calling out from male to female and back again.

I stood staring at him as though he were the last shrimp on the buffet table and I hadn't had fresh seafood in a while.

Clearly I was deprived of far more than sleep when the mere presence of a male made me jittery and breathless. *Get a grip, Jayla*, I told myself sternly, determined to raise my eyes above his waist and act like I had some good sense.

When I finally lifted my gaze back up to his face, his eyes had gone from casually friendly to heatedly curious. It wasn't until the drool was literally pooling at the corners of my mouth that I regained any semblance of composure. "Oh, I'm sorry, long day," I lamely explained. "I'll just get out of your way so you can close up." I smiled sadly, tentatively as I turned back toward the door. Was I so starved for male attention that I had manufactured chemistry with the coffee guy?

"Hey," he said softly, his voice deep, velvety, and smooth.

I looked back. "Hey?"

"I can always make just one more." He smiled with a flash of pearly white teeth that sent a tingle straight up my spine. "Do you mind if I make you my last customer?"

I don't mind if you make me your concubine. "No, no, that's fine. I appreciate it. I'm sure you're ready to get out of here."

His look was pensive. "Don't worry about it, you're a customer."

Right. Customer, here to buy coffee. "Well, thanks."

"Not a problem. Will it make you uncomfortable if I lock up?"

"Not at all, do what you need to do." I stood primly, clutching my case in front of me.

He brushed past me to lock the door and switch the OPEN sign to CLOSED. He slowly circled the store, pulling down shades and closing the drapes. It suddenly felt like a close and intimate space rather than a storefront. Walking back he paused beside me, close enough that the scent of him wafted to me. I took a deep breath. He smelled like coffee, cinnamon, chocolate, soap, and some sort of spicy musk. "So, what'll you have?"

You on a platter, please. . . . I looked up at him and saw by the slight glint in his eyes that he had heard me loud and clear, even though I hadn't said it out loud. Okay, maybe the chemistry wasn't so manufactured after all. "What's your specialty?"

"White mocha." Two words, innocent words at that, but I instantly shivered and flushed. His nostrils flared and his jaw tightened as he watched me.

"I'll take it extra large, extra hot." After the words left my mouth, I realized how they sounded. I was a little bit out of control.

He swallowed and blinked as if he wasn't sure he'd heard me correctly. "I beg your pardon?"

I took a step back and grabbed the last remnants of my composure. "The white mocha extra large, extra hot. To go."

He stepped back as well. "Oh, okay. Will that be all?" He started to move away.

I paused. What if I did what Kim suggested? What if I decided to be a little spontaneous, proposition the first guy I saw . . . this guy? Not ask his name, not care what his circumstances are, just ask for what I want in this moment, for right now. I trembled a little just in contemplation.

He saw the tremble, stopped walking, and looked me over from head to toe. Those ivy green eyes clearly missed nothing, noticing my tension, my fluttering pulse, and my parted lips. Green eyes heated to laser intensity before sending me a clearly appreciative look. He raised one brow, saying slowly, "Is there *anything* I can get you to go with that mocha?"

"Would you mind terribly if I had it here after all?" I said breathlessly, almost panting with anticipation and nervousness. I'd never propositioned a barista before; okay, or any stranger. What if he said no? Oh God, what if he said yes?

"The mocha?" He tilted his head and gave a look that said *if you want it, ask for it.*

"Yes, the mocha and . . ." I set down my purse and my laptop case and stepped to him in my black, figure-hugging sheath dress and peep-toe heels. "Listen, you don't know anything about me or what I'm going through and I don't know anything about you—"

"I do know something about you," he interrupted, meeting me until we stood toe to toe. "I know you are sexy and beautiful and you like coffee. I know you don't hook up with strange men often."

"Ever. I don't hook up with strange men ever," I corrected him. "And how do you know?"

He reached down and touched the fluttering vein pulsing at the base of my neck, caressing the area in soft strokes. "Because you're nervous and unsure. It's cute, sexy."

Cute. Sexy. I nodded with no clue what to say next. *Should I, shouldn't I?* I had re-engaged my brain and it was getting in the way of what the rest of me wanted.

He grinned at me. "Let me get you that coffee."

Coffee. Yes. That is what I came in here for. I stood there and continued to argue with myself. Was I really going to make a move on some strange guy at the coffee house? I mean, really? I sighed. I was bold, but I wasn't that bold. Tonight, the only craving I was going to assuage was for flavored, expensive caffeine. I watched while he measured beans, steamed milk, and mixed syrups in a cup. I could watch him all day and feel it was twenty-four hours spent productively. I sighed again.

He looked over at me with a look that sizzled. "So . . . just the coffee?" He was giving me every opportunity to make a move.

Wimpy Jayla beat Wanton Jayla down. I shrugged. "Just the coffee."

With a final stir, he capped the beverage and handed me the cup. "Tell me what you think."

I took a sip, my eyes slid shut, and I moaned. It was the best white mocha on the face of the planet: sweet, fragrant, hot, rich, and strong. The chocolate flavor didn't battle the coffee; it was a heavenly marriage of taste, texture, and spice. I took another sip and enjoyed the flavor of it exploding on my tongue and sliding down the back of my throat. "Oh my God." When I opened my eyes, his face had taken on a predatory gleam. "What?" I asked him.

"Your face when you drank the coffee . . . that was a look I'd like to see again. And again."

I took a shaky breath and vowed to maintain some semblance of control.

"It's okay, you know."

"What's okay?"

"I'm not going to do anything you don't want."

Ha! If he only knew. . . . "Thanks."

"Do you work around here?"

"Across the street. Are you new here? I haven't seen you before."

"I'm just helping to close tonight; I'm usually at one of the other stores."

I nodded. "This is the best white mocha I've ever had. There's something different about it. It's not like the others I've had here."

"I added a little something extra. It's my own private formula."

"Is that right?"

"Indeed."

"What would a girl have to do to get the formula?"

"What would a girl be willing to do to get it?"

I let a slow smile spread across my face. This guy was trouble. In all caps and bolded. I liked it. I took a final sip of the brew and set the cup down. "What do I owe you?"

"It's on the house."

"I can't let you do that."

"Come back and see me. That's payment enough."

I flashed a grateful smile and gathered up my things. Nothing like stellar coffee and harmless flirting with a good-looking man to reinvigorate you. He came around the counter to unlock the door for me. As I walked past I said, "Thanks. For everything."

"You're welcome." He took a step toward me and leaned down to whisper in my ear. "Just so you know . . . I would've given you anything you asked for."

I paused midstep and shifted toward him a little. "Anything?"

"Absolutely."

I lifted my eyes to his and we shared a smile as though we knew far more about each other than we really did. I nodded. "Good to know." I moved forward.

"Have a nice night."

"You do the same." I strolled out into the night wondering if I'd just dodged a bullet or missed out on something potentially great. Only time would tell.

2

Strolling the Park

"What do you mean you walked out? Are you crazy?" My best friend Celeste was never one to mince words. Today was no exception.

It was a week after meeting Cute Coffee Guy and I had just finished sharing the story over cocktails. We were at a trendy new bar and grill that was ridiculously packed for a Thursday night. "Celeste, I'm not one for the casual sharing of body fluids. . . . You know this."

"No one is asking you to sleep your way down Michigan Avenue. I'm saying just once, do something outrageously fun and satisfying without thinking it to death."

Celeste was tall and willowy, and could've been a model if she hadn't been determined to save the world, one cause at a time. Currently, she was running a nonprofit to bring free fitness centers to areas of Chicago in need.

She was also a serial man-eater. She devoured them like potato chips and disposed of them like Kleenex. She was very much like the Samantha character in *Sex and the City*: a great friend but you would not want her to date your brother. Best friend or not, I would not be taking dating tips from her. Instead of sharing those thoughts, I diplomatically replied, "You aren't the first person to tell me that recently."

"How hot was he?"

"Blazing, smoking, evaporating-panty hot." I couldn't get the look of him out of my head.

"And yet yours stayed on."

"That they did." I finished my drink and pushed the glass away.

"Well, what held you back? He was giving all of the 'green means go' signals."

I had asked myself that question a time or two in the last seven days. "I don't know. Maybe that was the problem. Who knows how many women he's mixed a special mocha for? Maybe I'm just not that girl."

"Was he giving a smarmy 'notch on my headboard' vibe?"

"He really wasn't. Truthfully, I made the first semi-sort of move. And then I changed my mind."

"Or lost your nerve."

"Or both. But I can't stop thinking about him."

She arched a brow. "You've got a bad case of coulda, shoulda, woulda."

"Along with what-if-itis."

"Next time at least get the man's name, marital status, criminal history, something."

"Next time? I hardly think so. That was one of those now-or-never moments, I think."

"You never know what's around the next corner. Chicago is a big city but a small town."

"True."

"Speaking of which, remember that guy Wayne who hits on you every time he sees you?"

I groaned. "Ugh, yes, why?"

"He's approaching on your right in 3—2—1 . . ."

"Hey Jayla, looking good." Wayne, an accountant from the company where I used to work, was the very definition of persistent. No matter how many times I told him "no, thank you," he just seemed to pursue me more. He was a good-looking guy, great credentials, but . . . he was trying too hard. It made me uncomfortable.

Looking at Wayne made me realize one more thing that had attracted me to Cute Coffee Guy. He didn't try to engage me or attract me, he just did. It was effortless and that much more sexy because of it. Wayne suffered in comparison. "Hi Wayne, what's good?"

His smile broadened. "You and me given half a chance."

I exchanged a look with Celeste. She rolled her eyes. I was spared having to respond by the arrival of another man at Wayne's side. "Who's your friend?"

"This is Larry. Larry, this is Jayla and her friend Celeste."

Inwardly, I sighed. I saw the look Celeste gave Larry. She was going to invite him to sit down, which meant Wayne would sit down. Which meant I'd have to pretend to be interested in whatever he had to say. I wasn't in the mood. "Larry, why don't you take my seat? I have to head out."

"Where are you headed? I'll walk with you," Wayne offered.

"Oh, that's okay, Wayne. I'm not that far away. Larry, Celeste—have a great evening." Celeste was already giving Larry her patented spider-to-fly look.

"No way am I letting a fine lady such as yourself walk these streets alone."

I'm positive my face resembled a trapped deer in headlights at that point. Thankfully, Celeste stepped into the breach. "Why don't you catch a cab since you have that thing to go to way across town?"

"Right, right." I smiled an insincere apology at Wayne. "I'm just going to grab a cab. Don't worry about me. Great seeing you, though!" Before he could answer, I had my tote bag on my shoulder and was out the front door. Stepping out into the humid night, I decided a cab wasn't a bad idea. The suit and heels I'd put on hours earlier were great for the office, not the best for a long stroll. I flagged a cab and slid into the back. On a whim, instead of giving my home address, I said, "Grant Park, please."

It took less than five minutes to get there even in happy-hour traffic. For some reason, I just wanted to walk around for a minute. I switched into some ballet flats I had in my tote and started my stroll. I came to a hill overlooking the softball fields, sat down, crossed my legs, and closed my eyes. It was the first time in weeks that I'd just done nothing. Deep breath in, deep breath out. I could feel the tension melting away.

I'm not sure how long I sat there in the moment and at peace. But I liked the feeling. It seemed like I had spent the majority of my life just trying to get to the next, better place. I grew up as an only child raised mostly by my grandmother in the less than enviable neighborhood of Englewood, and scrapped and clawed my way through public schools before landing a scholarship to Duke University.

Duke had been both a blessing and a curse. For the first time I was surrounded by people who were unfamiliar. They didn't look or sound like the people I'd grown up with. But I was in an atmosphere of learning, excitement, and growth. I blossomed. I soaked up alternative cultures and ways of life, understanding that I could live any one of them that I wished to live.

I had wanted to pursue an advanced degree, but my grand-mother had fallen ill. I came back to Chicago and took an entry-level position at a nonprofit company, where I met Celeste. She assisted me in finding live-in care for my grand-mother.

Then came the men. The string of "looked good on paper, just okay in bed, and not ready for prime time" boyfriends. By the time I met Joseph, I was ready to be dazzled and swept off my feet. He did just that. As my career was progressing and taking off, he was there with the encouraging word. Mostly, he was just there. In my house, eating my food, "borrowing" my money without my knowledge.

The last straw came after a grueling two-week period on the road meeting my people in the BeniCareCo field offices. As I sat in the airport waiting to get home, my phone rang. It was American Express, curious to know why I was charging business expenses in Denver and pleasure expenses at a five-star resort in the Dominican Republic at the same time. I had no idea what they were talking about. They gave me the resort name, phone number, and the room number I was supposedly staying in. When I called down there, Joseph answered the phone and there was the sound of girlish giggles in the background. I was too through. I called the front desk and let them know that none of the charges would be honored. I called the airlines and let them know the tickets were fraudulent. I called my bank and had them begin a fraud investigation.

When I got home, I packed up Joseph's stuff. I didn't realize that he had virtually moved in. I suspected he didn't even have a place of his own to go to. I sent his things in a prepaid taxi to his mother's house, changed my home number and locks, advised the doorman to never let him back in, and decided that was that. I had no idea how or if he got back from the Dominican Republic with his beach mate and I frankly didn't care. That let me know the reality of that relationship. I never missed Joseph, I just missed having someone there.

I heard a loud cheer go up below and I was startled out of my reflection. The sun was starting to set as I opened my eyes to see someone sprinting around the diamond. The cheers amplified as he slid into home. With a smile, I gathered my things and started to turn away. The logo on the front of one of the team shirts caught my eye: JAY'S COFFEE CAFÉ in a familiar blue and green. Impossible. But now I had to take a closer look.

I walked to the edge of the field and peered over at the players. In the center of the celebratory group was Cute Coffee Guy, wearing the number 00 on his uniform. He wore the baseball shirt and athletic shorts well. Yeah, he looked just as good as I remembered. I watched him laughing and talking with his co-workers before I reluctantly turned back toward the path.

Walking away briskly, I started talking to myself. "You are the biggest idiotic wimp on the planet! Seriously. I mean the man was right there. Did you NOT see that man? You couldn't even wave, say hello, and see if he remembered who you were? No, not you. You have to slink away into the night all safe and stupid. This is how it's gonna be, huh? Look but don't touch? Coulda, woulda, shoulda INDEED."

"I don't mean to interrupt while you are clearly in the middle of an important discussion with yourself but—"

"Ah!" I swirled around, raised my fists, and shifted my stance.

"Hold up there, killa." Cute Coffee Guy smiled at me.

"Oh, sheesh. You scared me to death. Hey."

His grin widened. "Hey yourself. Those are some serious survival instincts you have there, Ms. White Mocha."

"It's Jayla."

He extended his hand. "Jason."

I put my hand in his; there was that chemistry thing again.

"Jayla, what brings you out?"

"Believe it or not, just a mental-health break. For some reason I wanted some fresh air and found myself sitting on top of the hill over there."

"Do you believe in providence?"

"Not so much."

"Fate, karma, destiny?"

I laughed. "Maybe."

"Are you headed home?"

"I am."

"May I see you home?"

I looked at him in the fading light of day. There was something about him I trusted. Then again, he was a stranger. So I hesitated.

He turned back toward the remaining team members on the field. "Guys, am I not the safest, nicest man you know?"

"He really is." "You're all good, girl." "Too nice for his own good." He turned back toward me with a smile and a shrug.

Take a chance, Jayla. "All right Jason, I'm taking a chance."

"Do you want me to wait for you to finish your conversation?"

I gave him a look. "I'm good." I started walking and he fell into step with me.

"I've no doubt." He reached over and took my hand in his.

Since the hand-holding felt right, I decided to ask a personal question. "How old are you?"

"Thirty-five. What makes you ask?"

He seemed supremely comfortable in his own skin.

"Just wondering."

"Do you mind if I ask your age?"

"I'm thirty-three," I said with a slight wince. The years fly by when you're not paying attention.

"Why the wince? You wear it well."

I shrugged. "Thanks."

"You're welcome."

"So did you win?" I asked him, referring to the softball game.

"In fact we did. Are you a sports fan?"

"More football and tennis than baseball and basketball."

"A girl after my own heart. So you like coffee and real sports, what else?"

"Mexican food, gerbera daisies, vodka drinks, and Hitchcock movies. What about you?"

"Shrimp fajitas, long baths, ice-cold martinis, and classic blaxploitation films. Are you married?"

"I'm not."

"Neither am I." He flagged a cab. We slid in and I gave my address. "Oh, Wicker Park? We're practically neighbors."

"Where are you?"

"Lincoln Park."

I wondered how a barista could afford one of Chicago's toniest neighborhoods but I kept my thoughts to myself. I didn't want to disturb the vibe between us. We were still holding hands.

"Can I ask you something?" he said in a deep voice.

"Only if you know I might not answer."

"So cautious, Jayla."

"So I've been told. But go ahead."

"What did you really want in the coffee shop last week?"

I blushed, something I hadn't done since junior high. "I came in for coffee."

"And then, once you saw me?"

My face heated more, but I didn't answer.

He glanced at the driver then back at me. He lowered his voice. "Answer me this: I didn't imagine it, right? I'm not imagining it right now. There's a thing between you and me."

I nodded. "There's a thing."

He squeezed my hand. "A definite thing."

I nodded again.

"So what do you want to do about it?"

The cab pulled to a halt while I thought about my answer. A million thoughts raced through my head as he helped me out of the backseat. His hand slid along my arm and I gripped his hand tightly. I took a shaky breath and vowed to maintain some semblance of control.

"You don't have to, you know," he said quietly.

Glancing up, I asked, "Don't have to what?"

"Be all cool and in control."

"How did you know?" Did I have "uptight control freak" broadcasting from my pores?

He shrugged as he pulled me closer. "Just a hunch. Listen, Jayla—I'm single, disease free, relatively sane. I'm enjoying you.

I won't hurt you. I won't judge you. If you want me to walk away from here tonight and never see you again, I'll accept that."

"But?" I bit my lip nervously.

"But . . . I'd rather come inside with you tonight. Or have you come home with me. I'd like to spend the night buried inside you, seeing how many times you can scream out my name."

My eyes widened as I took in what he was saying. He clearly had no problem asking for what he wanted. This beautiful man wanted me. He was, in fact, my every fantasy. Something about him made me want to cede control, live in the moment—two things I rarely, if ever, did. But he seemed way too good to be true.

He shifted closer. "You're thinking."

"I'm overthinking. That's what I do." It was something I alternately loved and hated about myself. Everything was a Rubik's cube to me, a puzzle to be turned this way and that until it made sense.

He slid one arm around my back, leaned down, and placed a kiss to the side of my cheek. "Find me when you're ready. I'll be waiting."

I wondered if he really would be. Men like that, in my experience, did not sit home alone waiting for neurotic, wishy-washy chicks to look them up. As I watched him walk away, I wondered for the second time in two weeks if I was being really smart or really stupid.

3

Special

"You are so distracted right now. And you say it's all because of some girl who tried to jump you in the coffee shop? Then she changed her mind and left. Fast-forward to you seeing her again in the park, where you take her home but she shuts you down again? I'm afraid I don't understand the issue or the fascination. What was so special about her that we can't just call this a walkaway and be done with it?" Jason's business partner, Rick, was giving him a baffled "please help me understand" look. They were sitting in a skybox at Soldier Field watching a Chicago Bears preseason game. The game was going great; this conversation wasn't.

Jason and Rick had known each other since meeting on the baseball diamond in the tenth grade at Fenwick High School, a private school in the Oak Park area of Chicago. Though the school had some diversity representation, they had still bonded first as minorities at the exclusive school. They were both half Spanish (Jason had a Spanish father and Rick had a Spanish mother) and half African American, so they had that commonality of culture and background. They were both strikingly handsome men with easy smiles, charming personalities, competitive natures, and brains to match.

Whereas Jason was tall, green eyed, and quick to laugh,

Rick was a few inches shorter, blue eyed, and quick to tell a joke. Rick was the big-picture person, Jason was the details guy. They both came from families of privilege. Jason's father was a dentist, Rick's father was a county judge. Rick was a Casanova racking up conquests, Jason was more of a Romeo interested in long-time monogamy. They had been fast friends for years. Rick was the one person Jason could count on to be absolutely straight with him about absolutely everything.

After prep school, Jason had gone to Columbia University, including a semester abroad in Spain, while Rick had attended Emory University in Atlanta. They reunited for graduate school at Northwestern, both earning MBAs. After graduation, they both launched small businesses. Jason's coffee shop and Rick's martini bar. They merged their interests into one large corporation. The number of businesses had grown from there. As part of an annual review of businesses, they took turns working in the businesses. This is how Jason came to be cleaning up coffee mugs when Jayla strolled in.

Jason continued his explanation. "There was just something about her. I don't know what to tell you. She spoke to me. Not just with words; I'm telling you there was a vibe or a spark or something."

"We call that 'sexual chemistry' and there's an easy fix for that. Find her, scratch the itch, and let's be done. We have to keep our heads in the game here. No time for nonsense."

Jason shook his head. "It's not just an itch, I'm telling you."

"Whatever, Jay, this is a ground-breaking quarter for us. We have to decide if we're going to franchise nationwide or just broaden our local customer base. I need you at 100 percent."

Jason smirked; he was usually the one reminding Rick that the business came before the babes. "So *you're* actually telling *me* it's all work and no play?"

"Whatever it takes." Rick smiled back.

"No can do. Not when you meet a woman like this."

"Like what?"

"Special."

"From seeing her twice, you know this?"

"You know special when you see it," Jason said firmly. "Or rather, *I* know special when I see it. You're not really concerned about that."

"What I don't get—or should I say what I REALLY don't get—is how you of all people still believe in 'special' women after the hell you went through with Delia."

Jason's face fell at the mention of Delia. Delia was his exwife. He met her at Columbia. She was "that chick" on campus and he pursued her with a vengeance. Throughout their courtship, she appeared to be all the things he was looking for. And in those days he was looking for a lot, for what he thought made up the perfect mate. He had what he called the "Ten-Point Checklist" of must-haves for his future spouse. In those days, he believed that the future Mrs. Jericho needed to be model-quality gorgeous, sexually adventuresome, double-degreed, ambitious, savvy, well-traveled, impeccably dressed at all times; have a six-figure income and flawless social skills; and be from a family of means. He had been so intent on those ten things that he ignored the important five: someone who was honest, loved him for him, was attuned to his moods, knew how to communicate, and believed in mutual respect.

Delia had been great at the ten, terrible at the five. And he'd had to find out the hard way. The day after they exchanged vows, she turned into someone he didn't want to have a conversation with, let alone live with day in and day out. She quit her job and dedicated herself to shopping for designer clothing. She hated Chicago and constantly whined about moving back to New York.

She was all facade and no substance. She was a shallow, selfish shell of a woman lacking in empathy, sympathy, or moral compass. He recalled his mother saying the woman was a soulless pit where evil dwelled. He really couldn't argue with her. You name it, Delia did it. Overspend? Sleep with his friends?

Terrify the housekeeping staff? Trash his Gold Coast condo? All of that and more. The more unhappy she was, the more vodka she drank. His bill from the liquor store that delivered rivaled that of a restaurant with a robust happy hour.

A part of him wondered if it was his fault. Had he not been sensitive enough, supportive enough; had he not been clear about his expectations? Could he really not have seen that beneath the polish, there was nothing there? His parents' marriage, his grandparents' marriage, his uncle's marriages were all healthy and long lasting. He thought if he just hung in there, things would get better. They didn't.

When the end came, it came quickly. One day after a taxi brought her home drunk, half dressed, and smelling of another man, he decided that he'd had enough. There was no reason for either of them to be this miserable and, frankly, he was bone weary of all the drama.

The very next morning, he sat Delia down and asked her how much it would cost for her to walk away and never look back. She named a sum intended to shock him and asked for an apartment. She had no idea that he would have paid three times that much to be rid of her free and clear. Within forty-eight hours, papers were signed and he had her and her things packed and headed east to New York City. She left with a check in her purse and the key to her new residence in her hand. When he closed the door behind her, he thought *good riddance.*

He moved to his current townhome in Lincoln Park and rarely looked back. Which was why he was able to answer Rick's question with absolute clarity. "I've seen women who look shiny on the outside with nothing on the inside. I know the difference; this one is special."

"If you say so."

"I definitely say so."

"Okay, she's special . . . whatever that means. So what are you going to do about it?"

"Wait," Jason said with a secret smile.

"I beg your pardon?"

"I am just going to wait." Jason nodded, leaning back in his chair and closing his eyes.

"So, what? She's coming to you?"

"Yes sir, she is coming looking for me to see what's next."

Rick threw back his head and laughed. "This I would place money on. I wager that the Bears will go undefeated before this woman tracks you down. Five hundred dollars cash money, son." He reached into his wallet, pulled out four hundreds and two fifties, and slapped them down on the table.

Jason opened one eye and eyed the cash. "You just lost a half grand, Mr. Santos. I'll be calling you shortly to collect." He closed his eyes again. When he received no response and the silence stretched on, he opened his eyes and sat up. Rick was looking at him with a strange expression on his face. "What? Mad you just threw away five hundred dollars?"

"Intrigued that you are this positive. I don't think I've ever seen you this enthused about the sheer prospect of getting to know someone. Maybe this girl *is* something special."

"See? Now you're on my page."

"Just one last question . . ."

"Half this game has gone by with you and your questions. What is it?"

"Does she have a sister?"

"Ha! I'll find out."

"Now . . . about this game. . ."

4

Come What May

It had been two weeks since I watched Jason walk away from outside my condo. The good thing was I had no time to dwell on it; work was kicking my ass. The bad thing was I had no time to dwell on it; work was kicking my ass. Even though it was early September, we had started putting together budget projections for the following year. That meant long days in meetings and longer nights in front of a spreadsheet. A glance at my watch showed that it was already eight thirty. I'd been at work since seven a.m.

"Ms. Lake, are you with us?" Charles, my executive vice president, was shooting me the evil eye from the head of the table.

I opened my mouth to say I was fine, but what came out was, "No. I'm not. I'm not even on autopilot anymore. Eight straight days of this pace and I'm fried. I can't be the only one. At this point, we're in danger of doing more harm than good. I could sit here and fake it and pretend that I'm giving you my best, but we're better than that. I'm sorry, but I for one need a break." Then I held my breath. *NOW is when I decide to get brave?* Charles's eyes narrowed and locked on mine.

Everyone around the table froze, looking from me to Charles and back again. I was all in, holding his stare, not giving a damn about consequences. We were all a day away from nervous breakdowns or stabbing each other over the last turkey sandwich. Enough was enough. If this cost me my job or his respect, this clearly wasn't the place for me. After a few more seconds where I swore my heartbeat was audible, Charles spoke. "Okay. Truth time: everybody's fried?"

"Hell yes."

"My kid forgot my name."

"I was burned out a week ago."

"My socks don't match today."

"What day is it anyway?"

The chorus of assenting voices rose. Charles held up his hand. "I got it, I got it. All of this yet somehow Jayla is the only one ballsy enough to say something?"

Silence.

He leaned back in his chair and closed his eyes. When he opened them, he had a weary smile on his face. "Thank you, Jayla. It's Friday night. Everybody get outta here and take a three-day weekend. I'll see you on Tuesday."

We sat in stunned silence, not sure we'd heard him correctly. I again spoke for the group. "Seriously? Monday, too?"

"Move it before I change my mind. Also, no laptops home, no BlackBerrys on. Just take yourselves and go."

His last words acted like a starter pistol at a racetrack. People hopped up and scattered as though running for their lives. Or in our cases, running *to* our lives. Such as they were. By the time I logged off, locked up my laptop, and put my purse on my shoulder, I had made up my mind. I knew exactly where I was headed. And I suddenly couldn't wait to get there.

At the elevator doors, I stood tapping my foot impatiently. *Let's go already!*

"Jayla, can we buy you a drink? Hell, two drinks and a lobster dinner? You've earned it." Two of my co-workers offered and raised their hands for high fives.

I slapped palms while shaking my head. "Rain check, fellas?"

Charles walked up. "Hot date?"

I just smiled.

"Really? The workaholic is getting a life?" he teased.

I raised a brow. "Have you heard the one about the pot and the kettle?"

We laughed as we stepped onto the elevator. We made friendly chitchat as we rode down the eighteen floors to the lobby level. It was just what I needed to keep from dwelling on the potentially reckless thing I was about to do. "Good night, all," I called out as we scattered in different directions. I headed toward the coffee house. Approaching, I noticed there were no customers inside. I glanced at my watch. It was a little after nine: their closing time. I reached to open the front door, but it was locked. I rattled the door a little in frustration.

"Sorry, we're closed," a familiar voice called out from the back of the shop.

I rattled the door again, this time with a little more noise and force. It became urgent that I see Jason. Right now. Tonight.

"We're closed!" he called out again. Then he stuck his head around the corner to frown toward the door. When he saw it was me, a slow smile spread across his face. I waved with a smile of my own. Setting down the towel in his hand, he headed toward the door with a gleam in his eye that I had to call predatory. He looked amazing in simple jeans and a black T-shirt with the café apron over it. My mouth watered just looking at him.

He unlocked the door and opened it wide. "Look who's at my door."

"Hey," I said softly and stretched up on tiptoe to kiss his cheek. He turned his face and grazed his lips with mine. All my senses went on high alert and I had to concentrate to pay attention to what he was saying at that moment. "I beg your pardon?"

"I asked if you would like some coffee?" he said, drawing me into the store before running his lips down the length of my jaw. He pushed the door closed behind me and I heard the click of the lock.

The edges of my mind got a little cloudy the minute his lips touched my flesh. "I'm sorry. What did you ask me?"

He laughed. "I asked if you wanted some coffee?"

"Maybe later."

"Ah. One moment." He hurriedly circled the room, closing blinds, flipping off the outside lights, and switching the sign to CLOSED. He turned back to me. "So then: tea?"

I shook my head, took off my summer-weight jacket, and dropped it onto a chair with my purse. I had on a sleeveless jersey wrap dress in crimson and taupe sling-back pumps. I walked toward him, putting a little extra sway in my hips. It was as if standing up for myself in that meeting had set me free. I was going to be the woman to say what I wanted . . . and get it. And right now, I wanted Jason. Come what may. "I just want you."

He flashed a smile that literally made me weak. "I know." He met me in the middle of the floor and let me take the final step into his arms. He stroked his hands up and down my back.

I wanted to purr under his touch. "How do you know?"

He trailed his finger down my neck and across my bodice before pausing, "May I?" His fingers paused as he waited for my permission.

"Uh, sure," I breathed.

He continued running his fingers down and around my chest, flicking a razor-sharp nipple as he went. When I gasped, he said in a low growl, "I know you want me because you are here and obviously aroused." He raised his other hand and flicked both nipples once, twice until my head fell back in surrender.

"Violently," I agreed as he leaned down and tasted the column of my throat that was exposed, leaving a trail of flames as he licked. I leaned into him, wanting to get closer, quicker.

"Can I . . . help you with that?" he offered, flicking faster, making my nipples painfully sensitized and all of me needy.

"Please." I untied his apron and palmed the contours of his hardness through the denim, stroking and exploring.

He backed me farther into the store, pressing his hips forward and continuing to tease my nipples, first the left, then the right, in strokes and circles and perfect pressure. "You want this?"

"Um-hmm." I squirmed impatiently.

He slid one hand under my dress and up my thigh, sending a long finger beneath my panties and between my swollen lips, his hand instantly coated with my juices. "Quickly?" He asked the obvious.

"Oh God, please," I begged, starting to pant in earnest. My deprivation, his hotness, my wetness, his skilled fingers: I knew it wouldn't take long.

He lifted my right thigh and slid two fingers into me, stretching and teasing while his thumb zeroed in, pressing down in a quick circle. I came instantly, breath stolen at the intensity of sensation. He stroked me through every tremor before lowering my leg back to the ground, wrapping his arms around me, and lifting me onto the low counter behind me. "So, now that we've taken the edge off . . ." He tilted my hips forward and pulled my panties down while I shimmied to help him.

I was a whole new Jayla. I felt powerful, womanly, and in charge. Reaching forward with no shyness, I grasped the waistband of his jeans and carefully unbuttoned the four fastenings. Pulling the denim and black cotton down past an erection of impressive proportions did nothing to lessen my eagerness to have him inside me.

Kicking out of the clothing and stepping between my thighs, he waited until my eyes were on his before he spoke.

"Are you ready?" He canted forward until the tip of him teased my entrance.

"Yes." I scooted forward and rubbed myself against him. We both groaned as my juices moistened the head of his shaft. He backed away, plucked a lemon–lime–colored condom from the promotional display behind the counter, and quickly sheathed himself.

"Safety first. Now, if you're sure you want this?" He slid his hardness against me, hitting every nerve ending before pressing the head against the most sensitive part of me.

"YES!" I grabbed his rear in my hands and tried to pull him forward.

He held back. "Be sure." His voice was deep, his tone was firm.

Through the hormone haze I became aware of his meaning and my circumstances. I was, for all intents and purposes, exposed in a public place, with a man I'd met less than fifteen days ago. Of the two of us, he was thinking with both heads. Here we were: his hands under my knees to hold me open wide, my hands on his butt to pull him near, staring into each other's eyes and contemplating sanity. "Are *you* sure?" I felt him twitch against me.

He smiled. "Clearly. I've been sure. I've been waiting on you. I want *you* to be sure."

What the hell, you only live once, carpe diem: all those convenient justifications suddenly made perfect sense to me. I kicked off my shoes, tossed my head back, and lifted myself onto his shaft.

He took the hint and slid the rest of the way into me, so slowly.

I gasped for breath as he filled me to the hilt. "Hello, Jason."

He smiled and rotated his hips slightly. "Hi, Jayla."

"Jason . . . more," I implored as he slid out and then back in with the same wickedly slow pace. "More."

He shook his head. "You like that, Jayla?" He tilted my hips and slid in at an angle that set off every bell and whistle on the way down before twisting slightly and hitting all the others on the way back up. Ever so slowly he slid in and back out as though there was all the time in the world to stay and tease and linger. In and back out, again and then again. He was disciplined, he was delicious, and he was demonic in his ability to maintain the same achingly slow pace. Instantly, I was hooked, craving the return of him each time he withdrew. I couldn't hide from the pleasure. I started to moan and he laughed low. "Yeah, Jayla likes it like that."

I was burning, bucking my hips, craving more, unable to get close enough. "Help me," I asked, leaning back to get more leverage. He lifted me off the counter altogether and held me in place against him, grinding up against me so the sweat and the juices and the skin all fused into a humid jungle. "Jason!" I cried out as he bounced me along the length of him, his length hitting inside me so deeply that I began to convulse against him helplessly.

He carried me over to a large purple couch in the corner and laid both of us down. "That's right, baby, you just let it go. I know you have more in you. Now, let's go." Sliding his entire body on top of me, he began to thrust in earnest. Using the floor and the back of the couch for leverage, he rode me hard and deep like a man on a mission. I wrapped my legs around him and hung on for the ride. The feel of him filling me was addictive. I wanted more, all he had to give. How had I lived without this feeling? Had I ever had this exact feeling before? Had it ever been this good?

I was pure sensation from the tips of my fingers to the soles of my feet as a monster orgasm built up in waves. Desperate, I ground up against him, meeting his strokes, and milking him with my canal. I was not too proud to beg. "Just give me . . ."

"Take it, baby, take all of it." He slammed into me harder and groaned so sexily in the back of his throat as sweat dripped from his brow. Leaning down, he placed his lips on mine and let his tongue mimic the rhythm of his hips.

It was too much. Too hot, too good, too full, too deep, and too sexy. He paused, reared back, and sank back deep, moving with an urgency and a force I loved.

"Now, Jayla, now," he said through gritted teeth, his hips pumping faster as his climax hit.

I screamed as I came apart, raw screams torn from me in rapid succession.

Slowly, we came back to reality. Two minutes, then five passed. The scents of sinfully steamy sex, chocolate, and coffee hung heavy in the air. There was the hum of the machines and the rasp of our breathing for sound. His lips pressed lightly against my forehead, my hands still clutching and unclutching on his rear. I closed my eyes to keep real life at bay for a few minutes more. The world outside did not have to exist in that moment.

My thoughts were everywhere. Why had I ever thought I wasn't that sexual a creature? Who would sit on this sofa tomorrow and would the wet spot still be there? What was he thinking? Could I ever buy coffee at that counter again without imagining myself impaled and dripping, wide open and begging for more? "Umm." I took a deep breath and wriggled a little, aroused by the thought.

"Unless you're ready for round two, right here and now, you better hold still," Jason said with a smile in his voice, as he hardened a little in response to my humid wriggle.

My eyes flew open. Now *he* was eyeing *me* like I was the last shrimp on the buffet. I felt him swelling up inside of me and my head fell back. "I should go, I should really, really go." My hips started circling of their own accord. His hips rocked slowly back and forth.

"Before you've had your fill?" He pulled his shirt off and tossed it aside, revealing a toned and chiseled chest with a light dusting of hair tapering to a narrow waist with washboard abs.

"Are we talking about coffee again?" I asked, running my hand down his chest as he pulled my dress over my head, unhooked my bra, and sent it flying.

"You haven't even tasted my cinnamon mocha yet," he said, shifting so he was more firmly atop me. "Don't you want to stay and taste it?" He leaned down and lifted my left breast, sucking the tip into his mouth, never losing eye contact with me. This for some reason struck me as inexplicably hot, his mossy green eyes watching my reaction while he pulled sensation after sensation from me. Switching to the right side, he asked again, "Do you, Jayla, do you want to taste it?"

Keeping my eyes on him, I pulled away and maneuvered until he was below me. Licking my way down his torso, I whispered, "I do, Jason, I do want to taste it." Tossing my hair to the side, I took him deep in my throat and watched as his pupils expanded before his eyes closed shut.

It was his turn to moan. "Please say you're not talking about coffee."

I cupped him in my hands at his base and massaged while continuing suction. "I'm not talking about coffee." With every touch, stroke, taste, and texture I was killing shy Jayla and emerging a brand-new person.

"Jayla," he gasped, fists balled by his side, hips straining as my tongue caressed him.

I smiled. "Yes, Jason?" I wrapped a hand around the base and squeezed while whirling circles around the head with my tongue. A drop of moisture beaded up on the tip and I licked it off greedily.

"Oh God, that's it." He reached down, lifted and turned me clockwise before dropping my still-weeping opening over his lips.

At the first lap of his tongue, I froze, then went into a frenzy. My hips thrashed so violently, he was forced to hold me still, teasing and biting with darts of his tongue, nips of his teeth, and sweeps of his lips. His mouth explored every sensitive and swollen fold of my nether lips before dipping his tongue around my rim and darting inside. His thumb slid lightly over me and I shuddered.

It wasn't right that a perfect stranger knew my intimate needs, my personal rhythm, and gave them to me intuitively, unselfishly. Overwhelmed, I tried to lift away from his clever, clever tongue but he held me captive, a slave to his whim and my pleasure. But two could play this game. I matched the rhythm of my sucks to the rhythm of his licks and in no time we were writhing together with moans and sighs as the tension became unbearable. He became impossibly harder and larger in my mouth. I increased the pressure just as he took my nubbin into his mouth and sucked hard. Harder and higher until we broke, coming, him first spurting warm jets into my throat and me riding out the sensation. It seemed to go on and on, and I kept him in my mouth even after he softened, sucking the final drops from the very depths of him. His hips jerked convulsively. "Jesus," he said. "Jesus, Jayla."

I finally let him go and rolled to the side, trying to catch my breath. He reached out an arm to keep me from rolling off the edge. I put my hand over his and we rested there quietly, as if we had done this a million times before.

"Why did I have the idea that you were shy?" he asked me.

"I *am* shy."

"No woman who does what you just did that well is shy. You, Ms. Jayla, have hidden depths."

That flattered me immensely. "You think?"

"I was expecting a nice, fun time."

"And you got?"

"A mind-blowing thrill ride. Amazing."

"Well, you definitely know what you're doing."

"I could say the same for you. Wow."

No one had ever told me I was amazing outside of the workplace and definitely not in bed. Hmm, could it be that *I* wasn't the problem? Maybe I just hadn't been suitably inspired to perform at my best until now? I tucked that thought away for later.

"So how about that cinnamon mocha?" he asked.

I laughed, sitting up. "How about it?"

"Do you still want it?"

I met his gaze. "It's about the only thing I haven't had yet."

He raised a brow. "I wouldn't say that." His eyes ran up and down my form and he leaned over to gently nip at my shoulder.

My breath caught in my throat and I felt the warmth snake across my skin. "Don't start," I whispered, swaying toward him as if magnetically drawn.

His hand slid up my neck and pulled my face to his, dropping a light kiss onto my lips. "Who said I was finished?" His words sent a jolt straight to my epicenter as if I hadn't been satisfied, and well more than once, in the last half hour.

Okay, I had to get it together. I could not get used to feeling like this. Eventually, reality had to creep back in. I pulled back slightly. "You know, I think I will take that coffee."

He squeezed the back of my neck once and nodded. "You got it." He rose and handed me his T-shirt to tug on, then padded, gloriously and unabashedly naked, over to his jeans. I almost hated to see him pull them on. He walked to the back and emerged with a clean, damp towel, which he handed over to me before moving behind the counter to start measuring coffee beans.

After cleaning up as discreetly as I could in the middle of a coffee shop in front of a semi-stranger, I walked around scrounging for my scattered clothing items. "What would the store manager say about your extracurricular activities?" I asked in the wake of not knowing what to say as I shimmied into my panties and began unraveling my twisted bra straps.

He looked at me and smiled slightly. "He'd probably say, 'Way to go, boss.' "

I paused as his words sunk in. "You own this place?"

He nodded while steaming some milk. "And twelve others," he said.

That explained the Lincoln Park address. "So you're Jay."

"I am Jay."

I gave up on the bra and pulled my dress over my head while he poured a fragrant concoction into a cup.

I sat down at a bar-height table near the counter and smiled at him. "What are you doing making mocha at nine o'clock at night?"

"Enjoying myself." He walked over and handed the cup to me with a grin. "It's on the house."

I took a sip and closed my eyes in ecstasy.

"There's that look again."

I opened my eyes and smiled slowly. "This is almost as good as sex."

"Oh, honey, you haven't been having enough sex. My mocha is great, but sex like we just had? Now, that's downright addictive."

"You think so?"

"Want me to prove it to you?"

"Here? Again?"

"Take me home with you. Or come home with me. Spend time with me, Jayla. I'm not ready for you to fade away yet."

"Do I fade away?"

"So far. With me, you kinda do."

"I'm sorry. It's not you. You're gorgeous and sexy, amazingly hot and talented."

He came and sat down in the stool beside me. "All that, huh? And what are you?"

"I'm cautious and tired and gun-shy and wary."

"We should work on some of that."

He always said the right thing in the right way at the right time. It made me slightly uneasy. But new Jayla needed to spread her wings a little. I thought about it. And almost immediately decided why the hell not? I deserved a little fun. And he was certainly capable of providing it. When I met his gaze, my answer was in my eyes.

He tilted his head to the side and we both started smiling as we read each other's expressions. "So . . ."

I leaned toward him and whispered, "I wonder how many times you'll make that sound?"

"What sound?" His voice was rough as he leaned forward to swirl his tongue across my upper ear. Who knew that was an erogenous zone?

"That groan you make in the back of your throat right before you lose control." My own tongue flicked out to lick the side of his neck. "Jason?"

"Yes, Jayla?" His hand slipped up my back to cup my neck again in a way I was finding ridiculously sexy and addictive.

"Come home with me . . . now."

5

The Morning After

There's a feeling when you wake up after a great night wrapped in the arms of somebody who seems happy to be there. I woke up immediately aware of my surroundings and bed partner. I was in my condo, which I had slaved for, labored over, and renovated myself. When the whole Tiffany blue and chocolate brown craze exploded in decorating, I went all in. Richly stained Brazilian cherry on the floors and cabinets. Icy gray granite and stainless steel in the kitchen. Chenille L-shaped sofa in a misty green, patterned pieces to match. It was an open floor plan with a great room that incorporated the living room, dining room, guest bath, and kitchen. To the left was a guest room I used as an office, to the right the master suite where I currently lay smiling in my queen-size sleigh bed.

It was Saturday, I'd spent an amazingly energetic night with Jason, and I didn't have to be back at work until Tuesday. Life was good.

Jason's lips brushed the back of my neck: "Good morning, beautiful. Can I fix you some breakfast?"

Correction: life was great. I had to blink a few times to make sure I wasn't dreaming. His hand stroking down my arm assured me this was the beginning of a lovely reality. "You don't have to do that."

"I want to. I get the feeling you haven't been spoiled a lot."

A lot? Think: at all. As a matter of fact, I could not think of the last time anyone offered to cook for me, let alone spoil me. "Well, feel free. My kitchen is your kitchen."

He gave me another quick squeeze before rolling out of bed. As he pulled on his jeans, he said, "Tell me something." He stood there with his hands on his hips with the jeans pulled up but not zipped or buttoned. Lord have mercy.

I propped up and tried to keep from reaching for him.

"Jayla?"

"Um-hmm?"

"I'm up here, honey. Eyes up." He laughed as I dragged my eyes upward and laughed.

"Sorry, momentarily distracted. You wanted to ask me something?"

He slid his thumbs into his waistband. "Well, now, if you're hungry for something else, we can put this food thing on hold. You tell me what you want."

"Just tell you what I want." That was a foreign concept to me.

"That surprises you?"

I shrugged. "Let's just say it's not something I've heard often."

"Hmm. Interesting." Jason looked like he was filing that away for future reference. "If you ever want to share relationship battle scars, just let me know."

It occurred to me that there was a lot we didn't know about each other. Before I started overthinking and wondering how much I needed to know and what any of this meant, I stopped myself. "Breakfast sounds great and you had a question?"

"Question is: what do you have to do today?"

"The only thing I absolutely have to do is go see my grandmother. I usually take her some groceries and spend a little time. Why?"

"I would like to spend the day with you, if that's okay?"

"I would love that. But be forewarned, my grandmother is going to hit on you." She would, too. Sassy loved the pretty boys. She had been married three times, starting at age 16 and each of her marriages lasted exactly fifteen years. Old age hadn't diminished the twinkle in her eye one bit. If anything, it made her more outrageous.

"Let Grammy get her flirt on. If she's anything like you, I won't mind at all. Where does she live?"

"Barrington."

"So far?"

"She insists. She's got a little house there that her husband left her; her church; her senior center; a little walking trail. I've tried to move her closer in but she's not having it."

"We'll take my car. Start at the farmers' market, swing by Whole Foods, and head out on the 90."

Either Jason was a complete and total fraud or he was hands down the most charming, likeable, and considerate man I'd ever met. I was praying mightily for the latter. I smiled at him. "Sounds like a plan, but first, do me a favor?"

"Anything."

"Can you please button those jeans or we are never getting out of this bed."

"What's wrong with that?"

"I'm hungry . . . for food. How are your French toast skills?"

"Are you the kind of woman who keeps the ingredients for real French toast handy?"

"I am. It's my weakness." Looking at him shrugging into his shirt, I had to add, "One of them anyway."

He looked over at me. "Come on, woman. Let's get some sustenance before you lure me back into your sex lair."

"Me? Sex lair? Ha!" That was the first and only time my bedroom had been called that . . . but I liked it. When he headed for the kitchen, I got up and headed for the bathroom.

When I emerged from a hurried shower twenty minutes

later in jeans and a T-shirt, he was sliding crispy golden toast next to bacon on a platter. This was a man who knew his way around a kitchen. It was almost as sexy as his bedroom skills.

As I slid onto a stool at the breakfast bar, he turned around. "Wait, get up a second."

I got up, looking around, thinking I'd forgotten something. "What?"

He came around and looked me over, from my shower-flattened hair, past dangly earrings, lightly glossed lips, form-fitting pink T-shirt, dark wash jeans, and peep-toe ballet flats. He reached forward, took my hand, and twirled me in a circle. "Ni-ce. Very nice."

I looked at him with blatant skepticism. "It's jeans and a T-shirt, Jason."

He shook his head. "It's *you* in jeans and a T-shirt, Jayla. You are a beautiful, beautiful woman."

Suddenly, I felt very emotional. I knew that I was attractive, but it had been so long since it had been acknowledged from a purely appreciative perspective that it shook me a little. I took a step forward and hugged him tightly. "Thank you. I needed that. As a matter of fact, you've given me a lot that I needed this weekend. In case I forget to say it, 'I appreciate you.'"

He hugged me back. "You are more than welcome."

We stood in that warm embrace for more than a few heartbeats. It was the first time in years that I was in a man's arms just for comfort and appreciation. I liked it . . . a lot.

"Come on, girl, let me feed you before we get all mutual admiration weepy around here."

I stepped away from him and slid back onto the stool. Within moments, he had a plate of French toast, bacon, and fresh fruit in front of me. When I looked up he was handing me a cup of coffee. I grasped the handle and sniffed. "You found this coffee in my house?"

He sent me a sly smile. "I added a few things to it, trade secrets."

I took a sip. "Wow, I should say so. This is delicious. You know, you keep treating me this well and I may have to keep you around."

He raised a brow. "Were you planning on tossing me back?"

I paused with my loaded fork halfway to my mouth. Was I planning on tossing him back? "Good question, I hadn't thought that far. I hadn't thought beyond . . ."

"Having your way with me?"

"Is that what I did?" I bit into the French toast; it was excellent. I began to suspect that this man did everything well.

He slid onto the stool next to me with his own plate. "I think we had our way with each other, don't you?"

"Complaints?"

"Not at all. I plan for us to have our way with each other a few more times this weekend."

"And then?" I just wondered where his mind was.

"And then whatever you're comfortable with. I'd like to keep seeing you in whatever way you'll let me."

"You always say the right thing."

"You say that like it bothers you."

"It does a little. I was in a relationship with a smooth-talking guy and he turned out to be a dirty dog. Any time I see similarities, I get nervous."

"Well, maybe we were in relationships with two sides of the same dirty coin. I only say things I mean and if you need clarification, don't hesitate to ask."

He and I locked eyes for a second. I saw no deceit or guile. I nodded slowly and raised my coffee cup. "Here's to what comes next then."

He touched his cup to mine. "Can't wait."

6

Rich Boy

Jayla grew quieter the closer they got to Jason's house. By the time they walked up the stone steps and he opened the front door she was just standing there with her mouth open.

"Toto, I don't think we're in Kansas anymore," Jason heard Jayla mutter as they entered his town house.

He knew his home made a statement. He'd planned it that way. After his failed marriage, he wanted a home that was traditional, not trendy. One that would look good today and twenty years from now. It was a three-story restored home built in 1910. The color scheme was very traditional in gold, navy blue, and tan. The first level housed an open kitchen as well as the formal living and dining areas. The bedrooms were on the second floor. And the third floor, where Jason spent most of his time, held the office, media room, bar area, and a flight of stairs leading to a rooftop deck. There was a tiny side yard and an attached two-car garage. The entire house screamed understated elegance and casual wealth.

"Did you say something?" Jason asked, just to see if she'd say it again.

"How many of those coffeehouses did you say you owned?" she asked, looking around.

"Twelve, but I have interests in a few other businesses."

Jason thought it best to downplay the scope of his holdings; Jayla seemed overwhelmed enough by his success.

Walking up the stairway to reach the bedroom, she stopped dead on the landing. "Is this an original Jacob Lawrence?" She goggled at a painting, referring to the renowned African-American Harlem Renaissance artist.

Jason shrugged. "My father bought it for me at auction when I graduated from business school."

She nodded. "I see . . . and your father is a . . . ?"

"Dentist, retired now. Plays a lot of golf."

"Golf?"

"Yes, golf. You whack a little white ball toward a hole in the ground, perhaps you've heard of it?"

"Ah, you've got jokes. Just reflecting for a moment. I doubt my dad even knows where the closest golf course is."

"Your dad's not a sports enthusiast?"

"He's not much of anything."

Jason turned on the landing to study her face. She looked tense. "Touchy subject?"

"The touchiest."

"So we'll move on. Come on in to my room. There's another gift from my father here before you freak out. It's a Hepplewhite side table."

"How many cavities paid for this?" Jayla wondered out loud.

"I can ask him if you'd like," Jason teased.

Her gaze met his and her face relaxed into a smile as he intended. "I don't think that will be necessary." She walked into the middle of the room and turned in a circle. Jason's room was a man's room, no doubt. Massively heavy furniture in dark wood accented with shades of blue and tan. A monstrously large TV took up one wall. A sitting area with buttery leather seating filled one corner. "You know that half of my condo could fit into your bedroom alone. And is that a wine fridge, player?"

Jason rolled his eyes and came up behind her to wrap his arms around her waist. "It's a beverage fridge that sometimes houses wine but usually holds bottled water. By the way, Ms. Jayla, I am not a player. You are about ten years too late for my doggish days."

"Interesting."

"You doubt?"

"You were ready to do me on the coffee counter the first night we met!"

"Not until you sent out the 'come get some' vibe. I was in there minding my own business and you came striding in. You ate me up with your eyes and fairly scorched my pants off, woman. You should know that you have a very expressive face."

Jayla threw her head back and laughed. "My face was saying all that?"

"Girl, you know you were beaming ready, willing, and able signals my way. Admit it."

She turned in his arms. "I might have been thinking it but I didn't make a move."

"Neither did I. I'm a gentleman, ma'am."

"We'll see about that. Let's get you a change of clothes, rich boy."

"Oh, it's like that?"

"It is most certainly like that."

"Hmm, well, I have to take a quick shower. Maybe you should come in with me and soothe my hurt feelings?"

Her voice was husky when she answered. "Well, we can't have those feelings hurt."

Jason took her hand and led her toward the master bathroom. "We really can't. I'm sensitive."

"Sensitive, gentleman, not a player. Cooks, loves Mexican food, wealthy. Excellent in bed, not married or gay, makes a perfect mocha. What's wrong with you?"

Jason started to laugh until he realized she was serious. "Does something have to be?"

She nodded seriously. "Something always is."

"Well, I'm not perfect, but I'm not a bad guy. Kinda like you."

"Me, what do you know about me?"

"Coffee drinker, owns her own place, ambitious, and career focused. Burned before but not bitter about it, plays her cards close to the vest. Lady on the outside, freaky on the inside, loves her grandma, and knows her sports. And you have good girl/good woman written all over you."

Jayla was impressed, but tried not to show it. "Do I, now? Well, let's see what I can do to show you how bad I can be right quick, sir."

"Do your worst."

"I do love a challenge."

7

To Grandmother's House We Go

Due to obvious reasons, it took far longer than expected to "change Jason's clothes." It was well into the afternoon when we climbed into Jason's Mercedes Hybrid SUV. I had been peppering him with questions about his childhood for the last fifteen minutes.

"So you grew up in Oak Park and went to Fenwick?" I said incredulously as we rode in a car that cost about four-fifths of my salary . . . and I was very well paid. Oak Park was a neighborhood known for an extremely high median income. Fenwick was a private school.

He glanced over at me. "I'm a child of privilege from a two-parent household. I know I was blessed and treasured and loved. But I'm not obnoxious about it. I take it this was not your childhood?"

"Ha!" I laughed shortly and without humor. "I grew up in Englewood and went to public high school. One day when I was five, my mother dropped me off to visit my grandmother and just never came back. My father visited at Christmas and on my birthday. My mother on Thankgiving and Easter. So no, I was neither privileged nor treasured."

"Your grandmother?"

"Okay, I was treasured. Ethel Joy, also known as Sassy, thinks I hang the sun in the morning and the moon at night."

He smiled. "Ethel Joy. I like it."

"She's my rock. She made so many sacrifices to make sure I got out of Englewood and got my degree."

"Where did you go?"

"Duke."

"Ah, southern Ivy League. Did you like it?"

"I loved it."

"Graduate school?"

"I was going to go to Northwestern but Ethel Joy was diagnosed with lupus and I had to make some money."

"Wow." He shook his head in amazement.

"Wow?"

"You're a special person. I knew that."

"I didn't do anything that anyone else wouldn't have done."

He sent me an odd look. "You'd be surprised."

"Anyway, so no advanced degree and I've been too busy just getting to the next place to go back."

"It's funny. I went to Columbia, then Northwestern. If our lives were different, we could've met each other ten years ago."

"Oh, you wouldn't have given me the time of day. I'll bet you were the big man on campus."

Jason smiled wryly. "I might have been a little popular, but believe me, you would've caught my eye."

"I was the studious, oversized-cardigan, glasses-on, hair-in-a-ponytail type."

He shrugged. "It's not how you look, babe. It's that spirit. It calls out to me."

I was stunned speechless. There he went again, saying the perfect damn thing. I stayed silent while he battled for a parking space near the farmers' market.

We wandered through the market and stopped to sniff,

sample, squeeze, and select. Shortly we had three baskets going. One for him, one for me, and one for Ethel Joy. At one stall, he attempted to pay for my vegetables and I slapped his hand away. "Oh no, moneybags. I've got this," I told him. I paid and moved on to the next stall. When I looked back he was the one looking stunned. "What's wrong with you, Richie Rich?"

"You're just different from most women I know."

"Because I pay for my own kale?"

"Because it never occurred to you not to pay for your own kale."

"You've known some unfortunate-minded women in your day."

"You have no idea," Jason said in a tone.

"Uh-oh. That's your 'bad relationship memories' voice."

He smiled wryly. "We all have them. Unfortunately."

"Unfortunately." I sighed deeply.

"We'll compare tragedies on the drive to Barrington. You take twenty minutes, I'll take twenty minutes, and then we'll set it all aside."

Again, he stunned me with his straight on, no chaser approach. He was just without guile. I had no experience with a man who wasn't all about the games. "You're going to take some getting used to," I told him as we headed back to the car.

"So start getting used to me so I can stick around a while," he said simply while holding open the door for me. "Whole Foods next?"

I nodded without acknowledging the first half of his statement. I just didn't know what to do with that yet.

He climbed into the driver's seat and fastened his seat belt. "That is, if you want me to stick around?"

"I hadn't thought beyond the weekend," I answered honestly.

"That's right. You're cautious. Extra wary and cautious."

"Never met a man who didn't warrant some extra caution."

He nodded slowly and started the car for the short drive to the market. "Well, that puts me in my place."

"Jason! I didn't mean it that way. I'm good just in the moment. I don't need an idea of what tomorrow is going to bring. Okay?"

"Okay, if that's what Jayla wants . . . Jayla gets the moment."

We rode the few blocks in silence. He found a space on the third level of the parking garage and I dug in my purse for the list Ethel Joy had given me earlier in the week. It wasn't until we got a cart and headed for the butcher's department that I realized he hadn't said a word. I shot him a look and found him watching me intently. I tilted my head to the side in inquiry.

"Why do I have the feeling that you're going to break my heart?" Jason said seriously.

I was alarmed and appalled. "Oh no, not me! I'm not a heartbreaker. I'm really not."

He mimicked my tone from a few moments ago. "I never met a woman who thought she was."

"So just agree with me. We're taking it as it comes—no expectations, no strings, and no heartbreak." I said that not knowing whether or not that was even possible. But I needed him to agree.

"Let's give it a shot." He put out a hand to shake on it and I slid my hand into his and squeezed.

"Thank you."

He linked our fingers and we got started.

Jason, as I should have suspected, was a brilliant shopper. He knew half of the "foodie specialists" who worked there and before long we had Ethel Joy's list handled and an interesting assortment of foods for me packed into insulated cooler bags. When he reached for his wallet at the checkout counter, I shot him a look. He backed away with his hands up and let me handle it.

On the way out of the store, he stopped in the floral department and picked up a huge bouquet of roses, orchids, and daisies in a bright blue glass jar. "A little something for Ethel Joy." He smiled at me.

"Oh, you're determined to have her fall in love with you. I see you, Jason. I see you."

At long last we were in the car headed to Barrington. Jason had keyed the address into his GPS system and put some old-school R&B on the satellite radio. "All right, we're on our way." He headed toward I-90.

"At this point I think there's something I ought to know," I said seriously, sliding on some sunglasses.

He stilled. "Well, as I said earlier—I'm disease free, straight, not married . . ."

I laughed. "Me, too; not that—your last name?"

He laughed. "Oh, Jericho."

I barked out a laugh. "Seriously, you are not real." I looked at him over the top of my glasses.

"I know, Jason Jericho." He rolled his eyes.

"Sounds like a porn name." Apropos, I thought to myself, turning to lean against the car door to watch him.

"You're one to talk, Jayla Lake. Sounds like a comic book damsel in distress."

"How do you know I'm not?"

"Oh, you're no shrinking damsel waiting for a superhero. Damsel in distress? No. Stressed-out diva? Yes."

Amazing how perceptive he was. "Think you know me, huh?"

"Working on it."

"So this is the part where we swap relationship horror stories?"

"Let's not do a historical dissertation. How about you tell me your worst, I'll tell you my worst, and we won't have this conversation again."

"You go first," I challenged him.

He took a deep breath. "Here we go . . . in less than twenty minutes. Her name was Delia and she was without a doubt the biggest mistake and regret of my life." With that first sentence, I was hooked.

He told the terrible tale in tragic detail and my heart went out to him. And he was just as empathetic when I told the equally tumultuous story of Joseph.

Dirty laundry aired, we fell into a companionable silence for the rest of the ride, both of us thinking about what we'd just shared and heard. Like he'd said earlier, it was like we'd been involved with two sides of the same trifling coin. We'd both been through a lot to get where we were today. It made me more determined than ever to live in the moment and concentrate on one experience at a time.

8

Ethel Joy

Ethel Joy's house was a three-bedroom two-bath ranch on a quiet cul-de-sac in the drama-free town of Barrington. The lawn was immaculately groomed and I could see where she had started switching out the summer flowers for fall color. She swung open the door and grabbed me inside into the hug that I had come to expect and love. It was warm, tight, close, and lengthy. Ethel Joy Lake Henderson Sweatt was a gracious and loving lady. She stood five foot five inches on a trim frame that still wore a petite size four. Her face, still unlined, brought to mind the timeless beauty of a Lena Horne or a Diahann Carroll. Her long silver hair was pulled back in her customary bun. She was dressed in a turquoise-colored camp shirt over a long, chocolate-colored broomstick skirt belted at the waist with a silver belt. She had silver ballet slippers on her feet. Ethel Joy might have been well on her way to eighty years of age but she was still fly. "No need to let yourself go on your way to the other side. Might as well show up on Gabriel's doorstep in style," she always said.

Suddenly she kissed my cheek and moved me behind her as her eyes landed on Jason. "Now, who is this tall, handsome man you have brought with you? Girl, got this good-looking man on the doorstep waiting. Know I taught you better than this. Come on in, sweetie."

Jason's eyes went into full twinkle as he stepped forward. "My name is Jason, I'm a friend of Jayla's. These are for you, ma'am."

Ethel Joy twinkled back as she accepted the huge arrangement from him. "You can call me Ethel Joy and come on in."

"Well, let me get your groceries out of the car and I'll be happy to do that, Ethel Joy."

The minute his back was turned Grammy turned to confront me. "Oh girl, I could cut a step right here! Tell me everything: where did you meet him, what's his story, and can I read something into the fact that you brought him to see me?"

I rolled my eyes. I should've known having Jason with me would cause a stir. I'd never brought a man to her house. If pressed, I couldn't say why I decided to bring this one. But he was here now so I had to explain. "No need to dance, I met him at a coffee shop, he's an entrepreneur from Oak Park, and he offered to drive me so I let him. Don't get any ideas and don't grill the man."

"Dear God, he's a handsome one, isn't he?" Ethel Joy placed her bouquet on a side table and was peering out of her front window. "Ooh, look at him just leaning forward into that fancy car. Um, um, um. If I were thirty years younger . . ."

"You'd still be a cradle robber. Please don't let him catch you gawking, Grammy."

"I beg your pardon. I do not gawk, young lady. I appreciate a well-formed masculine specimen. Oak Park, you say? He comes from money?"

"Bucketfuls."

"Does anything good with it?"

"Owns a string of coffee shops and a whole bunch of other stuff if his Lincoln Park home is any indication."

"Well, don't hate the man for being beautiful and loaded. He's got a nice spirit about him."

"Funny, that's what he said about me. My spirit 'calls out to him.' "

Tears welled up in Grammy's eyes. "Did he? Did he say that? Those exact words?"

Alarmed, I walked over to her. "Yes, Grammy, why? What's wrong?"

She patted my arm. "Nothing, baby; that's real good. That makes Grammy happy. You go help that young man and I'll check on dinner."

"Grammy, you didn't have to cook. I keep telling you that. How are you feeling this week?"

"Little girl, I am fine. I sent that meddling LuAnn home for the weekend, I'm feeling so fine. Now go help your man." LuAnn was the full-time companion/nurse I had hired when Grammy first contracted lupus. She was in remission now, but I kept LuAnn on more to be a friend and a watchful eye than anything else. They alternately bickered and loved each other like family.

I had to clarify. "He's not my man and what am I paying LuAnn for if you keep sending her off?"

"Don't fuss, baby." She smiled a secret smile and headed into her kitchen.

I rolled my eyes and turned toward the door just as Jason was coming in.

"So did I pass?" Jason whispered as he juggled the bags.

I took three of the bags out of his hands and whispered back. "You know you did with your charming self."

"I aim to please, ma'am. I will take that as a compliment coming from you." He kissed my forehead and walked past me toward the kitchen. "Ms. Ethel Joy, what is that heavenly smell coming from this kitchen?"

My grandmother giggled, a girlish sound I hadn't heard since before her last husband passed away. If for nothing else he had done this weekend, I would always think fondly of Jason for producing that happy sound out of my Grammy.

From that moment on, the evening was a lovefest between Jason and Ethel Joy. I was the fascinated bystander watching the two of them fall under each other's spell. I worked on my lemon pound cake while the two of them danced around each other at the stove. Grammy's face when Jason tied on an apron and offered to help was priceless.

Grammy had made a roast with potatoes and carrots. Jason sautéed a mix of greens with onions and spices. Grammy gave him the side-eye as he was cooking but when he handed her the spoon to taste, her face lit up.

"Baby, did you know he could cook, too?"

"Yes, Grammy. I know he can cook."

Her eyes narrowed. "Do you, now? Well, Jason, do you know that my baby can cook circles around me?"

Jason raised a brow and looked at me. "No, ma'am, I was not aware that she possessed that particular skill." I looked at him, blinking innocently.

Her eyes cut from him to me and back again. "Um-hmm. Jayla, you don't have to beat that batter to death. Put the cake in the oven and then go see why I can't get my e-mail to come up on that machine you insisted I have."

Leave Grammy alone with Jason? Where they could exchange all manner of information? Not likely. "Um, Grammy don't you need—"

"Girl, you heard me the first time."

I sighed. "Yes, ma'am." I poured the batter into the cake mold and walked over toward the double oven. I was close enough to Jason to whisper and have him hear me. "You behave out here, Mr. Jericho."

"Or what?" he said teasingly.

"You do not want to find out. You remember, I'm a hood chick. I'm tougher than I look."

"Bring it on, girlie."

I closed the oven door, set the timer, and turned to see Grammy giving me "the look." Feeling twelve years old all over again, I walked over and kissed her cheek. "You love me, Grammy." I walked across the living room to her little home office.

As I booted up her system I heard her start in. "Now, young man, my Jayla is a special girl."

"Grammy!" I called out, mortified.

"Mind your business, young lady," she called back.

"Yes, ma'am. That is the exact word I used to describe her to my best friend. She's special."

He did? I strained to hear more of their conversation.

"Well, then, you're as smart as I think you are. Now, her parents were never worth a damn. It always shamed me that I raised a daughter as flighty and useless as her mother, but I've given that situation up to God. When Janet left Jayla with me, I felt like I'd been given a chance to do it right. And I did. That girl is a product of me getting it right the second time around. Do you understand?"

"Yes, ma'am, I believe I do."

"Her father was little better than a pretty sperm donor and only turns up nowadays when he needs a loan or to pretend he has a paternal gene in his body."

Jason didn't say anything and I felt myself getting a little misty.

"I don't know all the details, but the last few boys she's messed around with ain't been a bit of good either. What I'm saying is . . . my girl is due some goodness. Someone real and someone who sticks. Is that you, or are you just a pretty face?"

"Ma'am, I stick. Given the opportunity, once I'm in. I stay."

"You sound like you've been around a block or two yourself."

"At least once or twice, Ethel Joy."

"Well, all right then, nothing wrong with a little life experience. Helps you recognize landmarks on life's little highways. Now, let's get some food on the table. You do set tables?"

"Like a pro."

"Baby, you can stop straining your ears and come get the napkins."

I dried my eyes with a Kleenex. There was no one like my Grammy. "Yes, ma'am, on my way."

9

Sunday

Sunday night Jason and I were just getting back from Ethel Joy's. She talked us into staying the night (in separate rooms, of course) and going to church with her in the morning. We had brunch, took her to the movies, and played Scrabble. I couldn't remember the last time I had enjoyed myself that well. Great company, great conversation, great food, and all without the spectre of having to be in the office at the crack of dawn the next day.

It was the most relaxed I had been in months, maybe even years. But by the time Jason and I got on the road and headed back to Wicker Park, the sexual tension between us had blossomed again. Stronger than ever.

You could ask me under oath to recount how we got from the parking garage around the corner to the bed inside my condo, but I could not tell you with any sort of clarity. What I can say is within thirty seconds of entering my home, we were both naked. Less than one minute later, my back hit the mattress and Jason was protected and inside of me . . . hot, hard, and deep. He swelled inside of me for a perfect, snug fit.

"Yes," I hissed under my breath. He gave me exactly what I needed exactly when I needed it. No preliminaries, no foreplay this time, just that scorching friction and fullness scraping those sensitive nerve endings. Testing the both of us, I squeezed my internal muscles on his next upstroke.

He grabbed my hips and tilted them upward. "Oh, you want to play?" He ground down on me, hitting my G-spot from the inside and my pearl of pleasure on the outside. Circling his hips out, he slid down and repeated the motion, lifting my hips with the next stroke.

I strained my hips upward and circled tightly in the opposite direction, still squeezing him from the inside. My wetness was everywhere, running down my thighs and his, scenting the air.

"You *do* want to play," he gritted out and slid a finger in between us to press teasing flicks against me.

Not even a full stroke later, I started convulsing. "Jason!"

"God, baby—you are so hot, so responsive, don't close your eyes. I want to watch, I want to see." He slowed his strokes to draw out my climax as he rode me gently, rhythmically.

My eyelids rose slowly and I met his gaze, allowing him to see the helpless passion exploding, the satiation flowing through me. My flagrant satisfaction triggered his response, and with a low groan, he began to come. Our eyes stayed locked on each other as we shuddered through to completion. The moment was electrical, sensual, and very intimate, especially for two people who were strangers three weeks ago.

Startled by the unsettling feeling of rightness, I snapped my eyes closed and turned my head to the side. I was unnerved. I felt exposed and vulnerable, not like myself. Breathing deeply, I struggled to come to terms with the events of the night and the whole weekend. It had been quite the ride. In more ways than one.

Jason rolled off me and lay on his back beside me. We both rested silently, staring at the ceiling. After a moment, he shifted onto his side and ran a finger down the center of my chest, down my stomach before circling my belly button. His hand

rested low on my abdomen, fingers splayed wide. "This is . . ."
He sighed, seemingly at a loss for words. His thumb stroked
lazily back and forth, each time passing deliciously close to the
top of my pouting, swollen lips. Unconsciously, I arched upward into his touch, causing that thumb to graze me in just the
right spot. His thumb paused and pressed once as my juices
flooded his hand.

We both groaned and I turned to look at him. "This is
crazy." I had never responded to anyone like this. Yes, it had
been a while and yes, I was needy, but not even at my most
passionate had I been this open, responsive, and insatiable.

He nodded. "It is crazy, mind-blowing, confusing, exhilarating . . ."

"Addictive and scary," I finished for him, shivering a little
before I rolled away.

He took my hand to stop me from going too far. "Are you
scared, Jayla?"

I looked down at our joined hands before meeting his
eyes. "No, I'm not scared. I guess I'm embarrassed." I dropped
his hand and walked into the bathroom to run a bath. My
body ached in delicious places while my mind raced from
thought to thought. Adding cucumber-melon-scented foam-
ing salts to the water, I turned as I heard Jason come into the
room.

Holding up a cold bottle of water, he said softly, "I'll share
the water if you share the bath." He stood there waiting for my
response.

I liked that in spite of all I had allowed this evening, he still
respected boundaries. It was sweet. And it probably would've
seemed old fashioned if we both weren't standing naked in my
bathroom like longtime lovers even though we were working
with less than a month of acquaintance.

Settling into the large tub, I held out a hand. "Come on in,
the water's fine."

He grinned, passing me the chilled bottle. "You reachin'

for this or for me?" He climbed into the tub and settled in behind me as if we'd done this hundreds of times before.

I took a long drink, set the bottle on the ledge, and leaned back against him with a sigh. The warm water felt great between my legs, soothing the swollen skin.

"Sore, baby?" he murmured, cupping water in his hands and sloughing it over my shoulders. His hands slid down my arms before landing on the top of my thighs.

"Just a little," I responded, letting my head fall back against his shoulder. "It's been a while." As soon as the words came out of my mouth, I sat up and moved toward the middle of the tub. "I can*not* believe I just told you that."

He scooted forward and used his hands on my thighs to nestle me back up against him. "Jayla, relax. What did I say earlier?"

"Uh, which time? When you said, 'Jayla likes it like that?' " One of the hottest things anyone had ever said to me.

He chuckled. "That, too, but seriously—I said I wouldn't judge you and I won't. So stop worrying about it. Stop being embarrassed, just enjoy."

I liked that he was witty, and sexy, and gorgeous. "You can't be real."

"Why do you say that?" His long fingers traced circles on the inside of my thighs and I suddenly found it hard to concentrate on the conversation.

"You seem like a dream," I said lazily, not really censoring myself. "You look like you look, you say those things you say, and the way you make love to me . . ."

"Yes?" His fingers stilled on my skin under the silky water.

I rotated until I was facing him, placing my legs on either side of his hips. "Something about you just makes me want to say things and do things . . . that I never ever do." I leaned forward and licked his lips until he parted them. "You make love like one of my best dreams ever," I whispered against his lips before plunging my tongue inside. I was aggressive with my kiss, diving in and darting my tongue around before nipping at his bottom lip with my teeth.

He wrapped his arms around me and dragged me closer, changing the angle of the kiss and giving me as good as he got. Crossing my legs behind his back, I brushed against his quickly hardening dick. I wrenched my mouth from his and leaned back, breathing deeply. "You kiss like a dream, too."

My chest was rising and falling, my heart beating quickly. Without warning he tilted his head forward and took one of my nipples into his mouth, sucking it to pebble hardness. He traced the tip with his tongue, teasing and nipping with his teeth. Greedily, I held the other one up for his ministrations. "Jason, please." As he switched to lathe the other nipple with his tongue, his hand came up to lightly pinch and twist so both nipples were attended to. Jolts of pleasure shot straight from my nipples along already jangled nerves. My hips started gyrating of their own volition.

Replacing his mouth with his hands, he sucked my bottom lip into his mouth. "You are so responsive, liquid. So damn hot. How are you holding all of this in, baby?"

"I'm never like this, I'm not like this. . . . It's just you," I whispered against his lips.

Reaching underneath the water, I grabbed hold of him and began squeezing rhythmically while sliding my hand up and down.

His hips twitched and he groaned in the back of his throat. Sliding backward, he stood up and pulled me with him. Grabbing two fluffy towels, he wrapped one around his waist before lifting me bodily out of the tub. Securing the towel around me, he carried me out of the bathroom, focusing on the quickest path to my bed.

"Oh my," I said under my breath, literally swept away. It should have been incredibly corny and overdone that he was carrying me to bed. Instead, I thought it was hot and romantic.

He raised a brow, smiled, and looked down at me. "Oh my?"

"I don't believe I've ever actually been carried off to bed before." I glanced up at him through my lashes.

He stopped by the side of the bed. "Jayla likes that?" He set me down on the bed and started drying me off in soft, circular strokes.

I all but purred, "Oh yeah, Jayla likes that." Leaning back, I took a second to appreciate the sight of him. Sculpted torso with arm muscles rippling as he leaned forward to tend to me. My glance fell lower and I saw the rigid outline of him at full attention, tenting the towel. My mouth went dry before watering. Reaching up, I slid my hands up his damp abdomen, trailing up over his pectorals, feeling across his shoulders, down his arms, and back up.

He paused and took a deep breath. "That's nice."

"Jason likes that?" I whispered.

His gorgeous lips quirked upward. "Jason likes that."

"You're really going to like this then. . . ." I put my hands behind his neck and pulled him down, twisting and angling so he was lying back on the bed with his legs dangling off the side. I unwrapped the towel like a child with a gift on Christmas morning, eyes sparkling, and breathless with anticipation. I reached down and took him in my hands, my eyes floating up to meet his eyes, which had darkened to an almost forest green color. Trailing my fingers up and down the shaft, I didn't wait another moment before leaning down and taking him in my mouth. We both groaned in appreciation.

I alternated techniques, taking him deep into my throat with slow strokes before squeezing his base with my hand as I licked and flicked my tongue up the length, following with a quick nibble at the tip before starting the whole process over again.

"Jesus, Jayla."

"Hmm." I paused teasingly. "You want me to stop?"

Wordlessly, he reached down, placed his hand on the top of my head, and urged me back to task. I laughed quietly before sucking him back deep. As I pumped and sucked, his hips rose up to meet me and his quiet sighs became words of pleading.

"That is so good, Jayla, hmm—don't stop, baby."

The more he talked, the faster I went and the hotter I became.

"God yes, just like that," he growled. "You suck me just . . . like . . . that."

Giving him so much pleasure increased my own and I felt my body quickening again. At the same time, he reached down and tweaked my nipples with his long fingers. His fingers and my mouth echoed the same frantic rhythm and within moments he began to come. The thick fluid sliding down my throat triggered my own climax and I sucked him harder and deeper as I rode the sensation.

"Jayla," he screamed as I determinedly sucked every last bit of fluid from him. He continued to shudder with aftershocks as I held him in my mouth. Finally, he reached under my arms and lifted me off of him. "Lord, woman, you could kill a man like that."

I curled up next to him. "You'd die happy."

He kissed the top of my head and my eyes drifted shut for just a second.

10

Back at Work

My eyes opened like a déjà vu. I registered a few things at once: It was very light outside, I was naked and neatly tucked into my bed, and the scent of chocolate and coffee was in the air. In other words, not a normal morning. I sat up and long-neglected muscles twanged in symphony to remind me of my extended weekend's activities.

Monday, Jason and I had lounged around his house watching old movies before coming back to my place. Jason had spent the night teaching me things about my body that I had never known before and was determined never to forget. We had had another go-round in the bathtub and it was quickly becoming one of my favorite ways to get clean and be dirty all at the same time.

With a deep sigh, I realized it was Tuesday morning and time to get back to reality.

"Jason?" I called out to no response. Turning to my bedside table, I saw an insulated travel mug from the coffeehouse with a note propped up in front of it. Bold masculine handwriting filled the small sheet.

"Jayla, you looked so sweet sleeping; I didn't want to wake you. Brought you some of my special white mocha, hop-

*ing after the past few days you haven't had your fill. Thank
you for an incredible weekend. See you soon, Jason."*

I read the note a few more times as an increasingly large
smile spread across my face. He'd underlined "incredible" three
times. Classy note from a classy guy, I thought. I flicked open
the lid on the coffee mug and moaned . . . instant flashback.
Cool green eyes smiling into mine, hot body pressed against
mine, the thick feeling of fullness. Shaking my head, I took a
sip. It was perfect, of course. And no, even after the past few
nights, I had not gotten my fill. Not of this coffee or of Jason
Jericho. I sat savoring the flavors exploding on my tongue and
the memory reel playing in my head until my eyes fell on the
clock.

Choking on my mocha I blinked, squeezed my eyes shut,
and blinked them open again—8:15? I couldn't even think of
the last time I wasn't at work by 7:30. I shook my head as if
clearing it from a dream and headed into the bathroom with
my coffee in hand. I saw that the bathtub had been drained
and the towels from last night folded and stacked neatly on the
counter. Jason wasn't a dream but he was definitely too good
to be true.

Jetting into work over an hour and a half later than usual
had its benefits: I was so far behind schedule that I had very little time to dwell on my evening. Trying to play catch-up all
morning, Kim had no time to do more than spend odd moments eyeing me suspiciously. At close to one o'clock, she
came in with two salads and bottled tea. Closing the door behind her, she waited until we were situated at my small conference table to start the interrogation.

"Okay, what's up?"

Innocently I blinked at her as I spritzed vinaigrette dressing over the spinach leaves. "What?"

Her eyes narrowed. "You were two hours late, you've been

smiling all day, your hair is fluffy, and your eyes are shiny. . . . What's up?"

I smiled. "I finally got a good night's rest."

She waved her fork at me. "That's not it." Popping the top on her peach tea, she stared harder at me.

"Seriously Kim, I really just got—"

"Laid!" she screamed out.

I turned bright red. "Shhh! Kim! Stop—"

"That's it!" She hopped up like she'd won the lottery and started dancing around the office. "Oh my God! It all makes sense; you come floating in all smiley and stress free. Yes, finally got some. And from the looks of you it was good, too, girl. Um, um, um. Wasn't it, girl? Tell me everything. Who was he, how was he? What did he look like? How'd you hook up? Oh girl, ended your drought—high five!" She held her hand out.

Through the glass panel, I could see co-workers glancing in. "Kim," I hissed, "if you put your hand down and quit making a scene, I might answer a question or two!"

She held her hand closer. "Just one little 'got my groove back' high five?"

I sighed and laughed. "Fine, whatever." I slapped palms with her. "Now will you sit down?"

Kim sat down meekly before grinning triumphantly. "You go, girl; okay—now dish!"

Smiling a little dreamily I closed my eyes and thought about him. "It was a guy I met at the coffee shop. He was tall . . . ."

"With the body of Adonis, A-Rod kinda gorgeous, guys wanna be him, girls wanna be with him type of vibe?" she said in an awed-filled voice.

I frowned at the dead-on description and opened my eyes. "Yeah—but how did you know?"

She pointed out toward the cubicles. "Your coffee-man cometh . . . bearing gifts."

My head swiveled. Sure enough, Jason was walking up and

down the aisles with some of his staff, handing out coffee sam-
ples and muffins while chatting up my co-workers. And yes, he
charmed men and women alike. I pushed my chair back and
stood up. Kim had already gone to the door and swung it open
to get a better look.

He was in perfectly tailored khakis with a polo shirt adver-
tising the coffee shop logo, an outfit that would appear ordi-
nary on most other men. He smiled at my executive vice
president, laughing at what I'm sure was a completely lame
joke. I stepped into the doorway as he glanced in my direction.
He stopped talking in midsentence. Muttering something to
his staff, he handed over the tray of coffee he was carrying and
headed my way, purposefully.

"Oh my," I mouthed and saw his lips quirk upward in response.

Our eyes locked as he moved toward me and I was well
aware of the crackling electricity bouncing between me and
him. Everyone in the office was watching in interested silence
as he approached. His eyes raked down my body, then back up.
I had on a simple navy safari-style dress that buttoned down
the front with dark brown sling-back pumps. The outfit that
had seemed simple and professional a few hours ago now felt
sexy and amazingly "easy access" if the look in his eyes meant
anything at all. He raised his eyes back up to mine and gave the
smile that I now knew meant, "It's about to be on."

I froze completely, my breath catching in my throat. My
mind raced in a million different directions. What was he doing
here? Could I clear my calendar and take him home with me
RIGHT NOW? How long would it take to get there? How
soon could I press my naked body back up against his? How
soon until we made each other scream again?

I shifted uncomfortably with the now-familiar humidity in
my panties that he caused effortlessly. He was close enough to
see my telltale shift and his eyes did that heating-up sizzle
thing that they do.

"Damn, girl!" Kim said from beside me.

I jumped a little, having completely forgotten she or anyone else existed. I took my eyes off of Jason long enough to catch a breath and send her a glance. "Close your mouth, Kim."

"But, but—damn, girl!"

He was close enough to hear so I just nudged her in the ribs with one arm while reaching out for Jason with the other. "Hey you," I said, proud of my casual, cool chick voice. No need to advertise that this man had given me seven orgasms in one night. Or was it eight?

"Jayla," he said, taking my hand in his, his voice triggering all sorts of memories. Him slamming into me from the back, holding my legs open on the coffeehouse countertop, licking the dripping parts of me like a lollipop. He squeezed my hand in an I-know-what-you're-thinking way before turning to Kim.

"Oh, uh—Kim, this is Jason. Jason, Kim—my associate manager."

"Great to meet you, Kim. Beautiful name." He dropped my hand to shake hers as she practically bounced up and down with exuberance, looking from him to me and back again.

"Jason, so glad to meet you! So tell me—"

"Thanks, Kim. I'll finish up with you later." Practically shoving her out, I pulled him into the office and shut the door, locking it behind me. As I turned I noticed how many people were "casually" passing by the side of my office with the glass panel. Walking over, I pulled the privacy screens down before swiveling around.

"Hello, Jason." I smiled.

"Hi, Jayla."

"So this is a surprise," I said, still trying to play it cool as I took a step or two toward him.

He matched my steps with his own. "A good one, I hope."

Standing less than a breath from each other, I smiled up at him. "I think so."

Sliding his hand behind my neck, he leaned down and kissed me. Gently at first with lips closed until I sighed and wrapped my arms around his neck. With that signal, his tongue stroked out in a bold sliding rhythm that had me swallowing a moan and stepping back.

"So . . ." I breathed out.

"I didn't want to wait to see you. I had to leave early this morning. I really didn't want the morning-after, note-on-the-pillow vibe to linger so I thought I'd—"

"Track me down and disrupt my day?" I said with a smile so he knew I wasn't angry.

"Exactly. How am I doing?" He reached out and tucked a wayward strand of hair behind my ear.

My eyes threatened to close and I forced them open, giving him a decidedly "melty" look. "You can't touch me like that here."

"No?" he said softly, his hand drifting down my shoulder to rest above my heart. "Beating so fast, Jayla? Embarrassed again?"

I took a step back and fashioned a glare at him. "Hey, do I come to your workplace and make you want to get naked?" Realizing I had done just that, I blushed as he started laughing. "Okay, bad question—but you know what I mean."

He nodded. "Yes, you have to separate buttoned-up 'professional Jayla' from 'riding on my tongue begging for more Jayla.' " His eyes darkened in remembrance as he finished talking.

I leaned forward to rest my head on his chest. "You aren't helping."

He reached his hand down under my hem and slid his hand upward, shifting my panties to the side and sliding two fingers into my slit. He groaned. "You are soaking wet."

"You make me that way," I whispered, traced my fingers across his hardness currently twitching in his pants. *Just like that, less than two minutes and we've gone from zero to sixty.*

He flicked his thumb across me and I pressed my mouth into his shirt to keep from crying out. "Do you want me to make you come real quick?" he whispered in my ear, his thumb now moving in quick circles. His lips found a crazy-sensitive spot on my neck and he nuzzled it gently. My breath hitched as I felt more liquid gush out over his hand. "You only have to say the words, Jayla."

Here I was, at work—not ten feet from my staff and supervisors—and for the first time in a long time, my job was not the most important thing in my world. Five days ago, I hadn't known anything about this man, yet right this second he and what he could do were the only things that mattered. "Oh God, do it."

"What do you want me to do, baby?" he teased, sliding his middle finger inside of me.

"Do it, Jason. Make me come," I begged.

His thumb pressed once, twice on my sensitized button while his middle finger circled, hitting all the angles inside my walls.

"Yes!" I bit out before bringing his lips to mine as the orgasm slammed into me. He swallowed my cries as he kept up the pressure to let me ride out the pleasure as long as possible. Finally, I lifted my head and gasped for breath. "You're going to be the death of me," I said as he withdrew his hand. I grabbed some Kleenex and bottled water from the desk.

As I cleaned off his hand, he smiled. "But you'd die happy."

I smiled before noticing his still-impressive erection straining against the zipper. "Oh Jason, I'm so sorry. What about you?"

He shrugged. "You can make it up to me tonight."

I looked up. "What's tonight?"

"That's actually what I came by for," he grinned ruefully. "To ask you out on a 'real date.' Got a little sidetracked."

"Me, too." I grinned back. "Sure, did you have something in mind?"

"Thought I'd take you to a great little jazz club/martini bar that I know."

Something in his tone caught my attention. "Just happen to know a spot, do you?"

He shrugged modestly. "Okay, I own it—will you come with me?"

As if I could say no to anything he suggested. "Sure, why not? What's your specialty martini?"

He smiled. "White Mochatini."

Of course it was. "How can I refuse?"

"I really don't know," he said with a smile. "Pick you up at eight?"

"I'll be ready."

11

Date Night

Jason had been more physically and emotionally intimate with this woman in the last few days than he had been with anyone else in his life . . . ever. But he found himself unaccountably nervous as he stood outside her door. He had changed clothes three times, settling on a lightweight pair of flat-front pants and a mint green shirt (he was just vain enough to know it matched his eyes) and adding a perfectly tailored Italian silk jacket in an icy white color.

"It's just a date," he told himself. But he had the feeling that so much more was riding on this evening and he wanted it to be perfect. "Okay, Jericho—pull it together." He rang the doorbell.

Jayla swung open the door and his jaw dropped. Jayla had pulled out all the stops this evening. She was in a glittery skintight silver dress that showed off every asset she possessed . . . and those were considerable. Her hair was partially pinned up so that her neck was exposed, but wavy strands escaped here and there to tease against her skin. She was in sky-high silver shoes and smelled like an entire field of flowers. "Hi, Jason," she said with a sweet smile. "Do you want to come in for a minute?"

"Baby, the way you are looking . . . if I come in, we're not leaving tonight. Maybe for the rest of the week."

"Oh!" She turned around in a circle. "Jason like?"

"A lot. A whole lot. Grab your purse, woman, we're out of here."

Fifteen minutes later, he walked into the Gold Coast Martini Lounge with Jayla on his arm. He watched with pride as she looked around in admiration. "Okay, Jason, how many of these do you own?" She glanced at him over her shoulder.

"My partner, Rick, and I own four of these," Jason admitted.

She nodded slowly. "Do I even want to ask what else you own?"

"I'll tell you if you're dying to know, but I thought you might like this artist and want to enjoy the music tonight." He led her over to a booth near the stage but still to the side enough so they were semisecluded.

As they sat down, a waitress dressed all in black approached the table. "Hi, Mr. Jason," the young woman said. "Mr. Rick did not tell us you were coming in. What can I get you and your pretty lady?"

"The pretty lady will have the house martini and I'll have sparkling water. Thanks, Natasha."

"Do you want me to tell Rick you're here?"

Jason shrugged. "He'll be on the floor soon enough. No need to make a special announcement."

Jayla finished looking around. "This is lovely, Jason, you must be very proud of what you've built."

Looking at it through her eyes, he was. "Rick and I have done all right for ourselves."

"So this Rick . . . ?"

"Enrique Santos. He's been my closest friend since high school. He's also my business partner. So far it works."

Natasha brought the drinks back and Jayla smiled at her.

"That was fast." She raised the glass and took a sip. Her eyes widened. "Jason!"

Jason blinked innocently. "Yes?"

"Are you trying to get me drunk? When a drink tastes this smooth, it's got to be pure alcohol. What is in this?"

"Godiva White Chocolate Liqueur, Kahlua, vanilla vodka, and cinnamon schnapps."

"And you're drinking sparkling water?"

"Designated driver. I'm trying to be a responsible citizen and all."

Jayla leaned toward Jason after taking another deep sip. "Are you really?"

"Really what?"

"Trying to be a responsible citizen this evening?" Her voice turned husky and she slid her hand along his thigh.

"Maybe not." He rested his hand on her leg and slid upward. Just then, the lights dimmed and a voice came over the speaker system.

"The Gold Coast Martini Lounge is proud to present P.J. Morton and his band! Show him some love, Chicago!"

Jayla's mouth fell open. "What?! Did I tell you how much I love this guy?"

"It's your ringtone, it's on repeat on your iPod, and you've been humming songs from his latest album for four days straight. I got the message."

Jayla took Jason's jaw in her hand and turned his face toward hers. She placed a slow, seriously sensual kiss on his lips before leaning back. "You are too good to be true."

"As long as you think so."

They turned as the artist bounded onto the stage. For the next hour and a half, they enjoyed the show; singing along, getting up to dance once or twice, and clapping or swaying along to the well-played music.

When the show ended, they went backstage to meet the

artist. Jayla was still smiling and shaking her head fifteen minutes later as they headed back out front. Jason led her to the
door when they were stopped by a good-looking gentleman
with wavy black hair and blue eyes.

"Were you leaving without saying hello?" Rick asked
Jason.

Jason slapped his back. "Truthfully, I forgot all about you."
He turned back toward Jayla. "Jayla, my business partner, Rick.
Rick, this is Jayla."

Rick shook her hand and exchanged pleasantries, looking
from her to Jason and back again. "Wait a minute! Is this the
girl from the coffee shop?"

Jayla raised a brow and shot Jason a look.

Jason sent a warning glance Rick's way. "This is the young
lady that I met in the coffee shop, yes."

"So I guess I owe you five hundred dollars, you suave son
of a gun," Rick said.

"I beg your pardon?" Jayla asked.

"It's not what you think," Jason told Jayla and tugged her
toward the door. "Rick, you can keep it. Classy as ever, I see."

When they got to the car, Jason turned to Jayla. "Let me
explain."

"Please do."

"When you sent me home after that night in the park I
told Rick that instead of chasing you, I was going to wait until
you came to me. He bet me five hundred dollars that you
wouldn't."

"Huh. Pretty sure of yourself, were you?"

"Jayla, I wasn't sure. I was hopeful and I never took a
dime."

"Because I'm not about the game-playing."

"Neither am I, I completely understand. Rick can be a
thoughtless idiot sometimes."

"That was the only bet?"

"It wasn't really even a bet, but yes, that was it. Why?"

"I wondered if you'd bet him how many times we'd be together in a five-day period."

Jason smiled. "I never would have imagined. Are we going for a record?"

Jayla smiled back. "Take me home and let's find out."

12

All Falls Down

I woke at four in the morning in full freak-out mode. I had the overwhelming feeling that things were moving too fast and I was in over my head. Instead of being on a high from the amazing night Jason and I had, I was scared. Nothing this good could last, not in my world anyway.

I slid out of Jason's huge bed and pulled on a robe. Glancing over to make sure he was still asleep, I tiptoed upstairs to the media room. Clicking on the television for background noise, I allowed my thoughts to run free. This whole semi-sorta relationship was a disaster waiting to happen. Jason and I were from different worlds and I was not going to wait around like an idiot for the day that he figured that out. I was a woman who knew when to cut her losses.

Already it gave me physical pain to think of not having this man around. How much worse would it be one, four, six months from now? I curled into a ball with my head on my knees. My head and my heart hurt.

That's how Jason found me an hour later. "Whatcha doing?" he asked softly, sitting down next to me.

"Just thinking," I said in a subdued voice.

"Uh-oh. More like overthinking, unless I mess my guess. What's up?"

There was no easy way to do it, I just had to say it plainly. "Jason, I don't think I can see you anymore."

"You don't think you can or you're not going to?"

"Both."

"Is this about the bet, because I swear I never took a dime. It was Rick's idea of a joke."

"I know. I got that. It's not about the bet. I just can't be with you."

"Because?"

"I can't figure out what you're doing with me. And I can't figure out what's wrong with you, and the whole situation is destined to blow up in my face."

"You don't want to see me anymore because there's nothing wrong with me?"

"You're a little too good to be true. I can't trust it."

"You don't trust me?"

"I don't trust *me*. My instincts when it comes to men suck and I don't have it in me to be disappointed and hurt like that again."

"So you'd rather both of us be hurt and disappointed now than later. Is that what you're saying?"

"It sounds crazy put like that but that's what I'm saying."

"Well, that's an argument against which I have no defense. I mean, I don't know what's going to happen in the future, but right now we're good, right?"

"We're perfect."

"And that's a bad thing?"

"It's a bad thing for me. I don't trust perfection; it doesn't exist in my world."

"I'm not a perfect man: I don't always do or say the right things. It takes me a while to lose my temper but when I do, I hold a grudge. I don't fold my clothes when they come out of the dryer. I squeeze the toothpaste from the middle of the tube. C'mon, woman, I had sex with you in the middle of my business. Clearly I'm a degenerate sex fiend, and those are only the flaws I can think of in the thirty seconds since you said you're planning to kick me to the curb."

In spite of myself, I laughed. "Even that answer was perfect."

"What can I say, what can I do? I think we have the possibility of something really special here. If there's something I can say to change your mind, give me a hint and I'll figure it out."

"Jason, it's not you. It's me." I put my hand on his arm when he rolled his eyes. "Wait, I know that sounded completely lame, but let me explain."

"Please give me something better than that. You owe me at the very least something better than that."

So I gave him brutal honesty. "I'm just terrified. It's my phobia. You know my parents bailed on me, every man I've ever cared about . . . I just can't experience that again. Please understand."

"I'm trying, but please listen to it from my point of view. You're telling me that because I'm too good to you, you need to leave me before I leave you and there's nothing I can say to change your mind. What am I supposed to do with that? The only thing that will allay your fears is giving us more time, but you won't do it, worrying that more time will just make it hurt more later. It's a catch-22. You need to know me to trust me, but you won't allow yourself to get to know me in case you start trusting me."

"Don't get angry."

"Well, that's the one you've asked me that I can't do. I am angry. I know I didn't have the same hell growing up that you did, but I have worked my ass off for everything I ever got, Jayla. My life hasn't been all rainbows and unicorns. And I've never done anything to make you think I won't be good to you. Good *for* you. So yeah, I'm angry. I'm angry that you are ruining this before we even get started."

"I'm trying to save both of us some heartache down the line. You don't even know me well enough to know if I'm good for you. I'd rather cut my losses here before we get in too deep."

"Well, one thing you didn't factor into your formula? I'm already in. I've made plans in my mind and they include you."

"How is that even possible for you to be that sure?"

"Because I'm a grown-up. I know what I want. And until this moment, I thought it was you."

"Oh, Jason."

"I never suspected that you could be cruel."

"I never meant to be cruel."

"And yet here we are. I distinctly remember you telling me that you weren't a heartbreaker. This feels pretty close. But this is your decision, I'll respect it. One I think you'll come to really regret. I hope you change your mind and I hope you do it soon."

"I don't think I will, Jason."

"You know where to find me when you do. I'll call a cab to take you home."

Those were his last words before he walked out, letting the door slam behind him. I had either just saved myself a lot of grief in the long run or made the stupidest mistake in my life.

13

Convince Me

Six weeks later, I had decided—or rather, Celeste, Kim, and Grammy had forced me to decide—it was the biggest mistake of my life. Good Lord, what was wrong with me? I'd had an opportunity to build something with a man who took me at face value, flaky phobias and all, and I ran. As Grammy said, "Ran like a scared chicken with no head and no good damn sense."

She was right. It was a cowardly thing to do. Jason had showed no indication that he was anything like my father or Joseph yet I'd lumped him in with them and hadn't even given him a chance.

I was ready to admit my idiocy, but I wasn't sure how to go about it. I'd been dodging the coffee shop for weeks and was in serious mocha withdrawal to boot. I'd thrown myself back into work and we'd completed our projections. I came up with innovative cost-cutting techniques that would garner a larger profit margin for the next eighteen months. We were so far ahead of the workload that the entire department was working regular forty-hour weeks. My vice president was giddy. I was depressed.

Overall, life sucked. I couldn't imagine it getting any worse.

And then the phone rang. It was eleven o'clock on a Thursday night; I couldn't imagine who it could be. I glanced at the caller ID. It was LuAnn. Heart racing, I snatched up the phone.

"Hey, LuAnn. What's wrong?"

"It's Ethel Joy, baby. She slipped getting out of the tub and it gave her a little fright."

"Speak medicine to me, LuAnn. How bad and where is she?"

"Nothing broken, sprained hip, but she's having irregular heartbeats. They are worried that this could trigger a lupus flare-up. She's at Palatine Heart Center. She's asking for you."

"Oh Jesus, oh Jesus. Okay. Okay. I'm coming." I slammed down the phone and took two shaky breaths. "Tears won't solve da-da right now," I whispered to myself, repeating a line Grammy had said to me many times. I pulled it together and headed into the closet. It was downright cold outside so I put on wool pants, a thick sweater, and boots. I contemplated whether my car, an Acura that I rarely drove, had any gas in it. Looking down I noticed my hands were shaking. Not good. I snatched back up the phone and dialed a number.

Celeste answered on the first ring. "What's up? Did you go get the Mocha Man back?"

"Celeste, it's Grammy."

"I'll be there in five. Put on your coat and meet me out front."

True to her word, Celeste pulled up in front of the building in six minutes. I filled her in on Grammy's condition on the way out there. Even though she had the pedal damn near floored, it seemed to take forever to get there.

We found the closest visitor parking to the Cardiac Unit entrance sign and ran inside. We went up three floors and I located the desk. "Ethel Joy Sweatt?"

"Visiting hours are over."

The look that came over my face told the charge nurse all

she needed to know. "She's in room 412, but she's already over the limit on visitors. You're going to have to boot someone out if you want in."

"Fine," I said shortly and headed in the direction she pointed. Halfway down the hall I heard Grammy's laughter followed by masculine laughter. I exchanged a confused and relieved glance with Celeste and we picked up the pace.

Looking inside room 412, I saw Grammy propped up with a huge smile on her face. On the far side of the room sat LuAnn. At the foot of the bed stood Rick and right by her side, holding her hand and sharing a smile, was Jason.

Celeste nudged me forward. "I guess she's okay and in good company."

"Gram?" I said as I stepped into the room. My eyes scanned the monitors and then her form. If she was a cardiac patient, she was the healthiest-looking one I'd ever seen. Overwhelmed with relief, I flung myself next to her and started weeping. "Gram, you can't scare me like this, you're all I have." I kissed her cheek.

Celeste rounded up LuAnn and Rick and they stepped into the hallway, closing the door behind them. Jason stayed, holding my grandmother's hand. She patted my head. "Aw baby, now don't carry on so. Grammy ain't going nowhere quite yet, but you know what?"

"What?" I sniffled.

"I'm not all you have if you'd just give my friend a real chance."

I squinted up at Jason. "Hey."

"Hey, you. You want me to leave?"

I got up and walked around the bed and flung myself at Jason to commence weeping all over again. "No, I don't want you to leave. I never wanted you to leave. I'm just stupid."

He wrapped his arms around me and backed up to sit on the couch. He pulled me onto his lap and rocked me back and forth comfortingly. "Don't cry, baby, I'm right here. We're both right here."

"Now see, this right here does my heart good," Grammy said from her bed.

"Gram, are you sure you're all right?"

"Girl, I bumped my hip and got panicky. These folks just want to take a look at me overnight. I'll be back to whipping you two at Scrabble by the weekend, provided you don't go getting stupid again. In my day, we didn't let fine men get away. No, ma'am. We knew how to trap 'em and keep 'em. And there are damn sure better things to do in a man's arms than cry. . . . I know that."

"Grammy!"

She cackled. "What? I'm old, I'm not dead. Now you two get on out of here and let me get my beauty rest. I expect to see both of you tomorrow evening to spring me from this joint. The both of you, together. You hear me, Jayla Faye?"

"Jayla Faye?" Jason laughed.

I climbed off his lap and gave Ethel Joy a kiss. "You're evil, but I love you, grandmother. If Jason doesn't run for the hills, we'll be back tomorrow."

"Jason sticks, Jayla Faye," Jason said, leaning down to give Ethel Joy a kiss of his own.

"Get on, the two of you. Go on 'head, now."

Jason and I stepped into the hallway, hands clasped firmly together. LuAnn gave me a hug and went back inside the room. Celeste put her hands on her hips and gave Rick the look. "Jayla, I'll give this one a ride back to the city so you and Jason can talk."

"Uh-oh," Jason and I said at the same time at the thought of those two hooking up.

They walked off and Jason stood with me in the middle of the hallway. I sighed. I was exhausted. "You want to talk?"

"Maybe later. You look like you could use a cup of coffee."

I leaned against him. "I really could. I have missed my mocha."

"Did you know we have a shop here in Palatine?"

"You wouldn't happen to have the keys on you, would you?"

He smiled. "As a matter of fact . . ."

I smiled back. "You are so good to me."

"I'm about to be a lot better."

"Are we still talking about the coffee?"

"Whatever you'd like. One promise, though?"

"Okay."

"Don't break my heart again."

"I wouldn't dare. A man with your skills?"

"Are you talking about the coffee?"

I whispered in his ear. "Take me to the shop and find out."

"You're going to have to convince me."

"I'll do my very best."

We walked down the hallway hand in hand.

Wanted: You

Lutishia Lovely

Lois Edwards's jaw dropped, as did the paper from her hand. She surreptitiously looked around, as if her mother was lurking in the office and would catch and then chide her for reading porn. There's no other way to describe the contents of the note she'd hastily thrown on her desk, the note that even now silently taunted her to be picked up and read again.

Lois looked at the clock: 8:45. She always came in to work early, especially on Mondays. Her boss, whose weekend mail she was opening and to whom the letter was addressed, wouldn't be in until 9:00, at the earliest. There was no one else around. Her heartbeat quickened as she picked up the paper and read the letter again:

> *Dear Chaz:*
> *You don't know me, well, not really. But that's nei-ther here nor there when it comes to why I'm writing.*
> *I'm writing because, simply put, I can't get you out of my mind. This morning, while in the shower, I imag-ined you there with me, hard and naked. I imagined your thick shaft pulsating inside me, envisioned taking you full into my mouth. The water ran all over my body, and I imagined each drop was your tongue. I fingered*

my nipples, my nub, but in my mind, it was your hands that touched me. Chaz Covington, I want you. There, I've said it. And I won't take it back. One of these days, maybe my dream will come true.
Signed, Yours

Lois crumpled the paper and threw it into the trash. "That's where you belong," she hissed under her breath, rubbing her hands against her slacks as if the words she'd read had soiled them. *Mr. Covington doesn't need to know about this.* With resolve, she continued opening mail.

Lois had worked for Chaz Covington, the handsome, prominent thirty-nine-year-old attorney representing the poor and downtrodden in the state of Illinois, for two years. Her admiration bordered on idolatry, and where Chaz was concerned, she was loyal to a fault. He was constantly fending off interested females and Lois counted protecting him from these predators one of her duties—along with typing, filing, and opening mail. "They ought to be ashamed," she muttered, unaware of her facial expression or that she'd spoken out loud.

"That frown is fierce, girlfriend. Must have been some weekend."

Lois jumped. She hadn't heard her co-worker come in. "Hi, Gina." *Please keep walking. You're the last person I feel like talking to right now.*

"So what happened? Bad date? Oh, but wait. I forgot. You don't date." Gina Perez obviously didn't get the telepathically sent "keep it moving" message. She perched her perfectly round, silk-covered derriere on the edge of Lois's desk, her flawlessly made-up face still beautiful despite the smirk.

"I'm fine, just busy. You know how Mondays are." Lois underscored this statement and discouraged further conversation by turning on the shredder and feeding a pile of junk mail into the device. While she watched the paper being cut into miniscule pieces, she thought of the letter that needed to be obliterated as well.

"I know who'll put a smile on your face," Gina whispered conspiratorially, nodding in the direction of Chaz's office. "And one of these days . . . I'd like to put a smile on his." She slid off Lois's desk and continued down the hall, her waist-length hair swaying from side to side, much like her hips.

Lois's eyes narrowed as she watched Gina sashay to the break room, looking as if she'd slid off a page in a fashion magazine. Her thick ebony hair glistened with dark auburn high-lights, complementing the tangerine-colored suit that Lois felt fit much too snugly for the workplace. *And how does she walk in those heels?* One step in what she assumed were four-inch stilet-tos, and Lois knew she would keel right over. When she'd dressed for work this morning, Lois felt that her pink, polka-dotted, button-down blouse—a nod to the arrival of spring and the unseasonably high seventy-degree March morning—navy slacks, and sensible loafers were quite adequate. But with the whiff of Gina's floral perfume still tickling her nose, she now felt unfeminine, and underdressed.

Lois's eyes followed Gina until she'd turned the corner. She thought of the note lying in the bottom of the trash can, and thought that someone like Gina, who exuded sex appeal along with tons of confidence, could write something like that. Something bodacious and crass and . . . nasty. Her co-worker was always talking about men and Lois's boss was the man Gina talked about the most. "I'd do him in a heartbeat," she regularly admitted. Lois's face showed her disgust. She believed she'd just read exactly how Gina would "do" him.

After fishing the note from the wastebasket, Lois hurried to the restroom. *I'll flush it down the toilet . . . make sure no one else reads it.* Passing the mirror on the way to a stall, she saw her reflection and stopped.

She stepped toward the glass, put a hand to her face. Her

fingers idly stroked the smooth tanned skin, thin lips, and puffy cheeks. She stepped back, cocked her head, and saw breasts that were too small and hips that were too big. *I'm average-looking,* she concluded, before going into a stall and flushing the note. "Average, but decent," she whispered, watching the torn paper pieces swirl around and go down the toilet. *And probably the only thirty-one-year-old virgin in Chicago.* A virgin whose body now shivered from the impact of the words contained in the note she'd just destroyed.

2

Personal-injury attorney Chaz Covington was a household name. His television commercials were legendary: actual testimonies from rags-to-riches clients whose cases he'd won, followed by an impeccably dressed, confident-looking Chaz delivering the tagline straight into the camera: *If you don't get paid, I don't get paid.* Today, Chaz entered the office wearing a tailored navy suit, expensive cologne, and an award-winning smile.

"Good morning, boss," Gina said, not even trying to hide her lust.

"Good morning, Gina," Chaz replied, with a wink:

"Good morning, Mr. Covington." Lois's face was somber as she handed Chaz his mail. "I'll get your coffee."

"Make it green tea," Chaz replied. When Lois looked questioningly in his direction—because she couldn't look him in the eye—he added, "Trying to cut down on the caffeine." Chaz took a step toward his office and then turned around. "Are you all right, Lois?"

"Uh, sure, Mr. Covington. Why do you ask?"

Because you can't look at me, is what he thought. "Just checking," is what he said, accompanied by his signature killer smile.

He looked intently at Lois another moment. "On second thought, I'll skip the tea for now. Come into my office and give me today's schedule."

Lois grabbed her iPad and followed Chaz into his office, noting a broad back and long legs that supported a six-foot-two-inch, mocha-colored frame. She took deep breaths to still her pounding heart and tried to put a casual look on her face, to act as if it was just another Monday—business as usual. A difficult task, since every time she looked at Chaz, she saw the acts described in the letter she'd destroyed.

"What are we looking at so far?" Chaz asked. Always the multitasker, he turned on his computer and checked e-mails while listening.

"You have two conference calls and a Skype meeting with the litigator for the Jimenez case," Lois began, forcing herself to focus on the task at hand. "The interview with Roy Jones is scheduled for one o'clock this afternoon—"

"Police-chase victim, correct?" Chaz scrolled through his e-mails, deleting several without opening them.

"Yes," Lois answered. "And then there's the celebratory meeting with Mrs. Smith at three o'clock." Delicia Smith had been severely injured due to a machine malfunction at the plastics manufacturing company where she'd worked. She'd lost the use of her left hand, but gained two and a half million dollars.

"Did you order the champagne?" Chaz clicked on another e-mail, his finger hovering over the DELETE button as he scanned its contents. "What the . . ." Chaz sat up and straightened an already perfectly aligned designer tie.

Lois's heart raced. *Did the person who sent the nasty letter e-mail him, too?* The ringing office phone interrupted her thoughts. She reached over and picked up the call from Chaz's desk. "Covington Law Offices, this is Lois. How may I help you?" She paused. "One moment, please." Lois put the call on hold. "It's Jennifer."

At the mention of his ex-wife, a light frown scampered across Chaz's face. He'd just seen her yesterday, when he dropped off their children. *What does she want now?* He nodded curtly at Lois, who gave him the phone.

Soon, Chaz's one-sided conversation was drowned out by Lois's thoughts. *It could be Jennifer who sent it. Everybody knows she's still in love with him.* Lois had never cared for Chaz's ex-wife, and never bought the demure persona Jennifer tried to convey. She knew the truth: that at one time Jennifer Lawton Covington had been a "hostess" at a gentlemen's club. That's how she'd met Chaz. Lois believed that "ho" may have been a more accurate description, even though, being the church-going person that she was, she tried not to judge. Chaz's second line began blinking, and Lois hurried to her desk to answer the call.

"Elizabeth Stein for Chaz Covington," Liz's assistant chirped into the phone.

"Hi, Melanie," Lois answered, rolling her eyes. Elizabeth Owens Stein was the pampered and prideful daughter of Chicago real estate mogul Kenneth Owens. Stunningly beautiful, with bountiful blonde hair, turquoise blue eyes, and a model's physique, she and Chaz had met at a charity event a year ago. She'd been trying to make herself a permanent fixture in his life ever since. "Mr. Covington is on the other line."

"Hold on a moment." After Melanie relayed this information to her boss, Elizabeth came on the line.

"Tell him it's me," Elizabeth said with authority.

I'd rather not. "Hello, Mrs. Stein." Lois almost choked on the respectful greeting. "Mr. Covington is on an important call at the moment. Is there some way I can help you, or a message I can relay?"

"Look, you simpleton, the only thing you can do for me is get your boss on the phone. Now!"

"If you can wait one moment, Mrs. . . ." The sound of a click in her ear told Lois that Elizabeth had hung up the phone. Lois rushed back into Chaz's office, sure that his cell phone would ring within seconds. She was right.

"Jen, I need to run." Chaz ended the call on the office line and reached for his cell at the same time. He looked at the number, waited a beat, and then answered. "Hey, beautiful."

Lois almost flinched at hearing the endearment. *That's why you're always knee-deep in women problems, Mr. Covington. You're a big flirt!* Chaz routinely addressed women as "beautiful," "lovely," "gorgeous," and with other terms of endearment. From another man, these words might be considered chauvinistic, inappropriate for the workplace. But from Chaz, they were embraced as the highest form of flattery.

"She spoke correctly, Liz. I *am* on a call, and have a conference call starting in ten minutes. Lois is just doing her job, trying to keep me on track." Chaz winked at Lois, who quickly averted her eyes. "No, it's busy all day, but I'll call you back if I get a minute.

"Another Monday, another round of madness," Chaz continued when he got off the phone. "Look, finish going through my e-mails and let me know if there's anything urgent. Oh, I probably should tell you that I just deleted a rather provocative one. It was probably an isolated incident, but I'm aware of your religious convictions and felt you should be forewarned. If you run across another one, just delete it."

"Some women have no shame," Lois said softly. "I'll promptly delete every single one of them."

"On second thought, you might want to save them in a folder. Like I said, it's probably nothing, but on the other hand, this could be a potential stalker."

Lois's eyes widened.

"Just kidding, Lois. About the stalker, that is. But if these e-mails turn into a form of harassment, I'll want to have kept track of the evidence."

Lois hesitated, wondering if she should tell Chaz about the

letter she'd flushed. *But like Mr. Covington said, it's probably nothing; just some bored bimbo who's seen him on TV.*

Chaz, who'd swiveled around to retrieve a case from his back table, was surprised when he turned back to the desk and saw Lois still standing there. "Is there something else, Lois?" he asked, remembering her fidgety demeanor when he'd first arrived at the office.

"Uh, no, Mr. Covington." Lois quickly left his office and headed for the bottle of aspirin at her desk. It was definitely going to be one of those days. Before she could retrieve it, the phone rang again. "For the love of God," she murmured when she saw the number on the caller ID. She forced a smile to her voice as she answered.

"It's me again!" Melanie said laughing, accurately visualizing the scowl on Lois's face.

"What's the witch want now?" Lois asked, in a whisper. Melanie's mirth was contagious; Lois smiled for the first time that day. She'd never met Melanie McDougal, but they'd developed a phone friendship based on their mutual despising of Melanie's boss, Liz Stein—or Elizabeth, as everyone who didn't call her "Mrs. Stein" was instructed to address her. Everyone, that is, except Chaz.

"Mrs. Stein would like to see if Mr. Covington is available for a dinner meeting, tonight if possible." Melanie's ultraprofessional delivery alerted Lois that Mrs. Stein was either standing directly in front of Melanie, or had come within earshot.

"One moment, please," Lois replied, matching Melanie's professionalism. She clicked onto Chaz's calendar. "His first available evening isn't until Thursday."

After placing Lois on hold for a moment, Melanie replied, "Mrs. Stein would like to know if this evening's appointment can be rescheduled. She would like Mr. Covington to meet a potential major donor for his foundation. He's only in town for one day. She asks to be called back ASAP."

"Will do, Melanie." Lois ended the call, moved Chaz's appointment with his accountant to Thursday, and placed Elizabeth's dinner meeting in its place. Next to defending those who'd been injured or wrongfully terminated, Chaz's foundation was his passion. He'd founded From the Heart five years prior, after losing his mother to a heart disease that went undiagnosed for years. Lois knew that meeting with a potential donor would take precedence over Chaz's monthly examination of the meticulous books maintained by his personal accountant. She knew that Elizabeth was also aware of the foundation's importance in Chaz's life. Which is why this shrewd, determined woman had played the heart card.

After returning from the break room with a bottle of water and downing four aspirin, Lois once again tried to concentrate on work. But all she could think of was the letter, and who could have written it. Almost every female she'd encountered today, either by phone or in person, could be the culprit. Initially, Lois had been convinced it was Gina. She worked in the office, was always flirting with Chaz, and made no secret to Lois that she wanted to sex her boss. But Chaz's ex-wife, Jennifer, still believed she could win back the husband she'd lost after having an affair. Melanie had told Lois that Elizabeth Stein's marriage was a sham. Maybe she was considering divorce, and eyeing one of Chicago's most eligible divorcés as her next prospect. *They'd make a gorgeous couple,* Lois begrudgingly thought. Elizabeth could walk the runway at fashion week, and Chaz looked like a leading man. *Maybe she wrote the letter. But why be anonymous?* As Lois opened a file and began typing up the latest brief regarding a hit-and-run, questions about the letter-writer's identity continued to swirl in her mind. But she was sure of one thing: protecting her boss and his reputation from she-wolves was part of her job. And when it came to doing her duty . . . Lois Edwards was on the case.

3

"Is that lipstick?" Reverend Beatrice Hallelujah Edwards, the world-renowned pastor of Save Your Soul Ministries, stared at her only child with hands on hips. "Lois Elaine Edwards, you know better."

"It's not really a color, just gloss," Lois replied. It was amazing how in the presence of her fifty-year-old mother, a thirty-one-year-old woman could feel more like five. But that's the way it had always been: Beatrice spoke, Lois listened. Though her mother was strict, Lois knew she loved her. Their bond was a close one. Lois had been born out of wedlock, and following her birth, Beatrice had given up everything to focus on God and her daughter's welfare. Everyone Lois knew respected her mother, even Chaz, who claimed he was "spiritual, not religious." He'd voiced this position during their singular meeting. Lois later learned that Beatrice had not been impressed.

Reverend Beatrice Edwards's rules were followed without question. Lois agreed with these rules, for the most part. But for the past two days, since reading the anonymous letter sent to Chaz, Lois had begun looking at herself differently—viewing herself the way she imagined Chaz viewed her. While no one could fault her top-notch secretarial skills, Lois concluded that her feminine wiles were nonexistent. Since Monday morning, she'd watched Gina with a shrewd eye, hoping to glean a smidgeon of the sensuality she exuded by nature—not wanting to be sexy, you understand, but just enough to show Chaz, and remind herself, that she was a woman after all.

"You not out there man-hunting, are you?"

"No, ma'am."

Reverend Edwards's narrowed eyes continued to scrutinize Lois. Aside from the lip gloss, she couldn't fault her daughter's appearance: shoulder-length hair pulled back in a neat bun; conservative black suit, the skirt of which hung two inches below the knee; and a floral-print shell that hugged her daughter's neckline. Still, a woman of God had to watch and protect her flock, especially her daughter. The devil was always busy. . . .

Satisfied that her daughter had not been unfrocked, Reverend Edwards walked over and embraced Lois. "I'll see you tonight at Bible study. You're leading the praise and devotional, so spend some time with the Lord."

"I will, Mom. Love you."

"Love you, too."

Lois placed a Mary Mary CD into the car stereo as she navigated traffic on the Dan Ryan Freeway. If she kept her mind on Jesus, she reasoned, it was less likely to stray to other things. Like the letter. So far, it appeared her boss's prediction was accurate, and that the e-mail he was aware of and the letter of which he had no clue were one-time sends from some chick with a crush. Lois breathed a sigh of relief and looked forward to an evening service filled with prayer and praise.

Lois had arrived at her desk and begun sifting through the morning mail when her heartbeat stopped. *Another one.* The envelope looked the same: blank, white, addressed simply to Chaz Covington, Attorney-at-Law, in a bold Arial font. Lois's

first thought was to shred it, unopened. But then she remembered what Chaz had said two days prior: *If these e-mails turn
into a form of harassment, I'll want to have kept track of the evidence.*

Lois placed the letter to the side, under a paper-laden ac-
cordion file folder. She forced herself to concentrate on the
other mail and, after finishing this task, walked to the break
room for a rare cup of coffee and a bagel. She wasn't hungry,
but was trying to postpone the inevitable—being tainted by
the contents of the anonymous letter waiting at her desk,
tainted by the nasty.

By the time she returned to her work station fifteen minutes later, Lois had convinced herself to not open the letter at
all. She'd simply place the letter in a file, as Chaz had instructed. This decision lasted for all of five minutes. With her
most pressing duties completed and her boss away at court,
Lois's thoughts zoomed like a laser to the paper that seemed to
burn a hole through her desk top. She reached for the envelope and her letter opener and, after looking around to make
sure no one was nearby, unfolded the paper and read its contents.

> *Dear Chaz,*
> *I thought that if I wrote my feelings down on paper
> and mailed them to you, it would be enough. It isn't. In
> fact, seeing my desire in the form of the written word
> only increased my ardor. I WANT YOU NOW!*
> *If you were here, I'd strip naked. Then I'd remove
> your clothes. We'd take a long, leisurely bath, where I
> would get to know every inch of your perfect frame. After
> drying off, I'd allow my tongue to travel where my hands
> had been, from your toes to the top of your immaculately
> shorn head. I would suck, and lick, and explore some
> more. I imagine our kisses, hot and wet, as you plunge
> your massive manhood—*

"Good morning, Lois." Chaz's voice was rich and deep and, Lois determined, entirely too close.

She gasped, hurriedly folded the paper, and turned around to face him. "M-Mr. Covington," she stuttered, guilt written all over her face. "I didn't hear you walk up."

"The carpet soaks up footsteps fairly well," Chaz said, a smile scampering across his face as he stated the obvious. "Besides, you seemed quite engrossed in whatever you were reading."

"Oh, it was nothing." Lois's mouth closed up tighter than a sprung mousetrap.

Chaz's face remained neutral but inside his mind churned. *What is going on with you, Lois? You've been skittish all week.* His investigative instinct kicked into high gear. Chaz was determined to get to the bottom of his usually unflappable assistant's rather flappable behavior.

"Is this all of my mail?" he asked, picking up the neatly aligned stack in Lois's outbox.

Lois simply nodded, still not trusting herself to speak.

"Great. I need to write a motion and wish not to be disturbed. Text me my schedule, and when I'm finished, I've several letters to dictate."

"Okay."

Lois waited until Chaz's door closed. Then she hid the latest nasty note in her pocket and hurried to the employee restroom. By the time she opened the lavatory door, her hands were shaking and she was precariously near tears. She clumsily toyed with the lock on the stall, finally pushing it into place. She sat on the stool, took several deep breaths, and tried to calm down. *So much for keeping my mind on Jesus.* She knew she shouldn't, but Lois couldn't resist unfolding the paper and finishing the crude yet necessary task her boss had interrupted. *It's my job to know what's going on,* she told herself as she skimmed the part of the letter she'd already read. *I will protect him from wenches like these who are up to no good!* Lois took a deep breath and continued reading a letter that was almost twice as long as the first one that had been sent.

> *. . . as you plunge your massive manhood into my heat. We'll make love for hours, and when we're done and you've rested, we'll begin again. I want to sip you like a fine wine, until you are thoroughly satisfied. You'll gladly return the favor, your tongue a sword as it laps my nether nectar.*
>
> *I am so hot for you, Chaz Covington. I don't know if I can keep my identity a secret much longer. But how can I possibly reveal myself? Is it possible that you'll be as attracted to me as I am to you? Maybe one day we'll see. If dreams come true . . .*

Lois only became aware of the tears as one fell from her cheek and plopped onto the paper. She shook herself, as if from a dream, and quickly brushed them away. *Why am I crying?* But she knew why. It was because of the writer's audacity to pen such crude messages to an honorable, respectable man. Lois placed the paper back into her pocket, and exited the stall. After dabbing her eyes with a moistened paper towel, she straightened her suit jacket and then her shoulders, determined to carry out her duties as executive legal assistant to Chaz Reginald Covington. *He needs me now more than ever.* Lois knew that she could not, and would not, let him down. *And I will not let a piece of smut-filled paper get in my way!*

4

"Mrs. Smith!" Lois was surprised to return to her desk and find Delicia sitting in the mini sitting area directly across from her workstation. She was even more surprised at Delicia's markedly changed appearance. "What are you doing here?"

"I know, I should have called first," Delicia said, a slight hint of red creeping into her butterscotch complexion. "But I just wanted to drop off this thank-you gift to Mr. Covington. He was so kind to arrange that celebration on Monday, and I felt just horrible that I didn't . . . thank him more properly."

"He's asked not to be disturbed. I'll be glad to take the gift on his behalf."

"Oh. Well, I . . . ." Delicia nervously twisted her purse handle. "Of course he'd be busy. It's just that I took the bus down here, and it will be a while before one comes that's heading back to where I live. Do you think I could wait? Maybe he'll take a break."

"His schedule is pretty full." Lois took in Delicia's crest-fallen face and continued. "But I guess it would be all right for you to wait a few minutes. If I get the opportunity, I'll tell him you're here. May I get you a cup of coffee?"

"That would be nice."

"Cream and sugar?"

Delicia nodded.

"Be right back."

After watching Lois retreat down the hall, Delicia hungrily eyed the closed door to Chaz's office. Since her father died in 1997, no one had cared for her the way Chaz Covington had. Thirty-eight years old, Delicia had been separated from a no-account husband for five years. The only thing that had stopped her from finalizing the divorce was money. But in a few short weeks she'd have more cash in her account than she'd ever dreamed possible, and soon after that, Delicia would be free.

Before her settlement, Delicia would never have considered herself worthy of someone like Chaz Covington. Not only was she poor, but she wasn't your typical Barbie-doll beauty either. Delicia had junk in the trunk and years of fries on her thighs. During the trial, she'd been too focused on the case to care about her looks. This had probably worked to her advantage in gaining the jurors' empathy. But things were different now. Life held newfound possibilities. Which is why she'd borrowed three hundred dollars from her sister to make sure she showed up for today's visit in style. She wore a simple, navy, jersey knit dress (that, thanks to Spandex, hugged her size-sixteen curves in all the right places), three-inch pumps (that were killing her feet after missing her bus stop and having to walk back two blocks), and a fried, dyed, and laid to the side haircut (the first such style sans braids or weave since Outkast apologized to Ms. Jackson). When Delicia had left the small, two-bedroom apartment that she shared with an eighteen-year-old daughter and ten-year-old son, she felt pretty good about herself. But now, in the midst of the elegance that epitomized the Covington law offices, she wasn't so sure she could ever belong.

Lois eyed Mrs. Smith as she brought back her coffee on a tray containing cream, sugar, and a choice of pastries. She saw the apprehensive way this former client eyed her boss's door, and her stomach clenched. *Of course! I should have known!* Lois found the thought of this overweight woman being interested in her boss repugnant. She'd always seen Delicia Smith as a struggling, middle-aged single mother who'd been dealt a raw hand, and for whom Mr. Covington had sought and found justice. Now Lois was beginning to see something else. When another thought popped into her head, Lois almost dropped the tray she carried.

"Oh! Are you all right?" Delicia asked, as she hurriedly placed a steadying hand on the tray, before taking it from Lois and placing it on the coffee table.

"I'm fine, just, um, stumbled." *You wrote the letters. That's why you're here!* Lois turned and walked to her desk, lest her expression betray the sudden contempt she felt for a woman she'd once pitied—and whom Lois realized that with this new look was not only rather attractive, but maybe not as old as she'd first believed.

I've got to get her out of here. After giving Delicia five minutes to eat her donut and drink a third of the coffee, Lois took action. "Mrs. Smith, I hate to rush you, but I shouldn't have told you it was all right to stay. It's really impossible to see Mr. Covington without an appointment, so if you'd—"

"Lois, I need the petitions that we filed on the Scott case," Chaz began, as he barreled out of his office.

"Mr. Covington!" Delicia said breathlessly as she stood.

Chaz turned around. "Delicia! What a surprise. And don't you look lovely." He walked over with an outstretched hand. "What can I do for you?"

"I know I shouldn't have come without calling, but"— Delicia reached down for her purse—"I have a gift for you, just a small token of my appreciation. I was just getting ready to give it to Lois to give to you. She said I needed to make an appointment. . . ."

"That's normally true. But I make exceptions." Chaz winked at Delicia, causing her legs to almost buckle beneath her. Chaz looked at his watch. "I have a couple minutes. Step into my office."

If looks could kill, Lois would have faced murder charges for the daggers she shot at Delicia's retreating back before Chaz closed the door. She opened her desk drawer, pulled out the newly created file marked "Miscellaneous—N" ("n" for nasty, of course) and fingered the lone paper inside. So far, Lois had thought Gina, ex-wife Jennifer Covington, or socialite Elizabeth Stein was behind the notes. But now she knew that another suspect's name needed to be added to the list.

5

"Why, if it isn't Chaz Covington calling, and after hours no less. Is this business or pleasure? I prefer the latter." Elizabeth fairly purred as she idly fingered a strand of perfectly shaped black pearls. She stood at the floor-to-ceiling windows of her ultramodern condo on Michigan Avenue and gazed at the striking nighttime view.

"Would you accept that it's pleasurable business?" Chaz answered, his voice unconsciously seductive. "I wanted to thank you once again for bringing our latest donor on board. His company's million-dollar pledge is unparalleled, and your father's offer to sponsor this year's fund-raising ball—well, Liz, I'm in your debt."

"Umm, and I know just how you can repay me."

"Really, how?" Chaz asked.

"Come over to my place. Dinner, and especially dessert, is on me."

Chaz loosened his tie as he leaned back in a chocolate brown, leather executive chair. He was in his home office, resplendently decorated in brown, beige, and ivory tones. Decor that relaxed him, as did the two fingers of vintage scotch he sipped from a crystal snifter. "A generous offer, but one I must decline."

"Why, Chaz?" Elizabeth asked, with a pout in her voice. "I'm at the condo. No one will know."

Chaz chuckled. "We both know differently. Your father has eyes everywhere. Especially anywhere you are."

"Then you name the place. We'll meet for a drink. That's all." Elizabeth sipped a drink as well, her third glass of wine. It was the only reason she had the nerve to be so brazen, intimidation usually barring her ability to do so. And Elizabeth didn't intimidate easily. Chaz had the kind of confidence and swagger rarely seen in men, combined with a shrewd mind and intellect honed since birth. It was one of the reasons Elizabeth's father adored him, and had made no secret of his desire for Chaz to run for office—state senator for starters, and then congress and beyond. Kenneth Owens was the one who'd suggested—translation: demanded—that Elizabeth cultivate a business relationship with Chaz, even as he'd warned against anything further happening between them. "The man has a stellar reputation," her father had said, his deep voice powerful and commanding. "I don't want to see it soiled." He'd then eyed his daughter in a way that reminded Elizabeth of her promiscuous past, a past her father was well aware of, having paid hundreds of thousands in "shut up and go away" money over the years. Elizabeth's husband, Max, also came from old money. Neither family would tolerate scandal.

"You're a smart, beautiful woman, Liz. Your husband is lucky to have you. But I've been on the other side of that unfaithful coin and, believe me, it doesn't feel good."

"I know how it feels. Do you think Max has been a saint? Ha! Far from it. He couldn't care less if I slept around."

"Oh, really? Then have Max call me and tell me that it's all right to meet you. And then have him hand the phone to your dad."

Elizabeth laughed. "You irresistible jerk. Just remember, I'm ready. Anytime, anywhere . . ."

Chaz's brow creased as he remembered the desire-laden

e-mails he'd read every day this week before placing them in a folder—at least five so far. *Liz?* After agreeing to meet the following week to discuss the holiday fund-raiser, Chaz ended the call. He picked up his drink, walked from his home office to his tastefully masculine master suite—heavy black furniture made lighter with tones of tan, gray, ivory, and strategically placed splashes of red. He finished his drink, undressed, and stepped into the shower. He was totally unaware of the picture he painted: a tall bar of chocolate that was toned without being bulky, with nice tight buttocks and a "package" that would make even Scrooge shout "Merry Christmas!" As he lazily soaped said package, he thought about the woman who zealously raised money for his foundation. Whatever the motive, her efforts gave her clout in Chaz's eyes because in helping the foundation, Elizabeth was helping keep alive his mother's memory. For Chaz, the sun had risen and set on Camilla Covington and all these years later, he still keenly felt the pain of her loss. But while he had a soft spot for Elizabeth and found her attractive, she was off limits to him. She was married. *Besides, Liz is too classy a woman to send me e-mails like the ones I read. Isn't she?* He began to harden as he recalled the words of the writer—the detailed explanations of what she wanted to do to him and what she wanted to have done to her. He switched the water from hot to cold and quickly finished his shower. After toweling off, he walked to the phone, not pausing to cover his near-flawless nakedness. There was someone he had on his speed dial for moments like this. It was time to give her a call.

6

Two hours later, a sexually satisfied Chaz lay next to the former girlfriend he'd known since high school, Taylor Bates. Taylor was the one married woman for whom Chaz made an exception and shared intimacy. They'd dated, briefly, while attending colleges on opposite sides of the country, but couldn't sustain the long-distance relationship. When Taylor moved to Chicago, after marrying a prominent doctor, they rekindled their friendship. The two couples had even dined together—Chaz and Jennifer, and Taylor and her husband, James. But three years ago, James was severely injured in a head-on collision and paralyzed from the waist down. He'd offered to divorce Taylor, but she wouldn't hear of it. She loved him and vowed to stay by his side. But unlike her unfortunate husband, Taylor had shared with Chaz that she was "very much capable of feeling below the waist." James did his best, and Taylor was grateful they could still share intimacy. But sometimes his tongue and fingers just weren't enough. She needed something to go deeper, and eventually even her vibrator wouldn't suffice. She didn't need something, but someone. After two years of stress, sacrifice, and pleading with Chaz, he agreed to sleep with her.

The arrangement had worked out for both of them. Chaz, with his high profile, was very protective of the image he'd cultivated since graduating law school. He was known as an honest, fair man of integrity. And he was. But he was also compassionate and discriminating. By the time he slept with Taylor, after her husband's accident, Chaz had been celibate for a year himself. The two didn't get together often, only every couple months or so. They were "in case of emergency" lovers, "take off the edge" partners, and the best of friends.

"How's James?" Chaz asked, turning on his side to face Taylor.

"He's okay. Some days are better than others. Today was a good day."

"Has he given any more thought to serving on my foundation's board?"

Taylor smiled, turned from her back to her side, and faced Chaz. "I think he's going to do it. Thanks again for thinking of him, Chaz. Sometimes he feels so worthless, even though he's still consulting at the hospital and now teaches at the university two days a week."

"I wish I could do more for him." Chaz sighed and flopped onto his back. Chaz had prosecuted the driver for negligence and won the case. But the perpetrator, a fairly successful businessman, filed for bankrupty. The Bateses had yet to see a dime.

"You're doing plenty, believe me. James enjoys the man-time he spends with you . . . attending the Bulls' games, your grueling chess marathons. And I . . ." Taylor rubbed a hand across Chaz's firm, flat stomach and peered into the distance. "I don't know how I'd do this without you." Taylor kissed Chaz's cheek. "So what about you? How are things?"

"I've got a stalker." A smile accompanied what could have been a rather serious pronouncement.

"A what?" Taylor sat up in bed. "Who? Where? When?"

Chaz laughed and joined Taylor in a sitting position. "Whoa, detective. There's not enough evidence to convict anyone, or to know their identity." He gave Taylor a brief rundown of the week's events.

"Who do you think it could be?"

Chaz shrugged. "It could be anyone."

"That's what you get for being so fine." Taylor gave Chaz a playful nudge.

"You're finer than I am. Do *you* have a stalker?"

"No, but I don't have a commercial on television either, running every five minutes." Taylor mimicked Chaz's somber punch-line delivery. "If you don't get paid . . ."

"I don't get paid," they finished together, and then fell out laughing.

"I know who it probably is," Taylor said, after a pause.

"Who?"

"Your loyal assistant."

"Lois?" Chaz asked incredulously. "That's ridiculous."

"You think so?"

"I *know* so. Lois is staunchly religious. I'd bet my next court victory that the woman is still a virgin."

"Those are the very ones who often do these types of things: those quiet, mousy, 'religious' women," Taylor said, making air quotes. "The ones you'd least expect. I saw her checking you out at the law firm's five-year anniversary party."

Chaz looked at Taylor. "You're kidding, right?"

"No," Taylor said with a chuckle. "She checked out your ass as you walked away from her. I saw it."

"Taylor Bates, you're nothing but trouble, do you know that? Lois Edwards is the last woman on earth who would write the type of notes I received. Trust me."

"Au contraire, my dear friend, it's you who needs to trust me. Lois is no different from any other human with a va-jay-jay and eyesight. We see you, we want you. Her close contact keeps her meow meow at a constant purr. If she is a virgin, which I doubt, she's ready for you to stroke her kitty."

"Geez, Taylor, you really need to stop it. I've never looked at Lois that way."

"But maybe she's looking at *you* that way. Don't be fooled."

7

"Whew! Thank God it's Friday." Gina leaned against the counter in the break room, casually shaking a protein drink. "Got any hot plans?"

"Yes, really hot," Lois replied as she dipped a tea bag into hot water. "I've got a date with Redbox and a few movie stars."

"We need to get you a life, girlfriend," Gina said.

"No, you need to get some business and stay out of mine. What are you doing that's so special?"

"Going on a blind date. Well, not blind really, I've seen his picture. But I've never met him."

"Where you'd see his pic?"

"Dating Web site."

"Oh my goodness, people really use those things?"

"I initially thought the same thing. Who in their right mind would go online for a date, the same as shopping for shoes, books, or a concert ticket? But my brother's best friend just proposed to a woman he met online two months ago! I know this guy: smart, good looking, not a perv or anything. So I figured if he was on the site looking for love, then maybe there are other decent men on there."

"Why didn't you hook up with him, your brother's best friend?"

"Felt too incestuous. We all grew up together. Rick's like my brother. Besides, you know who I'm holding out for. . . ." Gina let the sentence hang when another co-worker came into the break room. She waited until he'd gotten his coffee and left, and then turned back to Lois, with a look.

"Gina, you really need to let go of that fairy tale. I think *Mr. Covington* dates women on another level than you and me."

"Ha! If you think you and I are on the same level, sweetie, then you're the one who's delusional. True, there is that pesky rumor that in all the years he's had this firm, he's never had an office romance. But there's a first time for everything. I plan to be the first and the last."

"Good luck," Lois said sarcastically and left the break room.

Gina unscrewed the top on her protein drink, contemplating Lois's words as she sipped her drink. *I know some things you don't know, Lois Edwards. Like certain things no man can resist . . . not even the great C.C.!*

Lois returned to her desk and plunged into work. The cheery mood she'd felt in anticipation of a relaxing weekend had been replaced by a gnawing unease. First there were Gina's inappropriate comments about her boss. Then there was the letter. Another one. After a day of not receiving anything and hoping it was over, another anonymous letter had arrived with the morning mail.

Lois hadn't opened it. And while she wanted very much to throw it away, she hadn't done that either. She'd placed the unopened envelope in the file hidden in the very back of her desk drawer and tried to forget about it. Act as if the letters didn't exist. But they did. And now, with two said letters hidden away in a file, and several e-mails in a Web folder, Lois felt more and more uncomfortable not letting Chaz know about them. *I should have told him from the beginning.* Lois saved the brief she was typing, took a deep breath, reached for the folder marked "Miscellaneous—N," and crossed the hall to Chaz's office. It was time to tell her boss about the nasty file.

"Mr. Covington?" Lois inquired, having opened his door after a light tap.

"Lois, you're a mind reader. I was just getting ready to buzz you." Chaz opened a folder and began examining its contents.

Lois had used up her bravado in the six steps between her desk and Chaz's office door. So here she stood, frozen like a deer caught in headlights, seemingly unable to loosen her hold on the brass doorknob. She realized that she must look like a fool, but for the life of her, she couldn't move.

Chaz looked up and noticed Lois still by the door. "Lois?"

Lois willed her legs to move. And then her mouth. "I, uh, Mr. Covington, would you like some more tea before we begin?" Lois was quite pleased when she managed some semblance of a smile. Unfortunately, the expression she donned was closer to that of one about to pass gas.

"Lois, are you all right?"

Lois was literally saved by the bell. "I'll get that, Mr. Covington." Instead of answering the phone in his office, the way she'd usually do, Lois rushed back to her desk. "Covington-LawOfficesthisisLoisspeakinghowmayIhelpyou?"

"Excuse me?"

"I'm sorry." Lois took a deep breath. "Covington Law Firm. May I help you?"

While Lois handled the call at her desk, Chaz swiveled around and took in the impressive view of downtown Chicago from his lofty fortieth-floor law offices. His eyes narrowed, remembering the words Taylor had uttered a couple nights before: *If she is a virgin, which I doubt, she's ready for you to stroke her kitty.* Chaz steepled his fingers as he pondered the possibilities. He was a shrewd, detail-oriented attorney whose reputation had been built on his ability to leave no stone unturned when it came to a case. He hadn't thought so at first, but Taylor's words, Lois's odd behavior, and the erotically written e-mails he continued to receive were becoming a cause for concern. Chaz believed he needed to stop what had at first seemed harmless before it got out of hand.

Chaz punched the intercom line. "Yes, Lois."

"Mrs. Smith is on line one, Mr. Covington. And your accountant is on line two."

"Take messages for both calls and then come in here. There's something I'd like to discuss."

Lois opened her desk drawer and hastily placed the manila folder at the very back. Determined to control her skittish nerves, she reached for her iPad and water bottle, then slowly walked back into her boss's office.

"Close the door," Chaz said without looking up.

The heartbeat she'd just slowed with deep breaths sped back up. *Get ahold of yourself, Lois!* It wasn't at all unusual for her and Chaz to work behind closed doors, especially when he was dictating letters or discussing touchy or confidential issues regarding a client's case. Anger replaced anxiety as Lois sat in one of the chairs facing Chaz's desk. If she came face-to-face with the culprit behind the nasty notes, the ones that had her so discombobulated, she'd throttle her!

"Lois, what I'm about to discuss with you is strictly confidential. I don't want any of the other lawyers or employees at this firm knowing about this."

Lois worked to keep her face neutral. "Sure, Mr. Covington. What is it?"

Chaz leaned back in his chair and studied Lois a moment before he spoke. "As you know, I'm still getting the erotic e-mails that started on Monday."

Lois dropped her eyes. "Yes, I know."

"My first thought was to simply ignore them, that the sender would soon tire of the game and the e-mails would end. Perhaps that's still the case. But because of their increased frequency and . . . stronger content . . . I'm not so sure this is still harmless fun. I talked it over with a, um, colleague, who agrees with me.

"Like I told her, it could be anyone. A high percentage of my clients are female, and women lawyers make up twenty-five percent of our profession. Then there are the foundations and other social entities I'm involved with." Chaz rose from his chair and went to stand by the window. "It's time to try and learn who's behind this, before the situation escalates beyond e-mails."

"I'm afraid that's already happened, Mr. Covington."

Chaz turned from the window. "What do you mean?"

"I have something to show you." Lois went to her desk, re-trieved the file, and returned. She walked over and handed it to Chaz, then sat back down. Chaz opened the file and began ex-amining its contents.

"I'm sorry for not showing these to you sooner," Lois con-tinued, "but . . . I felt the same way you did, that you'd get one or two pieces of this . . . filth . . . and then it would stop. I know how busy you are with the Jimenez case and hoped to spare you from having to deal with this crazy situation."

Chaz sat down at his desk, and after scanning the first doc-ument, reached for his letter opener. "I see you didn't open this second piece of mail, though I totally understand why reading one was enough." He hid a smile.

Lois took a breath and confessed. "Actually, I read two." Chaz looked up, but Lois hurried on. "I was shocked when I opened the mail on Monday, and the only thing I could think of was making sure no one else saw what I'd seen. This was be-fore our meeting when you told me to keep them as evidence. I'm sorry, Mr. Covington, but I destroyed the first letter you received."

"It's okay, Lois. I'm sure it was much like these two."

"They are vulgar and crude. I . . . chose not to read any more. I did, however, notice that the postmarks are from differ-ent areas in L.A."

"Has my exceptional assistant turned detective?" Again, that merest of smiles, the kind that caused Lois's heartbeat to quicken, flitted across his face.

Lois warmed at the praise and at the way his newly grown mustache framed perfectly succulent lips. "Uh, not exactly. But I'm also curious about who is doing this."

Chaz nodded, rereading the last letter. He wanted to know this person's identity, and for more reasons than protecting his name and reputation. A part of Chaz was beginning to enjoy the sexy notes from this unusual suitor and was intrigued at whom she might be. He'd spent way more time than he should have last evening pondering the possibilities. Even now, he worked to keep his manhood in check as he scanned down the page and read the last lines of the letter he now held:

I want your thrusts to reach my core, and I will clinch my muscles to keep you deep inside me. I grow wet thinking about the taste of you. Yum!

Chaz's soft chuckle piqued Lois's curiosity. "What does it say?"

"Nothing that you'd want to hear."

Lois nodded, but said nothing. She couldn't even admit to herself that she'd like nothing more than to hear the contents of said letters being read from Chaz's thick lips, in his deep, resonant voice. She'd told herself for two straight years that she wasn't in love with Chaz Reginald Covington. But that lie was getting harder and harder to swallow.

"Needless to say, this could be an embarrassing situation for the firm if these notes ever became public. I realize you're here early most days anyway and are therefore often the first to get a look at the mail. I want that to continue, Lois, and for you to help me keep this under wraps."

"That's no problem, Mr. Covington. I'll do anything to help."

"I'm glad to hear you say that, because there is something else—another reason why solving this puzzle is important." Chaz's face hardened slightly, remembering an earlier phone call. "We need to find out who's behind this letter-writing campaign just in case this isn't some besotted female's harmless flirtations."

"What else could it be?" Lois asked, her expression puzzled until realization began to dawn. "Or maybe someone is intentionally creating fodder for a scandal. . . ."

"Someone like Pete Bennett, for instance, trying to drum up a way to smear my image."

Lois paused, then shook her head with resolve. "I don't think so."

Chaz's brow furrowed as he looked at Lois intently.

"I mean, well, of course I can't be certain." Lois swallowed the sudden lump in her throat. "Everyone knows that Mr. Bennett hates you."

"And you heard with your own ears the verbal threat he recently made."

Lois nodded. "Yes, I heard it."

"He still hasn't backed down. I just got off the phone with a buddy of mine who heard him on the golf course, maligning my name. I wouldn't put it past that scumbag to try something like this."

They were silent a moment, remembering how Lois had been in Chaz's office when Pete Bennett had called. Chaz had answered via speakerphone, allowing Lois to hear the heated conversation in its entirety. Acting intuitively, Lois had pressed the message center's RECORD button. Chaz never forgot a threat made against him, and Lois never forgot anything concerning Chaz.

Finally Lois spoke. "It could be Mr. Bennett, Mr. Covington. But I don't think so."

Chaz twirled a paperweight and once again Taylor's warning came to his mind. *Could you be right, Taylor? Could the woman who types my briefs now want to get in my briefs?* Chaz quickly thought back to the firm's social functions. Lois had come alone—except for last year's Christmas dinner, when she'd brought her mother. There were no personal pictures on her desk, and while their conversation was 90 percent business, he'd never heard Lois mention a man—boyfriend or otherwise. In this moment, Chaz realized that, aside from the fact that she was an exceptional assistant, he knew very little about the woman sitting across from him. Chaz had been honest when he'd told Taylor he'd never looked at Lois "that way" before: as a woman with sexual urges who thirsted for love. But perhaps, he concluded, it was time to view Ms. Lois Edwards in a different light.

8

Lois placed the bag of Chinese food on the kitchen counter. She reached for a plate and piled it high with sweet-and-sour chicken, beef with broccoli, vegetable fried rice, and crab rangoon. If not for good genes and a high metabolism, Lois knew she'd weigh two hundred pounds instead of the one hundred and sixty that covered her five-foot-five frame. Food was often her companion, assuaging hungers unrelated to diet. This wasn't a fact Lois acknowledged. Lois's lifestyle demanded that certain satisfactions be denied.

Lois placed her plate, glass of tea, and fortune cookie on a tray and walked into the living room. It was a rare moment when she had the house to herself. Her mother had gone to an out-of-town women's retreat and wouldn't be back until late tomorrow night. Because of this, Lois had decided to skip the Friday night service that Save Your Soul held every other week, even though she often enjoyed the associate minister's sermons. Where her mother's sermons were more "fire and brimstone," focusing on what not to do, Pastor Mack's messages were upbeat, often laced with humor, and filled with what was possible when one had faith. But the week had drained Lois's energy, physically and especially mentally. Lois looked forward to enjoying a delicious meal, a great movie, and a good night's sleep.

The comedy Lois had selected on Netflix was a good one. Tyler Perry was her favorite actor, one who could usually make her forget anything that troubled her mind. Lois often came home filled with anguish about the plight of the law firm's clients. Part of the reason she'd purposely chosen comedies tonight was because of Mr. Covington's last appointment of the day: a mother whose son had been seriously injured when an amusement-park ride had malfunctioned. Her son had been thrown from the roller coaster and had landed on his head. This massive brain injury had left her son in a vegetative state. While Lois felt Mr. Covington was certain to get a substantial settlement for the family, there were some things that money simply could not buy, or replace.

As horrific as this situation was, an injured child wasn't the main issue Lois was trying to forget. It was the words of the letters she'd finally read when Mr. Covington returned the file to her for safekeeping. Try as she might, for the rest of the afternoon she hadn't been able to stop the pictures from forming in her head. Ones of Mr. Covington. Naked. And on top of her.

Lois reached for the remote and turned up the volume. She forced herself to focus on Madea and her "big happy family." For a few moments she succeeded, laughing uproariously as Madea shook her signature gray wig, placed a hand on an ample hip, and read her poor victim the riot act. *He has another hit on his hands,* she concluded. Unfortunately, her joy only lasted as long as the movie, and began dissipating as the credits rolled. Even her fortune cookie's promise of a silver lining behind every cloud couldn't lighten her mood.

It was only ten o'clock, but Lois prepared for bed. She walked into the bathroom and, after brushing her teeth, decided to take a shower. She undressed and caught sight of herself just before stepping into the tub. She walked from the bathroom to the full-length mirror hanging on the back of her bedroom door. For the first time in years, Lois viewed herself completely naked.

Her assessment couldn't have been more clinical had it come from a doctor: small breasts, a pudgy stomach, hips bigger than she would have liked. She turned to the side, her mouth turning down as she viewed her less than ample—okay, flat—behind. Why was it, she wondered, that of all the things she'd inherited from her mother, Reverend Edwards's butt wasn't one of them? Granted, few people knew the extent of Beatrice's treasures. She preached in long robes and, when she wasn't dressed for ministry, wore loose, earth-toned caftans. But Lois had seen her mother's assets and now wished she had them.

After taking her shower, Lois sat at the desktop computer in her room. She stared for a long moment at the blank page in front of her. Slowly, almost mechanically, she placed her hands on the keys and began to type:

Dear Mr. Covington . . . Lois stopped, deleted the salutation, swallowed hard, and began again. *Dear Chaz . . .*

9

The weekend passed quickly, and Lois was glad to be back at work. It had been a frenzied Monday, and Chaz was uncharacteristically demanding. Lois didn't take it personally. She knew her boss was focusing on the final arguments of the Jimenez trial that had gone on for months. If Chaz won the case, it could potentially be one of the largest personal-injury settlements in the nation's history. So Lois understood why Mr. Covington was on edge. She was nervous, too.

"Lois."

That one word spoken through her phone's intercom brought Lois scurrying into Chaz's office. "Yes, Mr. Covington."

"Sit down. I need to dictate a letter that then needs to be sent across town by messenger."

Chaz had just begun verbalizing his thoughts, when there was a knock at the door. "Yes?"

"Sorry to disturb you, Mr. Covington," Gina said softly, as both she and the subtly provocative perfume she wore approached his desk. "But this FedEx came with special instructions to be delivered immediately."

Lois begrudgingly admitted that Gina smelled good and looked even better, taking in her fire-red suit—the short skirt and high heels emphasizing long, well-shaped legs. In that moment, Lois decided to stop by the mall on the way home and purchase some perfume.

"Thanks, Gina," Chaz curtly replied. The tone of his voice clearly indicated that now was not the time for flirtation.

Gina got the memo. "You're welcome," she said and quickly walked out of the room.

"This is probably the evidence I requested," Chaz said, quickly opening the envelope. He pulled out the single sheet of paper. Only then did he notice that a pair of wispy-thin lace thongs was stapled to the bottom.

"Geez, not today," he groaned, rolling his eyes. He placed the unread letter and scented panties back inside the envelope and handed it to Lois. "You know what to do with this."

"Yes, of course." Lois's hands shook as she took the envelope, remembering her miserable attempt over the weekend to write a sexy letter to Chaz. She hadn't even been able to mentally form the words, much less type out a message. As much as she despised the nasty-gram culprit, she begrudgingly acknowledged the writer's imagination, and guts. Lois now knew for sure that she could never do such a thing.

Once Chaz finished dictating the letter, he left the office to spend the rest of the day in court. The law firm's receptionist had called in sick, so on top of her other responsibilities, Lois was splitting phone-answering duties with Gina and two other secretaries. She didn't mind the extra work. It kept her focused on other people's problems instead of her own. She was almost at the end of her last phone shift when two disturbing calls came in.

The first call was Jennifer Covington, Chaz's ex-wife. "He's in court," Lois responded when Jennifer asked to be put through to his line. She wished she could be nonbiased where Jennifer was concerned, but the fact that this woman had committed adultery, and that she'd cheated on a stellar man like Chaz, put her below the bottom of Lois's loser list.

"Which court is he in? I need to talk to him ASAP."

"I'm not sure," Lois lied, a rare occurrence. "You can call the courthouse and speak with the docket secretary. Would you like the number?"

"Do I come off as stupid to you?" Jennifer asked, her voice full of attitude. "When it comes to his work, Chaz doesn't make a move without you knowing about it, and you're probably pretty up on his personal calendar, too. Whatever you think about me, you're talking to Chaz's ex-wife and the mother of his children. Don't think I can't get your pitiful butt fired, and don't think I don't know that you could reach Chaz if you really tried. I don't know what you think you're doing, withholding information that I have a right to know, but please believe me when I tell you that you do *not* want me for an enemy!"

Lois had barely recovered from this verbal thrashing when the second call came in.

"Elizabeth Stein's office for Mr. Covington," Melanie said. The cheeriness that usually accompanied her greeting was noticeably absent.

"He's in court, Melanie. May I take a message for Mrs. Stein?"

After writing down the message inviting Chaz to a weekend fund-raising dinner for an influential politician seeking a second office bid, Lois changed the topic. "Are you okay, Melanie? Your voice is missing its usual smile."

"Hold on a minute, okay?"

"Sure."

After a brief pause, Melanie came back on the line. She spoke softly. "I think The Ogre just left for a meeting, thank God. She's about to drive me bonkers."

"Is that why you're upset?"

"That's part of it." Melanie paused. "The other part is that my boyfriend and I broke up last night."

"Oh no, Melanie. I'm sorry to hear that."

"Yeah, me too."

"What happened?"

"I don't know. He just called and said he needed space."

Lois heard the tears that Melanie barely held at bay. She thought of the call with Jennifer Covington she'd just ended, and the reason that woman was Chaz's ex-wife. "Do you think there's someone else?"

"I don't know what to think. I—"

"Are you on a personal call?" Lois heard a shrill voice in the background. The same voice soon boomed in her ear. "Who is this?"

"Um, hello, Mrs. Stein. It's Lois Edwards."

"Is he in?"

"No. He's in court."

"Is that why you think you can sit here shooting the breeze during office hours? While the cat is away the mouse plays? Well, I won't stand for Melanie goofing off on my dime, and you'd better believe Chaz will hear about your unprofessional dallying as well!"

By the time Gina relieved Lois from phone duty, Lois had a mammoth headache. She'd just swallowed two aspirin when the phone rang at her desk.

"Chaz Covington's office, Lois speaking."

"May I speak with him, please?"

The hairs on Lois's neck stood up, and her hands went clammy. She knew this voice; had hoped she'd never have to hear it again. It was the one person in life she actually feared. Not for herself. For her boss. It was the one person Lois felt could bring down Chaz's empire with a whisper.

"May I ask who's calling?" Lois asked, feigning ignorance.

"Naomi Stone," was the nonplussed reply.

Even through her envy, Lois couldn't help but admire the woman's poise. They both knew Naomi's identity was no secret to Lois, that her voice would be recognized anytime, anywhere. Lois shut her eyes against the memory.

★ ★ ★

"What do you mean he's in a meeting? It's seven o'clock!"

"He's not available, Mrs. Covington. May I help you?"

"I don't care if he's in a meeting. I need to speak to him right now!" Jennifer fairly snarled into the phone.

"Seriously, Mrs. Covington, he insisted he not be interrupted for any reason."

"When Chaz finds out his son was injured and you didn't tell him—"

"Oh my goodness, forgive me. I didn't know this involved his child. One moment."

Lois walked briskly to Chaz's office door, opened it, and became paralyzed by what she saw: Chaz's body moving between the upturned legs of the woman laying on his desk. Fortunately for Lois, who'd never seen a man's behind, his was covered by an unbuttoned designer shirt. But the pants around his ankles, the rhythmic thrusts of his hips, and the low grunts told even this sexual novice what time it was.

"Ooh, baby, yes, right there," the female voice loudly whispered. "You feel so good, baby, I love your . . . ooh yes, right there . . . yes!"

Lois squeezed shut her eyes and turned her head. "Your son's hurt!" she eked out, her voice an octave higher than normal. "Jennifer's on line one." Then she hurriedly slammed the door and ran out of the building.

The next morning, Chaz summoned her into his office shortly after he arrived. "Please accept my most profound apologies," he said when Lois stepped into his office and then plastered herself against the office door. "There's nothing I can say to convey how embarrassed I am. I thought you'd gone home."

"I-I left, but came back for my cell phone. I'd accidentally left it on the desk."

An awkward silence filled the room.

"I got caught up in a moment of . . . unrestraint," Chaz

said, as if each word brought pain. "If I'd had any idea you were still here . . ." Chaz stopped, and wearily sat behind his desk. "I miss my family, but that's no excuse."

"Please, Mr. Covington. There's no need to explain. It will be as if it didn't happen, I promise. I won't say a word."

That incident happened a year after Chaz had separated from Jennifer and one month after Lois began working for one of the most prestigious attorneys in the city. Seeing the anguish mixed with embarrassment on Chaz Covington's face had pierced Lois's heart. In that moment, she'd realized that behind the strong, confident, charismatic persona that graced televisions nationwide was a sensitive, even vulnerable human being who could probably benefit from a good, sound hug. That's when Lois fell in love with Chaz Covington. It was also the first and only time Lois had heard Naomi's voice. But both women knew it was a voice she'd never forget.

"Be sure and tell your boss that I called and wish to speak to him," Naomi politely requested.

"Yes, Ms. Stone. May I have your phone number?"

After taking down the information and ending the call, Lois sat back in her chair as if sucker-punched. Her mind immediately went to the overnight envelope that had been added to the Miscellaneous—N file. *I wouldn't put it past a woman like you to send letters like those,* Lois concluded. From what she remembered, Naomi could wear the thong that had been sent with what Lois felt was the nastiest letter yet. Naomi had taken off her panties at least once for Chaz Covington. Lois was convinced that she was ready to do it again.

10

"A cell phone?" Lois's expression was baffled. Chaz owned an iPad, an iPhone, a smartphone, and two BlackBerrys . . . that she knew of.

"Yes, a prepaid. Make sure it has texting capabilities. I'll be in court all afternoon. If you leave before I get back, just place it in the top desk drawer."

"It's none of my business, Mr. Covington, but . . ."

"Most of what I do is your business, Lois. What would you like to know?"

"Does this have to do with the letters?"

"Yes. I want to communicate with whomever this is, but don't want any way for said communication to be traced back to me. Up the ante for both of us and hopefully get this person to reveal who they are." Chaz began shuffling papers and placing files into his briefcase. "Is there something else you have for me?" he asked, after noticing that Lois remained seated.

"Uh, well, I have some ideas about who the person could be, about who's sending these letters."

"So do I, and I'd like for us to discuss this. If you can work late, I'll probably be back around six thirty. On second thought, why don't we make it a dinner meeting? How about McCormick & Schmick's, seven o'clock?"

"Okay." Lois quickly exited Chaz's office, wanting to hide her sudden giddiness. She knew this offer was strictly business, but this knowledge didn't stop her heart from skipping a beat. She'd eaten with Chaz several times when he was deep into a case and worked through lunch. But those occurrences always happened in the office. This was almost like a date, and Lois could count on one hand the times she'd been on one of those.

Lois pulled into the restaurant parking lot at six forty-five. She viewed herself in the mirror and wished she had makeup, or something to make her look less plain. She remembered a pair of earrings that were in the glove compartment, stowed there because once out of the house, she'd thought them too flashy for choir rehearsal. *But they'll work with this,* she thought. She put them on and turned her head this way and that. The Swarovski crystals added a bit of festiveness to her otherwise drab gray dress with a white Peter Pan collar. Lois looked at her watch, then in the mirror again. "It will have to do."

Chaz arrived thirty minutes later, looking like a million bucks. He'd been in court all day, yet looked as fresh as a spring breeze. He wearily sat down in the booth, blessing Lois with a smile. "Sorry I'm late."

"It's okay. How was court?"

"Long. Sometimes I wonder if this trial will ever end."

"They're playing hardball, huh?"

Chaz's response was interrupted by an approaching waiter. He placed down the menus and took drink requests. Chaz ordered a scotch on the rocks. Lois ordered iced tea.

Chaz loosened his tie as he sat back against the booth's cool leather. "You don't drink, do you? Alcohol, that is."

"No."

"Is that because of your religious beliefs or that you don't like the taste?"

"I've never tasted it."

"You've never had a drink, ever?"

Lois shook her head.

Chaz wasn't much of a drinker himself, but was still surprised in this day and age to know someone who'd never tasted liquor. He found himself wondering if there were other things that Lois hadn't tasted. "You know, Lois, I realize that while I'm well versed in your professional attributes and work history, I know very little about Lois the person. Who are you?" An impish smile indicated he was joking.

"Not much to tell, really. I grew up here in Chicago, am an only child, and my life pretty much revolves around work and church."

"Ah, come on. You're a young, vibrant woman. Surely you make time for pleasure every once in a while."

"Not really."

"So, you don't have a boyfriend?"

"No." Lois was glad the waiter chose that moment to deliver their drinks. She felt uncomfortable sharing her personal life, or lack thereof, with someone like Chaz, who she knew for a fact had a social calendar that was overbooked, and women coming out the proverbial ying-yang. As soon as the waiter had taken their meal orders, Lois changed the subject. "Did you get the cell phone I left in your desk drawer?"

"Yes, thank you."

"I chose an out-of-state number, to further shield you from being found out."

"The person will pretty much know it's me, Lois," Chaz said with a chuckle. "They just won't be able to prove it with hard evidence. Hence text messages, instead of phone calls—it could be anyone's hands on the keyboard."

"Oh, right."

"Now," Chaz said, crossing his arms, "who are your suspects in this letter-writing scheme?"

"Well." Lois took a sip of her tea. "It could be Gina."

"Gina? Hmm." Chaz leaned forward, stroked his chin. "She's quite the flirt, I'll admit that."

"She has a huge crush on you."

"Is that so?"

"Yes. She's always talking about how she'd like to . . . go out with you."

"Gina talks a lot. But your suspicion is valid. Have you considered anyone else?"

Lois shared her thoughts about Elizabeth Stein; Chaz's ex-wife, Jennifer; and Delicia Smith.

Chaz listened intently without comment. "Except for Delicia, I've considered the women you mentioned," he said, when Lois became silent. "But honestly, Lois, it could be anyone." Chaz shared his thoughts about a sixty-year-old socialite who'd chased him for years; the prosecuting attorney who tried to seduce him in the courthouse parking lot; and several women with whom he'd had brief, nonsexual dating encounters. "I've had my share of zealous suitors over the years," Chaz finished. "But this is a new experience."

The two engaged in small talk as they finished their meals. Lois ate the last bite of her grilled swordfish. She finished her tea, wiped her mouth, and looked at Chaz. "There's another possibility," she said.

"Who?"

"Naomi," Lois whispered.

"Who?" Chaz had speared the last of his prime ribeye steak, but placed the uneaten forkful on the plate when he heard Lois's answer.

Lois cleared her throat. "Naomi Stone."

Fifteen years of courtroom cool was evidenced in Chaz's unchanged expression. Underneath, he waded through a myriad of emotions. Having Lois walk in on him pounding Naomi had been his singularly most embarrassing career moment. But there was more. Chaz felt that Naomi was his one true love. She was also proving to be the most elusive. When he'd gotten the message yesterday that she'd called, he'd been over the moon. It had been a long time since he'd heard from her, and he had no idea of her whereabouts. They'd talked on the phone for two hours, but when Chaz suggested they get together, Naomi declined, using work and an early flight out as the excuse for rejection. Lois's answer had shocked Chaz, but now, looking at it objectively, she could be right. There was something about Naomi's mysterious persona that could very well support this kind of behavior. That and the fact that Naomi had a kinky side, one that knew Chaz would be totally turned on by seemingly anonymous sex talk.

The more Chaz thought about it, the more he thought Lois was on to something. But this was a thought Chaz kept to himself. "I'm still mortified at what you saw that day," he said at last. "That was very uncharacteristic behavior, an action that hasn't been repeated."

"Do you think it could be her? Do you think Naomi could be the one writing those letters?"

"That's one of the reasons I asked for the prepaid phone, so that I can offer my cell number, get the number of whoever's behind this, and have it traced. I believe then the game will escalate. Hopefully, I can use my courtroom skills to trip them up in some way, to cause whoever this is to reveal their identity."

"In a way, I hope it's Pete Bennett."

"Why do you say that?"

"A fight in the courtroom may be easier to win than one in the bedroom."

"Ha! There's a reason I hired you, darling. You're top notch."

"Thank you." Lois lowered her head, embarrassed. Chaz's

compliments often left her flustered—partly because she wasn't used to receiving attention from men, but mostly because of how she secretly felt about this particular man.

They left the restaurant shortly afterward. Chaz headed to the gym for a much-needed, stress-reducing workout. Lois headed for the church to pick up the outline for a program she'd agreed to type up. These two people were headed in different directions, but they had their minds on the same question: would Chaz find out the sender of the nasty notes? Neither was sure about the answer.

11

Chaz felt better. The workout was just what he'd needed. Now, driving home from the gym, he felt calm, relaxed. Before dinner, he'd not looked forward to preparing the closing arguments for court tomorrow. But exercising had released those blessed endorphins. His mind was alert, and he was actually looking forward to composing a compelling statement that would lead to victory.

Chaz was halfway through said argument when his cell phone rang. He started to send it to voice mail, but smiled once he looked at the caller ID. "Baby . . ."

"Hey, Chaz." Naomi Stone's sultry voice poured into Chaz's ear like maple syrup—sticky and sweet. "Sorry I couldn't rendezvous with you. It's been far too long."

"That it has." Chaz rose from his leather swivel chair behind the desk, walked into his living room, and reclined on a chaise. "Where are you?"

"Vancouver."

"Is that where you live now?"

"No."

"Is where you live a secret?"

Naomi chuckled softly. "No." And then, "I still reside in Los Angeles. But I'm thinking of moving again . . . to Chicago."

"Baby, I'd love that."

"It doesn't mean . . ."

"Did I say it meant anything? Not that I don't want it to. You know how I feel about you, Naomi. I don't see why you keep adding bricks to the wall around that special heart of yours."

"I told you why. My ex took me through changes that have taken me years to work through. I don't think I could endure that kind of pain again, and with you . . ."

"With me?" Chaz asked, his voice barely above a whisper.

"I know I keep running away from us. But it's because you move me in ways I've never been moved before. Even after all this time, I get wet just thinking about you . . . hard, strong, pulsating inside me."

Chaz sat up. "Pulsating, you say?"

"Yes," Naomi murmured.

"Interesting choice of words." Chaz imagined Naomi pleasuring herself, but remained focused. Naomi's words sounded suspiciously close to those in some of the letters he'd received.

"Yes, Chaz. I've tried to tamp down these feelings, to tell myself differently but . . . I want you."

Chaz's eyes narrowed. *What type of game are you playing, my sweet?* Or was she playing a game? If Naomi was the letter writer, he'd be delighted. Given her skittish nature and the traumatic past that involved domestic violence, her tentative approach to renewed, ongoing intimacy could be understood. But if it wasn't her, he could utter a revelation that would be TMI for this tenuous relationship.

Chaz knew he had to play his cards right. "You want me, huh?" He lay back on the chaise and began idly stroking himself.

"Umm."

"How do you want me, Naomi?"

"I love it when you lick me, like candy . . . when your body covers mine. I feel protected and secure. Lately, not a day goes by that I don't think of you, of us, and how good it was the few times we were together."

"What are you wearing?"

"A thong. Nothing else."

Chaz closed his eyes, his manhood hardened. "What color?"

"Red."

The same color as the one that arrived at my office! "Baby, we both want the same thing. If I could, I'd come to you. But I've got trials back to back. I can't get away right now. Can you come to me?"

A long pause, and then, "Yes."

"When, Naomi?"

A longer pause. "Soon."

After ending the call with Naomi, Chaz needed another shower. The mutual masturbation had been pleasurable, but it had also made him acutely aware of his divorced status. He showered quickly and was thankful for the work that took his mind off himself for the next hour and a half. But when he lay down to sleep, the thoughts returned.

I'm lonely. I'm ready to do it again. Chaz had enjoyed married life. He'd met Jennifer when he was fresh out of law school, twenty-five years old, already on a solid path to success. He'd been recruited by a small yet prestigious law firm that specialized in personal-injury lawsuits. It was also a firm whose partners were well connected, both socially and politically. They adored Chaz, and showed him the ropes that he quickly and efficiently grasped. This is where he'd first met Pete Bennett, twenty years his senior, a fading star watching one on the rise. A lawsuit involving a politician's niece had come to the firm. Pete chomped at the bit for that case, made his desire known. They gave it to Chaz, the 4.0 "grad with honors" upstart. Chaz won the case and a political comrade, huge chips in Chicago where politics ruled. Pete left the law firm shortly thereafter and, five years later, so did Chaz—to start his own firm.

He'd known he wanted Jennifer with him, and after dating

five years, Chaz and Jennifer got married. His mother had op-
posed the union; told him she didn't have a good feeling about
her future daughter-in-law. But Chaz was deeply in love. They
hadn't planned it, but Jennifer got pregnant the first year they
were married. A daughter was born two years after the son.
Jennifer became a full-time mom.

Later, Chaz would realize that was when the problems
started. He worked seventy-, eighty-hour weeks building his
practice, leaving a former party girl with not enough attention
and too much time on her hands. By the time he noticed, it
was too late. She didn't deny the affair he'd discovered she was
having with a radio station's heartthrob disc jockey. The affair
devastated Chaz, especially since Jennifer made it known that
she wanted to be with the DJ. Shortly afterward, Jennifer
found out that the DJ wanted to be with her . . . and a few
other women as well. Belatedly, she realized the good thing
she'd lost and tried to get it back. But it was too late. The marriage was over.

As sleep eluded Chaz, he continued to remember all the
way back to his childhood, where he'd grown up in a traditional family. His father, who died when Chaz was a junior in
college, had been a welder by day and a barber in the evenings
and on weekends. His mother stayed at home until he and his
two sisters were teenagers, and then worked at the local Good-
will—a place that had helped clothe them when all the kids
were young—until her death from a heart attack five years
ago. He'd missed her immensely while going through his separation and divorce, and now, he missed the overabundance of
love that had exuded from the Covington household, especially between his parents; the love that had molded and
shaped the man he'd become. Chaz had one last thought before sleep finally enveloped him: *I want a love like that.*

12

It was eight p.m. on a Thursday evening. Lois was still at work. She was tired, but also felt triumphant: the jury had deliberated just two hours before ruling in favor of Chaz's client. Her boss's celebration had been short lived, however, because the decision was immediately appealed. Fingers played the keyboard at eighty words per minute as Lois rushed to finish the motion Chaz would file first thing in the morning. If she hurried, she'd make it home in time to see the Lifetime movie she'd seen advertised; ironically, about a female stalker in love with her boss.

She was surprised to hear the elevator ding, but assuming it was one of the other attorneys, she didn't turn around. Until she smelled the perfume. And then she knew: Jennifer. Lois rolled her eyes and kept typing. Until she heard the voices. Two young ones, one male and one female. Jennifer never brought the kids to the office. *What trick do you have up your sleeve?*

"Hi, C. J., hey Cherish," Lois said, addressing the children. "Don't you guys look cute!" Her pointed ignoring of Jennifer did not go unnoticed.

"You're a piece of work, you know that?" Jennifer spat, fixing Lois with a look like there was dooky on her face. Jennifer sidled up to the desk and lowered her face to within an inch of Lois's. "Here you are playing the loyal, dedicated secretary. Don't think I don't know that you have the hots for my ex. Forget it, sista. That's a pipe dream that you'll never, *ever* experience. I was and will always be a part of Chaz's life. And when he and I get back together? You'll be the first change he makes to the personnel."

Lois swallowed her anger, even as she took in a look that could only be described as "video vixen." Jennifer wore a tight black dress and high, jeweled sandals. Her makeup was flawless, as usual, and her legs were free of scars or blemishes. In a word, Jennifer looked perfectly decadent. Lois couldn't stand her.

"Is Mr. Covington expecting you?" she asked with mock politeness.

"No. Nothing like a surprise family visit to brighten your man's day. Is he alone?"

"Yes, but he's . . ." The rest of Lois's sentence died on her lips as she watched Jennifer prance to Chaz's office door, followed by two children that Chaz could have spit out, so much did they look like him. Lois reached for the phone but realized it wouldn't do any good to try and alert Chaz of his ex-wife and children's presence. Jennifer had already opened the door.

"Jennifer!" The frown on Chaz's face quickly turned into a smile when he noticed that his children accompanied her. He quickly opened and closed his drawer before standing up to greet them. "My two favorite people!" he exclaimed, his arms outstretched.

"Daddy!" Chaz's daughter ran and jumped into her father's arms. His son, Chaz, Jr., showed more restraint, but was equally glad to see him.

"We were in the neighborhood," Jennifer said, hugging Chaz and giving him a kiss on the lips before he could turn them away. "I called your house, and when you didn't answer, thought I'd surprise you by stopping by with the kids. Have you eaten? Because we brought dinner."

"No, in fact I'm starved." Chaz took in Jennifer's appearance. Sometimes he forgot how attractive she was. At one time, she'd had him wrapped around her finger. That time was gone. Wasn't it? "What did you bring me?" he asked his daughter, forcing unwanted thoughts from his mind.

"Lasagna!" Cherish chirped.

"Come over to the table. Let's see this spread. I'll have Lois bring silverware and napkins."

Jennifer stayed him with her hand. "That's okay, baby. I've thought of everything."

Soon, the sound of murmured conversation, punctuated by tinkling laughter, drifted out to Lois's workstation. She knew what Jennifer was doing—playing the mommy card—and hoped Chaz knew what she was doing, too. She remembered when she first started working for Chaz, his subdued countenance and quiet mood. At first, she thought that was his personality. It was only later, as he began to heal and regain his vibrant, self-assured personality, that she got an inkling about how his divorce had affected him.

He never talked about it. The divorce. But Gina had been more than happy to fill her in on all the ugly details. At the time, LIVE-FM had been one of her favorite stations, their "grown folks' music" format one that she preferred to its hip-hop-driven counterparts. She'd rarely missed the morning show. The DJ was funny, informative, and always dropped positive affirmations to get one through the morning. But after Lois learned that this DJ's penis had been the wedge that dislodged Chaz's happiness, Lois never listened to the man again.

Moments later, Chaz's office door opened and out walked her boss and his brood, looking like one big happy family.

"You're leaving?" Lois asked, surprised. She knew Chaz had planned to work a couple more hours.

"I've been roped into seeing a movie, the latest Pixar flick," he said. "I tried to get out of it but . . ."

"C'mon, Daddy!" Cherish said, her eyes glowing with admiration and love.

"Yeah, Dad, c'mon," C.J. echoed.

Chaz raised his hands in mock surrender. "What's a father to do?"

"Yes," Jennifer cooed, speaking to Chaz with words Lois knew were meant for her. "What's a daddy to do but hang out with those he loves most?" And then to Lois: "Thanks for all your hard work, Lois. We appreciate you."

Lois's disgust was enough to make her lose her lunch. She finished typing the motion and decided to call it a day. She'd have to come in extra early in the morning, but Jennifer had drained her energy. She tidied up her desk, then walked into Chaz's office to drop off the paperwork.

"He left in such a rush," she said, noting the messy desk that was a rare sight in Chaz Covington's office. She methodically began to straighten it up, putting files, pens, and other office accessories in their proper place. She opened the top drawer to put away his electronic calendar. That's when she saw the prepaid cell phone she'd purchased earlier.

"That's funny. Has it been here all this time?" Lois picked it up and punched a button. The screen lit up. *Oh, no! I didn't mean to turn it on!* She scanned the phone's face and was about to put it back into the drawer when she noticed an envelope icon, alerting the user that a message awaited. Obviously, the stalker had taken the bait and given Chaz her cell number. Lois didn't hesitate to open the text. She scrolled to the beginning of the exchange.

The first one was from Chaz: who are you?

The response: Is this really you?

Don't use my name, if you do, this is over.

Okay.

Who are you?

I want you.

I get that, but why?
I've wanted you for a very long time.
You're a creative writer.
You like?
Maybe.
Is there any way I can be with you? It would be so
good. . . .

Lois's jaw dropped as she read Chaz's answer: Anything's
possible.

13

Lois was still reeling the next morning. She arrived at the office at seven a.m., partly to finish the work she'd left last night and partly because she knew it would take her a couple hours to perfect the neutral face that would be necessary to greet her boss.

Since reading the last two lines of the text on Chaz's phone, the words had played like a mantra in Lois's head. The sender's blatant question: *Is there any way I can be with you?* And Chaz's unmistakably welcoming response: *Anything's possible.* Lois had spent part of the night and all of this morning trying to figure out why Chaz would have responded the way he did. She held him, his character and reputation, in the highest regard, and imagined him with a partner of taste and refinement. Sure, she'd heard the tales that men liked a lady in the living room and a whore in the bedroom, but Lois hadn't thought that applied to someone like Chaz. That's why she'd found the letters so intriguing, yet so ridiculous at the same time. They were just a joke, just fun and games. No one like Chaz would ever take such correspondence seriously. She'd expected Chaz to "rip the sender a new one," to tell them in biting and scathing terms that they must "cease and desist" immediately from their appalling behavior. But instead, he'd encouraged it.

It's only because he wants to catch the culprit. Lois's conclusion was logical, but it didn't make her feel better.

She finished the paper she was typing, looked at Chaz's closed office door, and then at her watch: 7:45. One of the attorneys was already in the office, but most other attorneys and all of the supporting staff arrived between eight and eight thirty. By the time Chaz arrived at his usual nine a.m. start time, the office was normally in full swing. *Don't do it, Lois. What's on that cell phone is Mr. Covington's business, not yours.* These were her thoughts, but her legs had other plans. Before she knew it, Lois had left her desk and walked into Chaz's office. She reached for the desk drawer key in its secret compartment underneath the desk, unlocked the drawer that she'd made sure was secure before she'd left the night before, and picked up the phone.

An envelope icon indicated the new message:

Why Mr. Covington, your personality is as sexy as I've imagined, and when it comes to you, I've imagined plenty. There are places I've never been before. I want you to take me there.

Lois squeezed her eyes shut, trying to block out the images that arose unbidden in her mind. Images created by the words of other letters and e-mails she'd read: *hard and naked, burning, massive manhood* . . . Lois stroked the edge of Chaz's desk, imagining it was his chest. The wood was hard and smooth, the intricately carved grooves at the edge felt similar to what she imagined the ridge of a penis tip felt like, after viewing one online a few nights before. She wanted to stop the thoughts but could not. She continued to stroke the wood, and the now familiar tingling that had started in her core began to spread lower. . . .

"You're here early!"

Lois's eyes flew open. *What in the world is Gina doing here this early?*

"So are you."

And Mr. Covington? Oh my God!

"Is that a new cologne you're wearing?" Gina asked Chaz, as Lois listened to the conversation happening just a few feet away. For the first time in her life, she was thankful for Gina's flirtatious nature. She hurriedly placed the cell phone back in the drawer, turned the lock, placed the key back in its holder, ran out of the room . . . and into the arms she'd envisioned seconds before. Her left knee and Chaz's heavy briefcase had a forceful encounter and her rather thick heel chose this most inconvenient moment to connect with the only snag in the carpet. The wobbling began and Chaz—whose hands were full with the briefcase in one hand and a smoothie in the other—helplessly watched the inevitable happen. Lois tried to right herself, but the law of gravity prevailed. She went down on the floor, her feet went up in the air, and the sound of ripping fabric suggested that Lois's humiliation wasn't over. If possible, Lois would have clicked her heels three times and been home. But one heel was still stuck in the carpet and the other heel dangled off Lois's nonmanicured toes—now exposed through a pantyhose run the size of Shaq's shoe. Lois prayed to God to die right then.

Chaz's firm grasp on her arm was the clue that she was still very much alive. "Lois, please, let me help you up."

"No!" Lois exclaimed, her exposed bare butt cheek making its acquaintance with the carpet. She'd purchased her second thong in her life the night before, and why she'd decided to wear it today was now beyond her. "I mean, thank you, Mr. Covington, but . . . I can't." Lois felt an ugly cry coming on. It was the last face she'd want her boss to see. And why was Mr. Covington groping her leg?

"Mr. Covington . . . please!"

"Lois, does this hurt?" Chaz squeezed Lois's calf and then her ankle.

Lois winced but not from the type of pain Chaz imagined. Chaz's touch was soft, yet firm. His hand was burning hot. Or was it her leg? All Lois knew was that she couldn't think while he touched her.

"Mr. Covington!" Lois shrilled again. The words were uttered more harshly than she intended. "I'm okay. It's just that, please, can you leave me alone?"

Totally unaware of the effect he was having on his employee, Chaz continued his chivalry. "It's okay, Lois. Let me help you." He moved closer, straightened out her leg, and reached for her foot.

A throat being cleared from the hallway deepened Lois's shame. *Great. Just what I need. Blabbermouth Gina as a witness to the worst experience of my life.* Later, she would wish that it *had* been Gina.

"Well, what do we have here?" Elizabeth Stein's voice was full of mock concern. "Your assistant where she always wanted to be: flat on her back with you hovering over."

Chaz whipped around just as Gina came up behind Elizabeth. "Sorry, Mr. Covington. I tried to ring you, but the phone was still on night service. I told her to wait, but . . ."

"It's okay, Gina." Chaz's voice was soft but stern. "Liz, wait outside. In the *main* lobby."

Elizabeth donned a smirk as she took a long, condescending look at Lois and then waltzed out the door.

Lois's eyes were wide as she looked at Gina, still standing in the doorway. As always, Gina looked impeccable. Today she wore an off-white pantsuit, accented by a strand of faux pearls. She looked liked someone Chaz would have on his arm, which made Lois acutely aware of the fact that the same couldn't be said for herself.

This realization was the last straw. Elizabeth Stein looked like a runway model, Gina could grace the cover of any fashion magazine, while Lois sat ass out, literally, suffering from rug burn and humility. Crocodile tears streamed from her eyes and pooled in her ear.

"I've got this, Gina," Chaz said, not missing the look of barely veiled glee on his employee's face.

"Okay, I'll get right back to work."

"Oh, and Gina? I don't want to hear about this incident from someone who wasn't here. This isn't to be fodder for the office gossip mill. Understood?"

"Yes, Mr. Covington." The teasing sparkle in her eyes effectively dimmed, Gina turned and went back to her desk.

"My pants are ripped," Lois said with a sob. "I'm ashamed to have you see me like this!" Her whiney voice resembled how Nettie sounded when Mister threw her off the farm. *Ain't nothin' but death can keep me from it!*

The lightbulb finally came on. "Oh my goodness," Chaz said. He rose quickly and turned away from Lois. "I was only trying to help." He walked to the door and stopped. "I'm going to the lobby to speak to Liz. There's an extra shirt in my bathroom. It should cover the, um, problem. Then you can go home and change. In fact, take the day off, if you'd like."

"No, Chaz, I mean Mr. Covington. I'll come back. I just need to change my pants."

"I'll be in court all day, Lois. I think you could use the break." He turned and left Lois sitting on his office floor.

Lois closed her eyes and waited until she heard the click of the door. Then she scurried to her feet and ran to the private bathroom in the back right corner of Chaz's office. When she looked in the mirror, only one thought came to mind: *I look even worse than I thought.* Her perfectly coiffed bun had come undone, her eyes were red, and a carpet burn scar graced her right cheek. As bad as she looked, it paled in comparison to how she felt. She'd made a fool of herself in front of the man she most admired. The more she thought about it, the better Chaz's offer sounded. "I need the day off," she murmured, remembering she hadn't taken a day off, sick or vacation, in a year and a half. Lois slipped her arms into the oversized sleeves of Chaz's shirt, making sure it covered the massive split in her pants. For a moment, she reveled in the feel of it, and in Chaz's scent that remained in the fabric. She started for the lobby and then, remembering Elizabeth Stein still lurked around, went out the rear entrance—all the while planning exactly how she would spend the rest of her day.

14

The sound of raised voices greeted Chaz as he rounded the corner into the main lobby of Covington Law Firm.

"I don't give a rat's ass who you are! I don't have to tell you a damn thing!"

"The 'no soliciting' sign is clearly visible as you enter the building, and you obviously have something you're trying to sell." Liz's clipped, East Coast boarding-school accent became more pronounced in anger.

The identity of the other voice dawned on Chaz as he rounded the corner.

"Bitch, I will wipe this floor—"

"Ladies! Get ahold of yourselves," Chaz ordered, stepping in between them. "Delicia, what are you doing here?"

"Yes," Elizabeth hissed, straining her neck to look around Chaz's broad chest. "What is a woman like *you* doing in a re-spectable establishment like *this*?"

"Do you have an appointment?" Chaz calmly turned and asked Elizabeth. She tossed a mass of blond hair, but remained silent. "Go wait in my office." Chaz watched her walk away, dispassionately noting how well her butt filled out the pair of rust-colored Anne Klein slacks, and how the color comple-mented her salon-tanned skin. He then turned to face Delicia

Smith, understanding Liz's assumption. Delicia wore a pair of white stretch pants that couldn't have been tighter had they been painted on. A set of forty-four double Ds wiggled like Jell-o above a bright red-and-blue-striped, low-cut baby-doll top, and Delicia's sudden growth spurt was explained when Chaz noted her size nine feet in five-inch stilettos. His expression made a verbalized question unnecessary.

"Uh, I was in the area?" Delicia offered in a soft, innocent voice.

Chaz donned a look of chagrin and crossed his arms.

"I bought a new car and wanted to take you for a ride?" Delicia's wide-eyed, "don't-know-nothin-'bout-birthin'-babies" look brought the merest hint of a smile to Chaz's lips, even as his eyes narrowed. "I wanted to see if you had any openings for a one-handed secretary?"

Chaz's stone face finally cracked and he laughed out loud. A sense of humor was probably one of Delicia's finest assets, and why she'd been able to turn tragedy into triumph. That, and a few million dollars.

"I'm sorry," she continued, her face sincere. "I know I need an appointment. I just . . . I just wanted to see you. And I did get a new car. The dealer gave it to me on credit, pending the arrival of my check."

Chaz gently grasped Delicia's arm and pulled her to the side as more employees entered the building. "Delicia," he began softly, and her nana tingled at the way he said her name. "I'm flattered at your interest in me, but I have a rule about not dating my clients. You're a smart, attractive woman, and now you have the means to transform your life in a way that will attract a man who's perfect for you." Chaz dropped his voice farther. "But I'm not him."

Delicia blinked away the tears that threatened. "Rules are made to be broken," she whispered. "It would be so good, Chaz. More cushion for the pushin' . . ."

Chaz's eyes narrowed once again, but Gina's voice interrupted his thoughts. "Mr. Covington, you have a call on line two. Also, I can call the temp agency if we need a fill-in for Lois."

Chaz gave Delicia's arm a final squeeze. "I have to go. Good-bye, Delicia."

Much as Chaz had done earlier with Elizabeth, Delicia watched Chaz's retreating form as he crossed the lobby. His pants were tailored to fit him perfectly, emphasizing the symmetry of his broad back, narrow waist, tight butt, and long legs. Delicia didn't realize her mouth was watering until she had to swallow.

Once he'd rounded the corner, Delicia turned and headed for the door. "Every good-bye ain't gone, Chaz Covington," she whispered to herself as she walked to her brand-new, white-on-white, customized Escalade. As soon as her onion touched the calfskin seat, she pulled out the pearl white Slide she'd purchased to match her car and began pecking out a text message using the thumb of her one good hand.

15

"You are way out of line," Chaz said, as soon as he'd returned to his office and closed the door. He'd told Gina to take a message, way too angry to speak with a client right now.

"I know." Elizabeth bowed her head slightly, a rare sight.

"This is my place of business and that woman you insulted, one of my clients. How dare you disrespect *anyone* who comes to my firm!"

"I'm sorry. I overstepped my bounds."

Chaz took a deep, calming breath. "I respect your commitment to my foundation and all of the contributions you've generated on its behalf. But that charity and this law firm are two different entities. Liz, if you need to see me at my place of business . . . make an appointment. Have I made myself clear?"

Elizabeth swallowed a sarcastic comment, as she correctly deduced that now was not the time for petulance. Instead she stated the reason for her impromptu visit. "I'm divorcing Max."

Chaz looked at Elizabeth a long moment, noting the sincerity in her eyes. "Your father would never allow it."

"This one's twenty-three," Elizabeth said, moving away from Chaz to stare out on a picture-perfect April day. "The granddaughter of my dad's best friend. The housekeeper caught them screwing in our bed, two o'clock in the afternoon." Elizabeth swallowed hard, trying to dislodge the sudden lump in her throat. "He's not even trying to hide them anymore."

Chaz came up and placed a comforting hand on Elizabeth's shoulder. He could more than relate to how she felt in this moment. "I'm sorry, Liz." Often viewed as a bitch on wheels, an emotionless vixen carved of stone, he was reminded of the truth: that Elizabeth Stein was an insecure, vulnerable trust-fund baby, who had hundreds of associates but very few friends. Whose looks made her the desire of men and envy of women, but whose life wasn't the fairy tale it seemed.

"Please, don't be," Elizabeth said, with a snort. Her signature hair toss and a squaring of the shoulders effectively dissipated the moment of vulnerability. "I'm going to pay him back by fucking his golfing partner's twenty-one-year-old son. And maybe the partner, too."

"C'mon, Liz, two wrongs don't make a right."

"No, but it will make me feel better. In fact"—Elizabeth's crystal blue eyes, darkened with desire, bored into Chaz— "there's someone else who can make me feel better, who can make me forget Max and all of his whores." Elizabeth walked up to Chaz, scraped long, manicured fingernails down his chest, and pressed her breasts against him. "I want you . . ." Elizabeth leaned in for a kiss.

He gently but firmly widened the space between them. "You really have to go, Liz. I'll call you later."

Fortunately for Chaz, a slew of work kept his mind off the women troubles that swirled around him. Perspicacious and cunning in the courtroom, only those closest to him knew Chaz's sensitive side. For the next eight hours following Elizabeth's departure, Chaz took calls, met with two potential clients, and spent the afternoon in the courtroom. He'd used his private bathroom to shower and change and now looked forward to an evening with the Bateses.

He was almost out the door when he remembered the prepaid cell phone he'd left the night before. He smiled as he sauntered back to get it, already anticipating what saucy comment his mystery writer had left for his pleasure. After retrieving the key from his hiding spot beneath the desktop, Chaz opened the drawer and picked up the phone. A slight frown creased his brow. *I thought I turned this off before I left.* He looked at the lit face another moment before slipping the phone into his briefcase and striding purposely away from the drama of the day.

An hour later, Chaz dug his fork into the dinner Taylor had prepared, and savored the bite. "James," he asked, after wiping his mouth with a napkin. "Did Taylor really cook this meal? The rice is cooked to perfection and the lobster rivals the best seafood in town."

"I was watching," James replied, around a mouthful of rice pilaf. "She did it."

"Well, I remember when she couldn't boil water. Man, you're a miracle worker to have turned her into a chef!"

"Uh, excuse me, but I'll take full credit for my honed cooking skills, thank you very much." Taylor's smile belied her words, and her face glowed at the praise. "I admit, I was a ramen-noodle queen back in college and served so much canned pasta during those first years of marriage that James used to call me Chef Boyardee."

Everyone laughed. "Yeah, but I knew my baby had potential," James said, picking up a lobster claw and sucking the juice. "Between my iron stomach and Taylor's addiction to the food channel . . . we not only survived, but thrived."

After a light dessert of raspberry sherbet, James and Chaz retired to the library, otherwise known as the "men's den." The entire room had been redesigned to be wheelchair friendly, with a bar, pool table, and cushioned dartboard all lowered to accommodate the new James. He rolled his chair over to the bar and poured two snifters of premium cognac.

Meanwhile, Chaz rolled and snipped two Cuban cigars. "I ran into one of your colleagues," he said, accepting the drink

James offered and handing him a stogie. "He said you're shaking things up at the school."

"How so?" James asked, even as his eyes sparkled.

"Said one of your students petitioned for and won a change in the grading process—something about using experience at a local hospital in lieu of finals. You wouldn't have anything to do with that, would you?"

"You know I was never one to stand on protocol, even when I could stand."

The men exchanged small talk and enjoyed their cigars in companionable silence. Chaz declined James's chess challenge, knowing that if the men started, the game would go well into the night. He looked forward to spending time with his children this weekend, even if he did have to pick them up at eight a.m.

James reached into a crystal bowl filled with nuts and changed the subject. "It's been a minute since a skirt has accompanied you on your visits. You losing your touch, or what?"

A lazy smile crossed Chaz's face. He blew smoke rings, and for the first time in hours, the earlier drama of the day—much like the blue-gray smoke from the Cuban classics—wafted away from him.

"I'm beginning to think my life would be much less complicated without skirts."

"Aw, shit. You ain't getting ready to switch hit are you?"

"Ha! Man, you trippin'."

James's rumble of a laugh was contagious, and soon Chaz joined in.

"What about that fine little filly you had over here a year or so ago?"

Chaz sighed. "Naomi."

"That's a fine sista right there. What's going on with her?"

"Galavanting the globe."

"What does she do again?"

"She's a retail consultant, helping small- and medium-sized companies establish their brands, design their stores . . . stuff like that."

"One of those independent types? Not interested in settling down?"

"She's moving back to Chicago soon."

"There you go, might be a chance there, brothah."

"Yeah, maybe."

"She had your nose open for a minute, I remember that."

"Listen at you, talking smack."

"Man, I'm just messing with you. Truth of the matter is . . ." James's voice trailed off into nothingness as he drained his glass and rolled over to pour another drink.

"What's the truth of the matter?" Chaz asked softly. Even after the accident, James was usually jovial and upbeat. One rarely detected melancholy in his voice.

"That girl out there is my heart," James said, his voice becoming gruff with emotion. "I'm already ten years Taylor's senior, straining to keep up with her . . . urges. She's a young, healthy woman . . ."

"She's committed to you, James."

James's voice dropped to a whisper. "I'm not the man she married."

"You're the man she loves. I've known Taylor since high school, brothah, and I've never seen her happier than the day you made her your wife."

James visibly swallowed. "Yes, but there are things I can't give her now, that I can't do. I wouldn't blame her for . . . seeking release, know what I'm saying? I'd understand."

Chaz simply nodded, resisting the urge to squirm. He believed he did know what James was saying—that he was either giving his blessing on Taylor having an affair, or worse, knew she was already having one, if the intermittent dalliances he and his best friend shared could be characterized as such. "Even with all you've endured, you're a blessed man, James," he finally said, and meant it. "It's not always easy to find love; don't ever take yours for granted."

They clinked and then drained their glasses. Shortly afterward, Chaz headed home. Again, the day's events and the women behind them drifted into his mind: Delicia Smith, an attractive woman with a good heart whose affections were well-intended if misplaced; Elizabeth Stein, dealing with what had been his lot a few short years ago; and Lois. Chaz turned up the jazz and pondered his capable assistant who had no life. He let out a gentle sigh, remembering how embarrassed Lois had been after losing her balance and falling flat on her rear. *She was sure in a hurry,* he thought, as he exited the highway and turned onto the boulevard where he lived. *You would have thought that . . .* Chaz's sharp lawyer mind sifted through the pieces that made up Lois's embarrassing incident. *Is that why she was in such a hurry? Because I arrived at the office unexpectedly early? I'm sure I turned it off last night, but my cell phone was on today. That could only mean . . .*

Chaz pulled into the driveway of his Hyde Park residence, his thoughts becoming crystal clear with each passing moment. Lois had seen the text messages, he decided. But a question remained: Was she reading the messages for the first time or reevaluating the handiwork she'd sent?

16

Lois was petrified, which was why she'd sat in the parking lot for the past fifteen minutes. *What will people think?* Lois pulled down the visor, checking her image for the umpteenth time. Then she looked at her watch—8:25. In two years, Lois had never arrived to work later than 8:30. And she wouldn't be late today.

Inside Covington Law Offices, someone else was a bundle of nerves. Gina had worked on this plan for weeks, had waited for just the right time to put it into motion. Lois's mishap and subsequent absence the previous Friday had given her the opening she'd needed. After settling in the temp who would answer Chaz's phone calls and handle light filing, Gina had sent Chaz an e-mail requesting a meeting. She'd been thrilled when he'd responded positively, instructing her to set up an unusually early Monday meeting at 8:15 a.m. Now here she sat, an outward sea of calm while her insides churned.

"Thanks again for taking the time to meet with me," she said as Chaz perused the proposal she'd given him. "I know how busy you are."

Chaz waved away her comment. "Frankly, your e-mail intrigued me. Just the other day, the partners and I were discussing how to restructure the office. We've grown exponentially in the last five years, barely able to keep up with the caseload, let alone oversee administration as a whole. An office manager, as you've suggested here, is just what we need." Chaz reared back in his chair and eyed Gina intently. "But what do you believe qualifies you for the job?"

Gina sat straighter in her chair, smoothing out a nonexistent wrinkle from the designer suit she'd purchased specifically for this occasion. It looked like a suit an office manager would wear: a rich navy color with a skirt that stopped just above the knee, paired with a light blue shell and understated jewelry. Her four-inch navy pumps with the silver heels gave a bit of sassiness to the ensemble, while the decision to pull back her thick hair into a ponytail highlighted big brown eyes and a mouth that made men think of doing things to it.

Gina demurely placed her hands in her lap and looked Chaz straight in the eye. "Mr. Covington, I have worked hard for everything I've ever gotten in life. This work ethic came from my immigrant parents, who fed a family of seven through lawn services and domestic care. I'm the first in our family to pursue a college education. I am very proud of my secretarial certification, and starting this fall, I plan to pursue a degree in business management from the University of Phoenix.

"Being the oldest in my family, I was often left in charge of everyone. This is where I honed my supervisory and organizational skills, and why I'm a very mature woman for being only twenty-seven years old. Having four competitive brothers is how I learned to wield diplomacy. I am bilingual, get along well with people of all backgrounds, am tenacious when I have a goal, and quite frankly, Mr. Covington, I'd like to establish myself as an invaluable member of your team." Gina crossed her legs, which caused her skirt to ride a bit higher on her thigh. Her face and look were the epitome of professionalism, but raw sexuality oozed from her pores.

You are an attractive woman, Gina Perez. And a smart one, too.

Chauvinistic or no, attractive women fared well in the legal environment. As in many professions, beauty and brains were often a formula for success. "What would you say to the fact that there are other, more qualified assistants here?"

"I'd say that they're not here, in your office, with a well-thought-out plan," Gina quickly retorted. "No one will work harder for you than I will, Mr. Covington. Not even Lois Edwards."

Chaz's brow rose. "Few people in this business, or any business for that matter, can top Lois's skills, Gina. You'd do well to steer clear of comparisons where she's concerned."

Gina had wondered how secure Lois's job was as Chaz's assistant, a job that she'd love to have even more than that of office manager. She'd just found out. "I don't mean to imply that Lois is anything but a first-rate assistant," she explained, a bright smile following the obvious faux pas. "I like Lois. Speaking of which, will she be in today or should I call the temp agency?"

"That won't be necessary, Gina," Lois said from the doorway. "I'm here."

Chaz looked up, Gina turned, and two pairs of eyes widened in surprise. Chaz spoke first. "Wow, it's obvious a day off agrees with you, lovely!"

The usually chatty Gina was at a loss for words. When she found her voice, her statement was obvious: "You've changed your hair."

Lois shrugged, yet displayed her nervousness by self-consciously running a hand across the newly cut do. She was still getting used to the silky tresses, permed to within an inch of their life. The asymmetrical cut framed Lois's face in a way that highlighted prominent cheekbones, and the freshly arched brows brought attention to almond-shaped eyes that before went unnoticed. "I went to the mall," she finally offered, with not yet enough courage to look Chaz in the eye. "They were offering free makeovers."

Thankfully, the phone rang, ending what was for Lois an

extremely awkward moment. "I'll get that," she murmured, rushing to her desk to do so. She'd been surprised to see Gina's computer on when she'd passed her desk, and even more surprised to hear voices from Chaz's office. Belatedly, she realized that in her nervousness, she'd paid absolutely no attention to what other cars were in the parking lot shared by several companies in the building. *What is Gina doing here this early?* she thought, even as she passed the call through to Chaz. The bigger question, Lois realized, was what were Gina and Chaz doing here *together* so early in the morning?

The early morning encounter with Chaz and Gina threw off Lois's rhythm. She went through the motions of her normal routine to try and get it back: going to the mailroom for the day's correspondence and then on to the break room for what had become a daily cup of joe. Everyone noticed the change in her appearance: some complimented, others commented, and a few simply stared. By the time she reached her desk, the butterflies had returned.

It seemed like a good idea at the time. After Friday's embarrassment, Lois had gone to the mall to get the kind of fix that only shopping could provide. She'd gone to a large department store to purchase a gift, and run into a company promoting makeovers for the summer. One of the promoters had taken one look at Lois and declared her a perfect candidate. Any other time, Lois wouldn't have considered such a thing for a second, but the rough morning she'd experienced had left her open for change. That and the fact that she'd have an entire week before she'd have to explain herself, since her mother was preaching at a week-long, out-of-town revival. In a rare moment of spontaneity, Lois had agreed to the makeover, and had spent the next three hours being pampered and prodded, scrubbed and massaged, and given tips on how to dress in a way that flattered her physique. She'd then bought two skirts that would dare show her knees for the first time since puberty, and a suit jacket with a flared bottom that covered her hips while giving the appearance of a rounder bottom. She'd also purchased a pair of flashy gold earrings that complemented her cross necklace, and a pair of spiked heels, a marked contrast to the clunky two-inch heels she preferred, and in which she felt most comfortable. That she'd still managed to stumble and fall in said clunky heels would have given a lesser soul pause, but Lois had made a decision while languishing on the floor in her boss's office: she wanted Chaz to notice her the way she believed he noticed Gina and Elizabeth and Delicia and Jennifer: as a desirable woman.

The perfunctory routine of opening mail began to calm Lois's nerves. She continued to ponder on the events of the morning, the way Chaz's eyes had widened noticeably when he took in her appearance. *Is it me, or did his eyes sparkle a bit?* Lois allowed her imagination free rein, imagined being with Chaz behind closed doors, sprawled beneath him for reasons other than a snagged heel. These types of thoughts were still uncomfortable for Lois, but the small trickle had become a torrent ever since she'd received the first anonymous letter two weeks ago.

Lois reached for the next piece of mail and her hand stopped in midair. It was as if she'd conjured it up with her thoughts. She instinctively knew what it was before she opened it—even though this envelope was larger and bubble cushioned. The familiar bold, Arial font lettering seemed to leap off the page. Lois closed her eyes, swallowed, and then opened her eyes once more. The envelope was still there: teasing, taunting. *Open me.*

It was the first physical piece of mail they'd received in almost a week, the writer having shifted to e-mails and text messages. Lois had been glad for the reprieve, even though she'd reread the letters contained in the Miscellaneous—N folder several times. It was a fact that embarrassed her, yet over which she seemed to have little control. With every word, every letter dripping with sexual innuendos and promiscuous promises, a part of Lois had seemed to come more and more alive. And later, with each word she'd typed, her soul opened up. Now there were feelings—vibrant, pulsating longings and needs—that Lois had previously pushed to the bottom of her heart. The times were still few and far between that she allowed herself to acknowledge these carnal urgings, after which she'd ask forgiveness for the sins of her weak flesh. But now, looking at the envelope that seemed hot to the touch, Lois knew it was one of those times when she would stop the judgmental thinking and simply allow herself to feel. She quickly looked around and, seeing that no one was looking at her or coming down the hall, Lois slipped the envelope into her purse and headed for the restroom.

> *Chaz, my soon-to-be-lover . . .*
> *I'm still reeling at the fact that you responded, that I'm actually exchanging words with my heart's desire. Said heart is pounding with excitement at the thought that we may soon be together, that I'll soon be writhing and sweating beneath you. My pussy tingles at the thought of your dick thrusting deep inside me. Ooh baby, I'm so wet, even as I write this.*

Lois squirmed on the toilet seat as she continued to read.

> *In anticipation of the inevitable, I've purchased a few playthings. I've said it before, but I'll say it again: our night together will be one that neither of us ever forgets.*
> *Signed, Ready and Waiting*

Lois quickly read the note a second time before placing it back inside the envelope. She checked herself in the mirror, thankful that how she felt on the inside did not show on her face. New hairdo, plucked eyebrows, and minimal makeup aside, Lois felt she pretty much looked like she always had. But inside, the changes felt immense. As she walked back to her desk, her mind stayed on what had been said in the letter, as well as the enclosures that had accompanied it. It was the first time she'd ever held a package of condoms; she hadn't known that they came in "magnum" size. Shortly after sitting down at the computer, she learned the use of the other item that had been enclosed. Forbidden images of Chaz leaped into her mind. She tried to shake them, but it was impossible. *Would Chaz ever really do such a thing?*

"Lois."

Lois jumped at the sound of Chaz's voice on her phone's intercom.

"Yes, Mr. Covington?"

"I need the transcript for the Jones' case. And have you finished typing that motion?"

"It's almost ready. I'll bring in the transcript now."

"Thank you."

A few seconds later, Lois walked into Chaz's office. She was keenly aware of how handsome he looked, impeccably dressed as always, in a chocolate brown suit paired with a tan shirt and pin-striped tie. "Here's the transcript on the Jones' case. And here's your mail." She placed it in Chaz's in-box and then hesitated. "You received another letter."

"Oh, really?"

"Yes, I filed it along with the others."

Chaz noted Lois's discomfort. "Did you read it?"

Lois nodded. "I scanned it. There were, it had . . . there were enclosures."

"Don't tell me. Naked pictures."

"No, Mr. Covington . . . other things. Look, I'd better finish typing that brief. I know you need it ASAP." Without waiting for a response, Lois fled Chaz's office.

She tried to keep the image of the Chaz she'd just seen in

the front of her mind: professional, respectful, but most of all, clothed. But another image kept flitting across her mental screen, the one that she could barely imagine: the one with Chaz using the items that the anonymous letter had contained, one of which she'd had to look up online to learn its use. Since reading the description, Lois couldn't stop imagining Chaz naked and wearing . . . a cock ring.

17

Chaz had purposely waited until he arrived home to examine the latest anonymous letter's contents. The look on Lois's face had definitely piqued his curiosity, but Chaz didn't want anything to take him off focus from what had been a full, yet productive day. The text messages between him and his mystery woman had gotten more and more provocative and, along with what seemed to be an insatiable libido, the woman had also displayed intelligence, creativity, and a sense of humor. While changing from his suit into a pair of sweats, he remembered her response to his request to tell him more about her:

I'll tell you a little, but not too much;
I'm firm to the handling but soft to the touch.
At first glance, you might consider me meek and mild,
But behind bedroom doors I will get buck wild!

Chaz chuckled at the memory, poured a glass of OJ, and then went into his home office. He laughed again when he pulled out the condoms and the cock ring. "A little freaky, huh?" he said to himself, while examining the sex toy. He wasn't a man much into sex aids, but after reading the description on the box, decided to be open to new possibilities.

After finishing the letter, Chaz reached for the prepaid

phone, which, after suspecting Lois of snooping, he now kept at home. He leaned back, got comfortable in his chair, and typed in a message: Thanks for the gifts.

Chaz sipped his drink and checked e-mails, waiting for a response. *She might not be near her phone.* He reached for the iPod that was banked in its dock, and turned it on. Soon, the classic sound of George Benson's *Breezin'* oozed out of the speakers. A second later, his message indicator beeped. Chaz smiled as he read it.

You're welcome . . . in every way.

You seem extremely adventurous, and experienced. Not professional, are you? :)

Ha! Not hardly. I just have a vivid imagination, like you have a big . . . I did get it right, didn't I? With the magnum condoms?

Yes.

::Smiling:: I want to be with you . . . now!

My curiosity is piqued, not sure meeting is wise.

Why?

You're a stranger.

Not so strange . . .

You like getting your freak on.

Yes. I want to get it on with you. When?

When what?

When can I feel your dick in my pussy?

Chaz shifted in his chair, and allowed more room for his burgeoning shaft. You're being a very bad girl.

Not as bad as I want to be.

I have a reputation to protect.

It will be our secret, promise.

How can I be sure?

You make the rules: time, place . . . whatever you want.

There are lots of successful men. Why me?

The response wasn't immediate. For a moment, Chaz thought she'd decided not to respond. But after a while, his message indicator beeped.

Because I respect and admire you. I adore you. You're a good man.

Thanks.

I meant every word. Can I be with you? Please?

I'll think about it.

Just say the word and I'm there, with legs spread wide. . . .

Chaz turned off the prepaid phone. He massaged his shaft, grateful when it finally began to lose its erection. He looked at the clock and thought to call Taylor. Even though it was only a little past eight, inviting her over was a short-lived idea. He didn't know that he would ever be intimate with Taylor again. After his conversation with James, and even with her husband's indirect blessing, Chaz felt guilty. He decided instead to take a quick shower. When he stepped out of the stall, his phone was ringing.

"I'm in the mood to be a bad girl."

Chaz's heart clinched. *Naomi! Using the words that . . .* He smiled, believing the identify of his mystery letter writer might not be anonymous for very much longer. "Hey, you."

"I called earlier, didn't get an answer." Naomi's voice was soft, sinfully sweet.

The sound reminded Chaz of the sticky bun he'd eaten that morning. "I was in the shower."

"Umm, and thinking of me."

"Always." Chaz didn't miss the fact that this was spoken as a statement, not a question. "When am I going to see you?"

"I've been asking the same thing."

"So," Chaz began, reclining on his bed. "Are you finally ready to acknowledge that you miss me and that you can't live without me?"

Naomi chuckled softly, her voice lowered even more. "Not exactly."

"Then tell me, Ms. Stone. What are you ready to acknowledge?"

"I'm almost done here."

"Another happy client, I'm sure?"

"This one was fun, actually. A young ex-punker who's trying to brand a style that is a cross between grunge and glam."

"Is that possible?"

"You'd be surprised how sexy crystals can look on a pair of well-worn jeans."

"Not if you were the one wearing them, I wouldn't. Baby girl, you'd look good in a paper bag."

"Thanks, baby. That's sweet."

"That's fact."

They chatted a little longer—Naomi inquiring about Chaz's children, Chaz explaining his latest legal victory. The flow of conversation was smooth and natural, and before long, turned sensual again.

"I'd better get off of this phone. I can see you're about to start something that you can't finish." Not only did Chaz have an early morning appointment, but he didn't want to have to take another cold shower. "Seriously, Naomi. When am I going to see you? I'm tired of going to bed and waking up alone. I want you here, now."

"I'll arrive when you least expect it," Naomi answered, enticingly. "Just know I'm on my way."

18

Delicia stood in the exquisitely manicured backyard of another potential new home. She'd been house hunting for almost a month, ever since the day the judge and jury had sided in her favor. It would be another six to eight weeks before she received the check, but based on the inevitable arrival of a big chunk of change, she'd found a bank willing to extend her a line of credit. Having grown up on the south side, Delicia had often dreamed what it would be like to have the type of home you wanted, the type of car you wanted, and all of the clothes that you could buy. She remembered watching *Lifestyles of the Rich and Famous*, had even made champagne her drink of choice for a while, inspired by the show's famous tagline: champagne wishes and caviar dreams. Now, she was realizing everything she'd wished for, and very soon would be living the life of her dreams.

"Country Club Hills is a wonderful community for your family," the realtor said as she continued the tour. "The streets are safe and the schools are excellent. This house is priced to sell, which means there will more than likely be several offers. If you're interested, I suggest we move fast."

Delicia nodded. She found it interesting, bordering on ludicrous, that a home listed at over three hundred thousand dollars was considered a bargain. But that's how the four-bedroom, three-and-a-half-bath, Tudor-styled home had been described. When she'd begun the search for her self-described mansion, the numbers had astounded her. Now she knew more about the market, and also what a generally solid investment a home could be. "A good place to put your money," the financial planner that Chaz referred her to had explained. Delicia agreed. If anything happened to her, her children wouldn't be homeless.

"Shall we go back inside, take a look at the guest bedrooms and the master suite?"

They walked into the home, passed the state-of-the-art kitchen and dining room where Delicia had already envisioned Thanksgiving dinner being served, and climbed the staircase to the second floor. They looked at two nice-sized bedrooms and a hall bathroom before walking to the master suite on the opposite end. The realtor opened the door and then stepped back to let Delicia enter.

"This is beautiful," Delicia said as she looked around. The first thing she noticed about the room was its size. The living room of her current abode could fit inside this space, with room to spare. Plenty of sunshine streamed in from three large windows while a cozy sitting area with built-in shelves anchored the other side of the room. But the jewel of the room, the master bath, is what Delicia would later say sealed the deal for her. Sea green and icy-blue glass squares were the backsplash to the oversized Jacuzzi that took up one corner of the large room. On the other side was a shower stall and next to it, a vanity complete with marble bench and makeup lights. A walk-in closet and dressing room was just beyond the vanity, and the toilet area was separate. Unexpectedly, tears welled up in Delicia's eyes. "It's really beautiful," she repeated, her voice hushed and reverent.

"Would be the perfect place for a romantic evening with you and your guy," the realtor said. Sensing a sale, she wanted

to paint pictures that her client could see and, just as important, feel. The smell of chocolate-chip cookies worked in the
kitchen; talk of love and romance usually helped sell the master suite.

"Yes, it would," Delicia answered, her finger skimming the
counter where the "his and her" sinks were housed. When
daydreaming about her and Chaz being together, she hadn't
been able to imagine him being in her cramped, inner-city
apartment. She could imagine him here.

"Well, what do you think?" the realtor asked as they walked
back through the house and stood in the living room, where a
beamed, vaulted ceiling offered an unobstructed view of the
dining room's crystal chandelier.

"I think I'd like to make an offer."

19

"Daddy! Can I get an ice cream cone? Please?"

"Of course, sweetie." Chaz's heart filled with love for his daughter. He'd readily admit that she had him wrapped around her finger. She was daddy's little girl, in looks and temperament. Chaz adored her. He pulled out a five-dollar bill and gave it to Cherish. "You want one, too, son?"

He gave his namesake a five-dollar bill, then turned and saw Jennifer's broad smile. "What about you?"

"What I want to lick is not in a cone."

"Ha! C'mon, now. Behave."

"I'll try," Jennifer answered. But her mischievous smile suggested otherwise.

It was the second two-parent family outing since the children's therapist had suggested it two months ago. There'd been little change in Cherish's demeanor following Chaz and Jennifer's separation and ultimate divorce, but Chaz, Jr. had become more quarrelsome and his grades took a dive. Since beginning the therapy, however, both parents had seen improvement. For Jennifer, the therapist suggesting outings involving both parents was an unexpected plus.

The family enjoyed a pleasant afternoon at Safari Land, a time filled with fun rides and junk food. As they walked to the parking lot with two satisfied yet sleepy children, both Chaz and Jennifer were remembering that there had been good times in their marriage, a time when they'd both been madly in love.

"I'd forgotten how much fun we could have together," Jennifer said, after the children had hugged their mother and gotten in the backseat of Chaz's car.

"I enjoyed it, too," Chaz answered.

"I'd do anything to have a second chance with you, Chaz. There isn't a day that goes by when I don't kick myself for what happened. You're an excellent lawyer, a wonderful father, and a good man. If I had it all to do over again—"

"Let's not dwell on what we can't change," Chaz interrupted, even as something she said niggled at his mind. "This was a good day, let's leave it at that. Your therapist deserves a thank-you. I can see a change in the kids, especially C.J."

"It does make a difference, doesn't it? The children seeing their parents together, acting civilized, happy. C.J. has a track meet in two weeks. Maybe we can—oh, hold on a minute."

Jennifer had felt her vibrating phone in her pocket. She read its face and smiled. "Hold on," she said, without looking at Chaz. Instead she focused on the keyboard, her thumbs moving rapidly as she typed in a message.

Chaz looked on with interest as his wife finished the message and placed the phone back in her pocket.

"Sorry about that," Jennifer said, still smiling.

"I never knew you to be a text messager," Chaz said, a myriad of thoughts racing through his head.

"I haven't been doing it long, only a few months."

"Couldn't tell it from how fast your fingers moved over those keys."

"You remember how I used to beat your butt at video games. This kind of stuff comes to me naturally."

"You don't say. Well, you're obviously good at it."

Jennifer hugged Chaz. He noted that her embrace was one

of familiarity, her right hand rubbing his back while her left hand squeezed the back of his neck in a way she knew drove him wild. The feminine scent of her musky perfume assaulted his nostrils, even as the feel of her soft breasts pressing against Chaz's chest became all too noticeable. Of their own volition, Chaz's arms tightened around Jennifer, his right hand inching precariously close to the butt he used to squeeze in the throes of lovemaking. He brushed her buns with the palm of his hand. Jennifer reacted by pressing herself into him and placing a light kiss on his lips.

"Mama, I have to use the bathroom," C.J. announced from the backseat window.

And the spell was broken.

"You come, too, baby girl," Chaz said to his daughter, as C.J. bounded from the car. Chaz punched his son playfully. "It would have been too much like right for you to use it before we left the park, huh?" Then he turned to Jennifer. "This was a good day, Jen. I hope it is reflective of the type of relationship we can have . . . for the sake of the children."

Jennifer stared at Chaz, not trying to hide the love in her eyes. "What time should I pick the kids up tomorrow?"

"How about I drop them off? Maybe we can even go out to dinner, us and the kids."

"I'd like that!"

"Okay." Chaz gave Jennifer another brief hug and then followed his children, who were already running back toward the restroom just inside the park's entrance.

After they'd all done their business, Chaz, Cherish, and C.J. returned to Chaz's BMW. All the way home, the kids chattered about how much fun they'd had and which had been their favorite rides. Chaz engaged them in conversation but at the same time, thought of other things. Like how good Jennifer had felt in his arms. And about her newly developed texting skills.

20

"Liz, I'm deeply grateful for this." Chaz looked up from the two-hundred-and-fifty-thousand-dollar check he held, and blessed Elizabeth with a smile.

"It's from the heart," Liz replied, purposely using the name of Chaz's beloved foundation.

"Even though you have a lot of it, there are many places you could spend your money. Believe me when I say that I truly appreciate it. Thank you."

"You're welcome."

Silence ensued, as Chaz and Elizabeth looked at one another with appreciation—for very different reasons. Neither would have disagreed that at another time, another place, they might have been one of Chicago's power couples. One of them still wished that, because it seemed highly unlikely that they'd ever *be* a couple, they could couple, at the very least.

"I'd like to have you over for dinner," Elizabeth said.

You'd like to have me for dinner, more likely. "I don't think the two of us alone, without a chaperone, is a good idea," Chaz responded.

"You're a big boy. And I won't bite. Not much, anyway . . ."

"How are things with Max?" Chaz asked, in an abrupt change of subject.

Elizabeth sighed, and the slightest hint of vulnerability showed in her eyes. "Well, you were right. We're not getting divorced."

"What exactly did your father say?"

"That hell would freeze over and the moon would fall before that happened. Oh, and he also included a pesky detail about me being cut off from my inheritance."

"Kenneth Owens is nothing if not exacting."

"My dad's a royal pain in the ass."

"He's a shrewd businessman who'd give his life for you," Chaz countered. "Looking at you and this check from your public relations firm, a business I know you built without your father's money, I'd say the apple didn't fall far from the tree."

Elizabeth glowed at the praise.

"So how did you and Max kiss and make up?"

"He bought me the vacation home I'd been eyeing in the Bahamas. The one I want to use for clandestine getaways." Elizabeth looked pointedly at Chaz. "And we agreed to formally have an open marriage."

Chaz Covington was shocked, and he didn't shock easily. "You're lying."

"Scout's honor. It's the only way he and I will be able to peacefully co-exist. This means we can be together, Chaz. I can have sex with you without breaking my vows."

"What happened to the golf-partner's son?"

"Oh, God. That little bunny rabbit came almost before he was in good."

"Ha!"

"Half my age and no staying power. But I'm sure you, on the other hand . . ."

"Excuse me, Mr. Covington," Lois interrupted, after tapping lightly on Chaz's closed door. "But your two o'clock appointment is here." She walked over to Chaz and handed him a folder. "These are the notes from your first meeting."

"Get them settled in the conference room, Lois. I'll be right there."

Elizabeth watched Lois walk out of the room. "She sure has a different pep in her step. What did you do?"

"Not what *I* did, what *she* did . . . got a makeover at the mall."

"Poor little thing. I hardly noticed. Then again, I guess it's the first time I saw her hair outside of a bun or ponytail. You know she's in love with you."

"So I've been told. But true or not, that has nothing to do with Lois's proficiency. She's an excellent employee."

"Yeah, one I just might steal from you."

"Oh, really? Why's that?"

"Melanie turned in her two-weeks' notice, right before I left the office to come here."

"Did she finally have enough of your verbal assaults?"

"The little twat was incompetent. And if it's left up to me, she won't get another job in this town."

Chaz stood. "Well, then, it's a good thing it's not left up to you."

"Oh, so you think you might hire her?"

"I have a couple of openings. We've promoted Gina Perez to office manager, so we need another secretary and a couple more file clerks." He came around from his desk, hugged Elizabeth, and gave her a kiss on the cheek. "Thanks again, Elizabeth. For everything."

Elizabeth kissed Chaz on the lips. She looked into his eyes and kissed him again. "There's only one way you can truly thank me, Chaz Covington. When the opportunity arises, and it *will* arise . . . don't blow it."

21

Later that evening, Chaz and Lois chatted in the sitting area of Chaz's office. They'd gone over the events of the day, Chaz's schedule for the rest of the week, and now discussed how Lois would be affected by Gina's promotion.

"So, she's like . . . my supervisor?" Lois asked, not aware of the frown that accompanied the question.

"You've only got one boss, and that's me," Chaz replied. "We've made it very clear in the job description that Gina is to manage the office, not the secretaries. All of you will still report to the attorneys you work for. Gina will oversee the file clerks and other supporting personnel—cleaners, maintenance, lawn services, temp services, and so on. She'll also be the liaison for social events and work with our public relations firm to heighten our profile, especially when it comes to community projects." When Lois remained silent, Chaz continued. "Lois, is this a position you would have wanted? If so, I offer no apologies. When it came to making this decision, I was very selfish. You're the best legal secretary I've ever seen, and I appreciate being able to bounce ideas off of you. As long as you're in this firm, which I truly hope is a long time, you're working for me."

Any resistance that Lois had to the idea evaporated in that moment.

"I'm thinking about having a meeting."

Lois knew Chaz had changed the subject, but didn't know in which direction. "A meeting?"

"With Ms. Anonymous."

"The person writing the letters?"

Chaz nodded. He was 98 percent sure he knew the sender's identity, but the remaining 2 percent was why he decided to tell Lois about his plans. He had to cover all of his bases, in case this was a setup.

"Do you think that's a good idea?" Lois tried but failed to keep from fidgeting in her chair.

"I want to know who it is," Chaz said truthfully, continuing to eye Lois intently. He'd noticed her fidgeting and wondered if the reason had anything to do with the 2 percent.

"But then would you . . . oh, I'm sorry. Never mind."

"Would I what? Act out the things she's written in the letters?"

Lois bowed her head, too embarrassed to speak.

"I doubt whoever it is would even show," Chaz replied, trying to prevent Lois from further embarrassment. "But with a meeting, there is one person I could effectively eliminate from suspicion."

"Pete Bennett?"

Chaz nodded.

"How could you be sure he wasn't behind whoever showed up?"

"I've thought about that. I have my ways."

"Pardon me for being honest, Mr. Covington. But you have a nationally recognized law firm with a staunch reputation to uphold. Any scandal resulting from a meeting would be costly and detrimental. If you decide to move forward, please make sure you've counted all the costs."

Chaz looked at Lois, respect in his eyes. "You'd make a good attorney, Lois. Have you considered law school?"

For the second time today, Lois warmed at her boss's praise. Later that night, she'd feel the heat a third time. And once again, thoughts of Chaz would be the reason.

22

"I need you, Chaz." Taylor toyed with the straw in her daiquiri. They sat on The Terrace at The Peninsula Chicago.

"I want you," Chaz replied. The weekend following the dinner at the Bateses, Chaz had told Taylor about his conversation with James and how uncomfortable it had made him. He and Taylor had continued to talk almost every day, but since that night this was the first time they'd seen each other. "How's James?" he asked at last.

"He's . . . okay." A wistful smile appeared on Taylor's face. "But lately he's become obsessed with sex, and the fact that he can't satisfy me . . . like he used to."

"But what about oral?"

"I try and reassure him that he's still handling his business, that I'm satisfied. And I am, most of the time."

"And those other times?" Chaz softly asked.

Taylor looked at Chaz. Her eyes shimmered with unshed tears. She shrugged, but remained silent.

"You know how much I love you, Taylor. You're my best friend. But James is also my friend. And while he thinks he can handle your stepping outside the marriage, and even encourage it to a degree, the reality of actually finding out would feel quite different. Trust me, I know."

"But Jennifer cheated on you. You had no idea there was somebody else."

"So what will we do? Go to James, announce our intentions, and make sure he's okay with the idea?"

"Well . . . when you put it that way, the idea does seem preposterous. But what if you didn't know?"

"What do you mean?"

"What if our meeting happened anonymously . . . like the person writing those letters?"

Chaz sat back and crossed his arms. "How could that happen?"

Taylor smiled. "It could actually be kinda sexy. You know: blindfold, handcuffs, soft feathers, and melted chocolate . . ."

"Whoa, where's my friend Taylor, and who's this dominatrix sitting in front of me?"

"Ha! What can I say, Chaz Covington? You're bringing out the freak in me."

"Freak" wasn't a word often bandied about in Chaz's circle. The fact that he'd heard it used recently from two very different women, whom he dearly loved for different reasons, wasn't lost on him.

"I told James I was meeting an old colleague and that I'd probably be late getting back." Taylor's eyes were searching, beckoning . . .

But a voice from the past pushed its way to the surface, the voice of another spouse explaining her lateness. "They're having a fund-raiser at the radio station," Jennifer had said, sometimes substituting "private party" or "meeting" for the event. "I offered to volunteer. I'll be home late."

While the circumstances were different, to Chaz the feeling was familiar and did not feel good. He was a viral man who needed release, and he would get it soon. But it wouldn't be tonight.

"I've got a busy day tomorrow," he said, hoping that this truthful statement would serve to let Taylor down easy. He stood and reached for his suit jacket. "I'm in court all day to-morrow. Best prepare myself with a good night's sleep."

"You're probably right," Taylor said, standing as well. "But remember one thing, Chaz. What James doesn't know won't hurt him. And it won't hurt you either."

Chaz nodded, but as he left the restaurant, he was more confused than ever. *What I won't know won't hurt me?* "What is it that I won't know?" he murmured aloud, as he waited for the valet to bring around his car.

The answer came as he tipped the driver and got behind the wheel. *You don't know the identity of who's been writing the letters.* Chaz didn't, but he knew one thing: he was about to find out.

23

Chicago's elite had turned out for the invite-only dinner, where the mayor of Chicago was scheduled to present Chaz and the From the Heart Foundation with a special award. The charity had formed an alliance with a local hospital that was committed to bringing a world-class team of scientists and cardio specialists to the Windy City. Chaz had made a one-million-dollar donation from his foundation to advance the cause. As he sat at the head table, along with the mayor; Elizabeth's father, Kenneth Owens; and other city notables, Chaz knew in his heart that his mother was smiling down from above. In her memory and honor, he'd had the place decorated in hues of yellow, her favorite color, and had devised a menu from her favorite foods: steak, potatoes, and pecan pie, but prepared in lighter, healthier versions. His memories were bittersweet, but he reveled in the fact that attention was being given to a hideous disease. If even one life was saved as a result of his efforts, he'd believe that his mother's untimely passing had not been in vain.

Chaz excused himself from the table and began to work the room. The speeches would begin shortly, but there were still a few people he hadn't personally thanked. He stopped at the table directly beside where he'd sat and thanked Max for supporting all of the time and money his wife, Liz, put into the charity. He noticed that Elizabeth smiled obligingly but it didn't reach her eyes. Later, he would wonder if her pout had anything to do with the gorgeous, twenty-something sistah who also dined at their table. Chaz waved at Lois, who looked out of place, yet happy, as she sat at a table with Gina, Melanie, and other members of the law firm staff. He acknowledged the attorney whose unrelenting advances could be labeled sexual harassment; the matronly socialite who'd offered Chaz five million dollars to bed her and, after he refused, had given only half a million dollars to the charity; and attorneys from his old law firm. After shaking hands with James and hugging Taylor, Chaz greeted news personnel, local talk-show hosts, and doctors from the partner hospital, and he finally stopped at a table that bore two of the people he most loved in the world.

"You are the belle of the ball, honey," he said, as he knelt down and hugged Cherish. He turned and hugged C.J. "I thought I was the most handsome man in the room," he said, straightening the collar of his son's tuxedo. "But I think you've got me beat."

"Oh, Dad," C.J. moaned. But his eyes beamed.

"Thanks for coming and bringing the children," he said, sitting at the recently vacated chair next to Jennifer. "You look good. But the jury is still out on that chump you brought with you."

"Antonio is a good friend," Jennifer responded, delighted at the thought that Chaz might be jealous. "And the children love him."

"Love him?" Chaz lowered his voice. "Is this guy spending time at the house? Around my kids?"

"Now, Chaz, I don't know that that is any of your business."

"If it involves my children, it's my business."

"No worries, darling. You and I still have unfinished business. If all goes well, we'll take care of it soon."

Before Chaz could respond, Jennifer's date returned with their drinks. Jennifer made the somewhat stilted introductions, and then Chaz was forced to return to his table. It was time for the ceremonies to begin.

Tomorrow, the events of the evening would be splashed across both the business and society pages. But tonight, as the evening came to an end and Chaz drove through the rainy Chicago streets, his thoughts weren't on his professional success but rather his life's personal puzzle. Underlying issues aside, seeing Elizabeth with her husband and Jennifer with a date served to highlight Chaz's loneliness in a room filled with one hundred people. He'd hoped that Naomi would return in time to join him. But the last two calls he'd made to her had gone to voice mail. Chaz knew that he was an eligible man who could get almost any woman he wanted. Yet tonight, he realized that the most intimate female interaction he'd had recently had been from a distance: through letters, e-mails, and text messages. By the time Chaz reached his home, he'd made a decision. It was time to get up close and personal. He unlocked his door, walked straight to his study, and picked up the prepaid cell.

24

Let's meet.

Even though it was after eleven, the response came almost immediately. When? Where?

Chaz typed in the information, a boutique hotel he often used for intimate business dinners and off-site meetings. The owner was a personal friend; the staff, people he could trust. He remembered this as he typed his response:

I've covered all my bases. If you don't show up alone, are working with anyone to make this a tabloid moment, or are trying to exploit me in any way, this meeting will NOT take place.

::Smiling:: Trust me, I want this meeting to be strictly between you and me. Though I must say . . . I didn't take you for the paranoid type.

But you do realize that I am the don't "f" with me type, right?

Of course. I have a request as well.

???

I want us to meet with the lights out until we've . . . you know . . . done it.

Why?

Contrary to what you may believe . . . I'm shy.

Ha! You're right. I don't believe you. Are you scarred, handicapped? Why continue the secrecy once we've met?
Just for the first time. After that I'll . . . be more comfortable.
I'll think about it.
I'm thinking of you and little else.
Will send instructions. From the time you receive them, the window of time to meet me will be narrow. Be ready.
Ready and waiting . . .

The next day, Chaz made a few calls to arrange the meeting. Explaining his visit to the hotel as "handling something of a sensitive legal nature," the hotel manager assured him that the utmost discretion would be practiced. Chaz would come in through a private entrance, sweep the suite for audio or video blackmailing devices, and then text his "date" that everything was ready.

He'd tossed the idea back and forth all day, but in the end, he decided to let one person in on what was about to happen.

"Oh, I see," Lois said softly, upon hearing the news. There was an unreadable look on her face.

"You disagree? Think that I shouldn't meet . . . whoever this is?" Chaz's decision to confide in Lois had been a calculated one. He closely monitored her reaction.

Lois fidgeted with a loose string on her blouse, a garment she'd had for years. She'd kept up the hairstyle and plucked eyebrows from the makeover, but when it came to her wardrobe, old habits died hard. She'd gone back to dressing the way she had before her big reveal two weeks ago. Today she wore a long-sleeved lavender blouse paired with a deep purple skirt that almost brushed the carpet.

Her heart hammered in her chest, and Lois worked to slow her breathing. "You should do it," she said with obvious effort. Lois looked at Chaz with widened eyes before quickly ducking her head, the double entendre almost causing this black woman to blush. "Meet with her, I mean."

A quick blink of his eyes was the only change in Chaz's neutral expression. *Why are you acting so strangely, Lois? Are you ashamed? Embarrassed? Eager?* This last possibility gave Chaz pause. He thought back to a conversation he'd had with Taylor and suddenly wondered if Lois was a virgin. And if he honored his blind date's request and allowed her anonymity until after they'd had sex, how would he feel to discover it was his secretary he'd bedded, that he'd taken her innocence and compromised an excellent working relationship?

After switching the subject to safer matters—clients, briefs, court dates, and the like—Chaz excused Lois from his office. He made a few phone calls, worked on a couple of legal briefs, and met with the junior partners of the firm. The day was another productive one, and Chaz felt great about the high-profile-type cases his firm was receiving, and especially about their 78-percent win rate. The success was heady, exhilarating; made him feel proud and powerful. By the end of the day, this excitement had turned into energy, energy that needed to be burned off. Chaz thought about putting a couple hours in at the gym, but knew that he was kidding himself with that idea. There was only one way Chaz wanted to release the pressure. It involved pumping, sweating, and using a piece of equipment that money couldn't buy.

Lois looked at her image in the full-length mirror. She wore the heels that made her feet hurt for only the second time since purchasing them that "makeover" weekend. But she had to admit, they gave her legs a longer, more flattering appearance. The dress that the saleswoman had talked her into buying was one that Lois would not have picked out on her own. It was more fitted than those she usually wore, with a golden tone that complemented her skin. Its belted design helped define her waist, while the flared skirt hinted at more in the back than was actually there. She'd combed her hair back away from a face devoid of makeup, save for a coating of shimmering lip gloss that gave her lips a pouty appearance. Lois took one more look at her appearance, picked up her purse, and headed to her car.

"No!" Delicia screamed, after hearing her son's question for the third time. "I want to go to the movies by myself!"

She'd spent all day at the salon, getting a fresh weave, a mani/pedi, and a facial. Then she'd stopped by the mall and picked up a designer warm-up that was casual yet elegant at the same time. Made from a satiny, stretch, burgundy-colored fabric, the pants were tight, announcing her ample behind to the world, while the V-neck top, of the same material, highlighted her bountiful breasts. Delicia knew that the Nutrisystem program she'd always wanted to try but until now could not afford, was working. It had felt good to walk out of Ashley Stuart with a size fourteen.

Delicia clipped on her earrings and splashed on perfume. She walked into the living room and was glad to see that for once, instead of fighting, both her children were engrossed in the DVD she'd purchased. "Keep an eye on your brother," she told her grown daughter. "Call if you need me." Delicia walked over and kissed each child on the forehead.

"When you coming back?" her son asked without taking his eyes off the screen.

"When I get good and ready," was her reply. "Y'all behave," she commanded, and left.

"Honey, that's great." Taylor sat in the living room, idly flipping through an *Essence* magazine. She'd been waiting on her husband, who'd just called to say he was going to hang out with the boys. The car they'd had customized to handle James's disability was one of the best investments they'd ever made. Now, he was beginning to make friends with some of the colleagues where he taught. He was getting his life back. Taylor was thrilled.

"So what are you going to do with yourself?" James asked. "Do you think you can handle an evening without me?"

Taylor smiled as she rose from the couch and headed to her bedroom to change clothes. "I'm sure I'll think of something."

On opposite sides of town, two women were doing the exact same thing. Elizabeth soaked in her oversized Jacuzzi tub in their home's master suite, while Gina luxuriated in a unisex tub at the gym. Both women had spent the day hard at work. And now, both women closed their eyes and thought about one man.

Naomi smiled as she walked through the hustle and bustle that was O'Hare International Airport. She'd traveled light and was able to bypass the baggage area and head straight for the rental car agency. Within minutes, she was headed to her destination—Chaz.

25

A light tap sounded on the door to Chaz's suite. His heartbeat quickened at the sound. Chaz Covington was a smart, sophisticated, ladies' man. It took a lot to make him nervous. Later, Chaz would liken the feeling to those he had in high school, when he'd made the game-saving midcourt three-pointer, or asked the homecoming queen to be his date for the prom. Ms. Anonymous had been right: there was something to be said for mystery. It heightened expectations and that, along with his need for physical release, was why Chaz felt this meeting was unlike any encounter he'd ever had.

He put down the glass of wine and walked to the door. He peeked out and wasn't at all surprised to see that the hole was covered to hide the identity of whomever was on the other side. It was okay. The hotel's penthouse suite could only be accessed by a special access card, a card that the hotel manager had given to Chaz's "client" personally after confirming a list of Chaz's foolproof safeguards for this clandestine rendezvous—including that she was female and had arrived at the hotel utterly alone.

"Hello there," he said, pressing his mouth against the door.

"You promised," the person whispered from the other side.

Chaz swore he detected a smile in her voice. *She's as excited about this as I am.* "Okay, I'm unlocking the door now, and then I'll step away. The bedroom is directly ahead."

Chaz unlocked the door and retreated into the L-shaped living room. Resisting the urge to peek, he instead picked up his glass of wine and walked to the large picture windows. Thousands of lights winked at him from all over Chicago. *Nice,* he thought—about both the stunning view and the exciting evening ahead. A rustling sound was heard as the front door opened and closed. The deeply piled carpet absorbed foot-steps, so Chaz was left to wonder whether the woman had sauntered or scampered to the bedroom. He forced himself to relax, calmly sipping the Pinot Noir. He looked at his watch. Five minutes had passed. He was just about to head to the bed-room when he heard the shower turn on in the master bath. Chaz had showered upon arriving at the hotel. He continued to sip his drink, and a couple minutes after he'd drained his glass, he picked up a tray and headed to the bedroom.

"Is it okay to enter?" he asked from the other side.

"Just a minute." Again, that whisper—sultry and a bit ten-tative. "Did you turn the lights out?" she asked after another moment.

"Yes."

"Okay, come in."

Chaz eased open the door and stepped inside the bed-room. His date had pulled the thick, silk curtains, which threw the room into utter darkness. Still, he could make out a silhou-ette lounging against the headrest in the center of the bed. *Is she naked? Nervous? Chaz, what in the world are you doing?*

"I brought some champagne," Chaz said as he walked over to the nightstand. He strained to see into the darkness and, while he could see her outline more clearly from this angle, any details as to age or ethnicity were still a mystery. He low-ered the tray onto the nightstand and poured two flutes. "You do drink, don't you?"

"I'll have some tonight," was the whispered answer.

Chaz deduced that her low, breathy answers were delivered in such a way as to shield the actual sound of her voice and prolong the mystery. He found the sound sexy, and that, combined with the secretive feel of the moment, turned Chaz on.

"To what shall we toast?" he asked, after pouring their glasses.

"You."

"That's a bit one-sided, don't you think? Let's toast to the moment: to mysterious meetings and . . . whatever unfolds . . ."

They clinked glasses and then sipped in awkward silence.

"I can't believe you're here," the woman finally said, still whispering.

"I can't either. But your letters intrigued me. If this was your attempt at using a unique and clever way to get 'one of the city's most eligible bachelors' in your clutches," Chaz said, making air quotes, "you've succeeded." There was silence, but Chaz imagined that the woman was smiling.

"I'm glad," she finally said.

"Would you care for another?" he asked, after they'd finished the drink.

"I'd like something else."

"What's that?"

"Your clothes off." When this statement was met with silence, the woman continued, "So that you can be naked, as I am."

Chaz hardened. "Cutting right to the chase, I see. Don't you think we should take some time to get to know each other, at least a little?"

A pause and then, "There are many ways to get to know one another. I'd like to use the one that requires no clothes."

Whispered in the soft, sultry voice she'd used all evening, the words still came out as a blatant dare. Chaz waited a beat before standing up and shedding the charcoal gray Armani knit top that he wore, and the black, tailored slacks. He hesitated just another moment before ridding himself of his undershirt

and briefs and was surprised at the vulnerability he felt standing naked before a stranger. But that's what he did: just stood
there.

There was movement in the room as the woman gently
pushed back the covers and rose to her knees. She ambled over
to the side of the bed where Chaz stood. And waited.

Chaz reached out and, as if by design, came in contact with
a hard, erect nipple. A short hiss was heard as he tweaked it, as
with his other hand he palmed the woman's face. *Soft.* That
was the first word that came to mind. *Very little or no makeup,*
was the second thought. He moved his hand a bit to the left
and felt silky strands bathing the shoulder. *Long hair.* He immediately thought of Gina. *But it could be a weave.* Chaz chose not
to continue to the scalp to investigate further. His curiosity
about the woman's identity grew, along with his manhood. But
his unease began to grow as well. While having anonymous
sex was a titillating thought, the reality of it was more sober-
ing. Sexing the wrong woman could have all kinds of reper-
cussions. Chaz had spent his entire adult life carefully crafting a
stellar reputation, both in and out of the courtroom. He'd be
damned if one woman would bring it down. *Who are you, my
pretty mystery? And is sex all you want from me?* Chaz knew that
before he went too much further, her identity would have to
be revealed, and both her short- and long-term intentions
would have to be made known.

A set of nails lightly raked his chest, and interrupted his
thoughts. Chaz stopped the hand before it could go any lower.
He sat on the bed, and his lean, hard thigh brushed up against
a soft one. A light, floral scent wafted past him, as the woman
gently turned his face toward her. She brushed his lips with
hers, wispy, teasing, her hand moving up and down his muscu-
lar arm. Chaz skimmed the woman's lips with his tongue, noting that they were full. She immediately opened her mouth.
And the dueling began.

Chaz wielded his tongue like a sword, darting in and

around hers, playfully increasing her arousal. He mimicked the sexual act with it, before pulling it out, nibbling her lips, and plunging in again. The woman moaned, turned herself more fully into him. She pressed her breasts against his hard chest, threw a supple thigh over his.

She'd never experienced such ecstasy and knew that if the man could get her this crazy with just a kiss, the night would be exceptional, beyond her wildest dreams. Her hand fell to his hard chest and her arm brushed the tip of his rocklike erection. Intuitively, she knew it was long and thick, and soon it would be inside her. There was no doubt that this man was an ardent, thorough lover. He would be the best she'd ever had. She reached for his massive weapon, but once again, Chaz stayed her hand.

"Please," she whispered. "I want to feel it, lick it, suck it into my mouth."

Chaz shushed her with a kiss, and as he did so, his mind was in overdrive, thinking of who might this be. Delicia was eliminated when he reached out for the woman's neck and then slid his hand down a slim, taut bare arm. The plush lips made Liz Stein an unlikely choice, since her lips were thin. Chaz continued swirling his tongue with the very capable kisser, and discovered he couldn't recall what Lois's lips looked like.

This thought brought Chaz out of the heated moment just as the woman tried yet again to stroke his prize. "Wait a minute," he said, his voice as soft as his dick was hard. "Before we go any further, I've got to know who you are."

There was a moment of silence before the woman removed her hand from where it rested on Chaz's thigh. "You agreed that that could come later, after we've made love," she whispered.

"I've changed my mind."

Another pause. "Why?"

There were a number of reasons, but being the diplomatic

debater that he was, he chose the most logical one. "It's not fair that you know who I am, but I don't know you. I find you mentally attractive, and can't imagine that I wouldn't find you physically so as well."

Another long, silent moment passed before the woman spoke. "Do you promise to make love to me, even after you discover who I am?"

"I can't promise that."

"Chaz, I've waited for a long time. Please."

"Look, I'm ninety percent sure I'll make love to you. It's what I want to do. But the remaining ten percent of uncertainty is why this is as far as I'll go, until I know you at least as well as you know me."

The woman sighed. "All right then." Her voice was low, though she didn't whisper. "Turn on the light."

Chaz rose from the bed and walked toward the lamp he'd spotted earlier when the room was being swept for devices. It sat on a nightstand next to the bed. He heard the sheets rustle and assumed that the woman had covered her body. Just before he turned on the lamp, Chaz reached down for his black briefs and did the same. The spontaneity of the moment was gone and part of the night's thrill followed closely behind it. Chaz almost wished it weren't so important to know the woman's identity. He was as hard as a rock, and knew that if he didn't have sex now, he'd have to see Taylor later.

"Are you ready?" he asked, his hand on the switch.

"Yes."

Chaz turned on the lamp, and then slowly turned around. For a moment he was speechless, not believing who sat before him, with large, bared breasts, hard nipples, and both lust and vulnerability in her eyes.

"It's nice to see you again, Chaz," she said, her voice husky and as loud as she'd spoken all evening.

"Reverend Edwards?" Chaz tried without success to keep the incredulity out of his voice. His hard dick twitched its frustration before deflating as quickly as a punctured balloon. Even in its limp state, the massive outline remained clearly visible, a fact that didn't go unnoticed by the lone observer.

Instead of showing what she initially felt, embarrassment, Reverend Beatrice Hallelujah Edwards defiantly tilted her chin, tossed off the sheet, and lay back on the bed—naked and not ashamed. "In the flesh," she answered, through nervous laughter. "Literally."

Chaz hadn't stuttered a day in his life. But there was a first time for everything. "I–I don't know what to say."

"Baby, I didn't come here to do much talking."

Chaz was glad he'd put on his briefs, and now he reached for his T-shirt as well. "But I don't understand. You're a preacher, a pastor, you're my assistant's mother for God's sake, you're—"

"A woman who hasn't known a man in almost thirty years," Beatrice interrupted. "Yes, a minister who has lived the life she's preached about, and a mother who's raised her daughter the best she could. But in the process, I've lost that person who is most important—me. I'd resigned myself to living a life of abstinence and was doing a pretty good job of it. And then I met you."

Chaz remembered their meeting at the Christmas party shortly after Lois was hired. They'd spoken only briefly, he recalled, and had not seen each other since that evening well over a year ago. He reached for his pants.

"Please, don't," Beatrice said as she sat up. "It's been so long since I've seen a man, so long since I've touched. . . ." Her eyes moved from his face to the bulge between his thighs. She didn't even realize when she licked her lips. Her eyes traveled upward. "I've got more to lose than you do," she continued. "There's no way I'd ever share what happens between us with anyone. You've got me so hot for you. Your kiss alone . . ." Beatrice scooted to the edge of the bed, reached out, and placed her hand squarely on Chaz's manhood.

Chaz backed up. He hadn't felt more like a piece of meat in his entire life.

"Please," Beatrice again pleaded, her eyes wide, begging as well. When Chaz remained where he was, she slid to her knees, placed her face against his groin and inhaled deeply. She licked his shaft through the thin, soft cotton. His hungry dick awakened quickly, and began to grow. "Lord have mercy," she said, reaching into his shorts like an excited child grabbing Halloween candy. She pulled down his briefs. His dick sprang up and popped her on the chin. "Ooh, Jesus," she moaned, before opening her mouth wide and taking in as much as she could. She continued to moan as she licked and sucked or, more accurately, gobbled him up. She'd never experienced oral sex in her life, but having faith that this moment would indeed come to pass, as had been her prayer, she'd covertly purchased a couple of instructional videos. Had there been grades given, Beatrice would have gotten an A.

"Reverend Edwards." The assault had happened so quickly, and felt so good, that Chaz's reaction was delayed. But now that his upper head was catching up with his lower one, he knew this had to stop. "Reverend Edwards!"

"No," she instructed, between licks, "call me Beatrice."

"Beatrice, stop." Chaz put a gentle, yet firm hand on Beatrice's shoulder and pulled away from her. He placed his once again engorged shaft back behind fabric. It stood out like a sore thumb; a very big, long, sore thumb. "I can't do this."

"Why not?" Still on her knees, Beatrice moved toward him.

Chaz moved farther away. "Because it's not right. I understand your wanting to feel like a woman again, but don't you think there's a better way? Like finding a Godly man and getting married, the way it appears you've taught Lois to do?"

"Let's leave my daughter out of this," Beatrice said in a tone that brooked no argument. She sat on the bed and wrapped the sheet around her. "I'm a grown woman who thought long and hard before writing that first letter. Actually, I'd written dozens of letters before then. It took me months to gather up the nerve to send one. But I'm glad I did. And I'll be even happier once we finish what we've started." She unwrapped the sheet again, exposing her furry, unshaven mound. "Come on, Chaz. It's my birthday. And I want you to be my gift."

Meanwhile, in various parts of town, there were other people thinking about Chaz, and at least one other person thinking about birthdays.

Delicia sat in a movie theatre pigging out on hot dogs, popcorn, nachos, and fries. She'd gone by the law offices hoping to catch Chaz working late, but had driven into a near-empty parking lot and a security guard who'd firmly informed her that the offices were closed.

Gina smiled as she chatted with her date from Match.com. He wasn't Chaz—her Mr. Right—by a long shot, but with his bald head, chocolate eyes, and smooth, dark skin, she believed that he might definitely end up being Mr. Right Now.

Liz sat across from Max at her parents' dining room table, wondering where Chaz was and wishing she were with him. But as she watched her father, husband, and in-laws engage in political rhetoric, she knew that that was a wish that would never come true.

Jennifer sat home alone, having broken up with Antonio earlier in the day. Her husband bar had been set pretty high, and she wondered if anyone would ever come close to what she'd had. Her earlier call to Chaz had gone to voice mail. She reached for her phone, and it rang in her hand. It was the DJ from LIVE-FM. He wanted to be with her. She agreed. He was a capable lover. Jennifer needed loving, plain and simple, and tonight, would get it from him.

Naomi Stone had navigated O'Hare, secured her rental

car, and now sang with the music as she drove toward Chaz's house. She was sure that her visit would be as she'd stated, "when he least expected."

And Lois sat in the church offices with Pastor Mack, trying for the third time to reach her mother.

"This is so unlike her," Lois said as she hit her speed dial.

"Maybe she made her own celebration plans," Pastor Mack suggested as he stared at Lois with newfound admiration. He couldn't get over how good she looked. And that dress! Being twenty years older than the woman sitting across from him, this associate minister had never considered the possibility before. But now he thought he just might be ready to put his widowhood behind him, and put some sanctified moves on his reverend's daughter.

"She never does anything special," Lois countered. "She's always here! And the one time I plan a surprise birthday party and have a dozen people waiting at the restaurant, she chooses to act out of character." Lois put up her finger in a shushing manner. "Mom, where are you?"

"I see you've called several times," Beatrice said, ignoring the question. "What's wrong, Lois?"

At the same time Lois answered her phone, Chaz's cell rang. He walked into the living room to answer it. "Hello?"

"Hey, baby. Where are you?"

"Naomi!"

"The one and only."

Chaz spoke quietly. "Baby girl, it's so good to hear your voice. Where are *you*?"

"In Chicago, across the street from your house."

"You're here?"

"Yes. I was planning to surprise you. Please don't tell me you're out of town."

"Even if I were, I'd charter a plane to get back to you. As it is, I'm less than twenty minutes away. Your timing is *perfect*.

And, baby," Chaz said, his voice dripping with desire, "when I get there, I don't want you wearing anything but a smile."

Naomi laughed. "You want me to get undressed here, in my car, in public?"

"You've got a point. I guess I can wait until you're one step inside my place. Then I'm going to wear you out."

"Is that a threat?"

"It's a promise."

"Umm, I like the sound of it. But hurry up, man! You've got me wet."

"And you've got me hard."

"Then stop talking and start driving. I want you!"

"I want you, too, Naomi Stone, in more ways than one. And I plan to have you." *Maybe even for the rest of my life.*

From One Lover to Another

Cydney Rax

1

If a Man Calls His Own Mama the B-Word, He Cannot Be with Me

At first she wasn't sure, but when Lorraine Eafford heard her ex call his mama the b-word *again*, she knew she'd made the most important decision of her life. She'd broken up with Posse late last year, but her ex kept dialing her number. It didn't matter that she told him, "That's not happening," when Posse asked if she thought they'd hook up again one day. He still called her using the sexy voice she'd previously loved to hear, and tried to coax her back into his life. Posse couldn't accept that when Lorraine moved away from her hometown of Dallas where *he* lived, to Houston where he *didn't* live, it was an indication she meant business. They were through. Period. Her feelings were cemented even more on a quiet Sunday afternoon.

Lorraine was at home alone in her one-bedroom apartment in the Westchase area of the city. She had just started running some steaming hot bathwater. The bottom of her garden tub was scattered with tiny lavender-scented body-soaking beads that when melted softened the water and provided relaxation for her aching slender body. Lorraine believed in working hard and staying busy, but there were times when she needed to de-stress and pamper herself. Sunday was one of those days.

While the tub filled with water, she rummaged through her walk-in closet searching for a sexy nightgown to wear once her bath was complete. But before Lorraine could pick out a cute nightie, her phone rang. She rushed to her nightstand where she last placed her smartphone. She thought it might be Joanna, her sister who still lived in Dallas. But when she noticed it wasn't her sister but an unrecognizable number, she answered anyway.

"What's up, my lady?"

Lorraine cringed when she heard her ex's raspy voice. "Posse? I am not your lady anymore."

"Man, don't say that."

"It's the truth. I told you I'm all about pure truth now."

"You need to get off the gas with dat new attitude, bring your fly ass back to Dallas, and chop it up with your boy." While listening to him, she struggled with a mixture of desire and disgust. She pressed the phone against her ear and recognized Posse's normal background noises. Familiar sounds that let her know that three months after their breakup, this guy was still caught up in the same old same old. Hanging out with five of his partners in a smoke-filled room. Playing dominoes. Getting high. Getting drunk. Talking shit. Wasting time.

Frustrated, she tried to respond, but he interrupted and ordered her to hold on. She heard a ringtone by Bushwick Bill of the Geto Boys, an H-town rapper who'd been known for his sexist and misogynistic lyrics. As soon as she heard the melody, she knew Posse's cell phone was ringing. He'd obviously borrowed one of his boys' phones to call her.

She listened in.

"Aw, Mama, you tripping. Nobody tearing up your damn house. Okay, okay, okay, we'll turn down the music. *Damn!*" The background noise grew quieter. So did Posse. Lorraine heard his mother screaming at him through the phone.

"Mama, I ain't trying to hear all dat, now I told you I—"

Mother and son continued to verbally sling it out. His volume increased a few decibels as he argued with the sixty-year-old woman.

Then Posse abruptly shut up.

Lorraine knew that, like a hundred times before, Posse's mama had rudely disconnected the call and left him looking stupid.

"Fucking bitch," she heard him mutter before he snapped the phone shut. He switched back to his boy's phone and resumed talking to her in a normal tone. Color drained from Lorraine's face. Posse's disturbing encounter with his mama reminded her why she had to get away from him. It wasn't that he'd ever referred to *her* by that awful name. But if a man called his own mother the b-word, she knew the name-calling wouldn't stop at the woman who gave birth to him. And if a man had the nerve to talk about his mama with blatant disrespect, he wasn't the man for her.

"Posse, may I ask you something?" she said, trying to shout over the din of all his partners, who began yelling and arguing with one another.

"Ask me anything, my lady."

"Why do you talk to your mother so horribly?"

"What? Dude, don't ask me something you don't wanna know the answer to."

Lorraine wanted to scream. He never answered a question directly. Or he'd often deflect her grilling. Lorraine wanted a man who wasn't afraid to speak his truth even if it was something she might not want to hear. In her opinion, raw truth was always better than a dressed-up lie.

Exasperated, she blurted, "This is exactly why I had to burn out," then realized her error. "I mean, this is precisely why I *broke things off*." She hated herself for letting him influence her enough to talk his gutter language.

"Like I've tried to tell you a million times," she continued, "we're on two different pages. You know that. It was never going to work for the long term. I simply can't handle your lifestyle."

As she admitted her truth, her heart exploded with pain. She didn't want to hurt him. But to not hurt him would mean hurting herself.

"So you sitting up here trying to tell me you didn't like rollin' wit me this past year, Lo? That you was acting fake all dat time we hung out, Lo?"

It hadn't been that long ago when Lorraine had loved for Posse to call her by that shortened pet name. Back then she'd craved his slight Southern twang, his unique way with words. The fact that they were so different intrigued her and she was all ears. But she didn't want to hear the slang anymore. These days she hated being called "Lo." It sounded so *ghetto*.

Not that Lorraine wanted to be known as a snob. She just knew she wasn't hood enough to feel comfortable dating a hood guy anymore. In the beginning of their relationship, Lorraine had a ball hanging out with Posse. He introduced her to a wild, adventurous, and borderline dangerous side of life that she had never been exposed to. The first time she visited him at brother Donnie James's, she saw things that made her eyes widen. Young men barely out of their teens openly sold drugs in the presence of innocent five-year-old boys. She was amazed and repulsed at the same time.

Lorraine grew up in an upper middle-class family on the north side of Dallas. Her parents married each other a few months after they both earned master degrees. They obtained good jobs as educators, saved their money, plunked a hefty down payment on a ranch-style house, and then had their two children: little Lorraine Yvonne followed by Joanna Marie three years later. Lorraine admired her parents for their strong values, sense of responsibility, and no-nonsense approach when it came to life. They held high expectations for their daughters, and Lorraine didn't want to let them down.

Of course, when she met Posse and began dating him, Lorraine was forced to keep their relationship a secret for months. If her Church of God in Christ mother knew she was hanging out with a man who wore his pants so low that everyone could see the color of his boxers, she'd have a fit, first calling on Jesus and asking him to save Lorraine from her sins, then pulling her eldest daughter to the side and asking her what her problem was.

"I didn't raise my girls to lay up with any old man," Francis Eafford would often say. But once Lorraine did start sleeping with Posse, she thought her mother didn't know what she was talking about. The sex that Lorraine had with Posse was oh-so-good: hot, wild, freaky, noisy, sweaty, lengthy, messy, impulsive, painful, and all consuming, just how Lorraine liked it. Outside the bedroom, she became addicted to Posse's streetwise ways, his playful swagger that kept her blushing and giggling. From his shoulder-length braided hair, to his piercing, light brown eyes that sparkled in the sun, to his chiseled jaw that made him look thug sexy—everything about Posse drew her. Because he was so unique, she felt that trying to explain her feelings to him was too overwhelming. And lately talking to him on the phone wore her patience. This evening she had had just about all she could take. Instead of hanging up in his face like she was tempted to do, she addressed his nonanswer.

"Posse, you talking bad to your mother has nothing to do with whether or not I enjoyed being with you."

"So you saying you *did* love me? And you *are* gonna come crawling back to Big Daddy? I'm still here, Lo. I'm ready for ya, legs spread, waiting for you to crawl on top—"

"Stop it, Posse, don't talk like that."

"Why not? Your pink thong getting wet? You want me to come to Houston and fuck the panties off you?"

"Oh God, please be quiet." Posse knew how much she adored pink undergarments; plus he knew all of her other likes and dislikes (NBA games, any movie with Angela Bassett, and sweet-tasting chocolate-covered strawberries). The fact he knew her so well sometimes surprised her. She didn't think a man like him could be so in tune to her, but he was. He knew the right dirty words to say to get her turned on; turned on until there was no turning back.

When they were an item, she used to love when he'd talk his nasty talk, but she despised when he opened up his nasty mouth in front of his nasty friends. It made her feel cheap, like a run-of-the-mill whore he could find on any city corner. Lorraine knew she was more than just some chicken head he liked to screw. She was Lorraine Yvonne Eafford, a young, black, female architect in the state of Texas. She had a Master of Architecture degree from Texas Tech University and she was thriving in her career.

It broke her heart that she had tried to make something work that was bound to fail. In retrospect, she could admit she lowered her standards to be with a man who probably couldn't truly appreciate a good woman like her. A man who didn't understand that calling his own mother out of her name was an absolute no-no.

And the fact that he made this mistake on more than one occasion made Lorraine realize that you can take a man out of the ghetto, but the ghetto will always be a part of that man. He'd constantly be drawn back to the familiar, even when he knew it wasn't good for him. And every single time that happened, Lorraine would lose hope that she and Posse could be together forever.

"Posse, I really wish you'd just answer my original question."

"Which was?"

"Tell me why you call your mama the b-word."

"*What?*"

"What kind of man calls a woman that?" she asked, almost shouting.

"A man whose long, tasty sausage you used to love to slobber on, dat's what kind."

"Ugh! Posse, this conversation is over. I've moved on. Don't call me anymore."

Hands shaking, Lorraine hung up. She rushed to the bathroom and felt grateful that her bathwater hadn't overflowed and was still hot. She slid off her aqua jersey tank and matching running pants, stepped over the edge of the tub, sank her body deep into the water, swiftly closed her eyes, and dreamed of better days.

When Lorraine finished soaking and felt refreshed, she lifted herself out of the tub, thoroughly dried herself off, and applied scented lotion to her entire body. When she returned to her bedroom, instead of getting dressed in a nightgown, crawling into bed early, and calling it a night like she'd originally planned, she threw on one of her favorite dresses, an outfit that made her feel confident and beautiful every time she wore it. She still felt on edge after talking to Posse and had an urge to get away from her apartment. But before she walked out her front door, she returned to the bathroom and gazed at her reflection in the wall-length mirror. Even without a hint of makeup, Lorraine's features showcased her attractiveness: round cheeks that expanded when she laughed, deep-set dark brown eyes that lit up when she felt joyous, and protruding soft lips that hinted of her occasional pensive nature.

With a quivering voice, she said, "I love you, Lorraine Eafford." She tried not to flinch as her voice grew stronger. "I love you, Lorraine. I love you, Lorraine. Love you, love you, love *me*." She gasped like she'd just spoken the most difficult words she ever uttered. But soon she detected an inner strength that had been missing from inside of her the past couple of months. She felt focused, centered, and more than anything, she believed she possessed the power required to move on from one lover to another.

Lorraine sensed that although it was true that she missed some of the unforgettable moments she'd shared with Posse, as good as things seemed during their best days, there was something greater ahead for her. Something she couldn't see initially, but a good thing that would be revealed in time.

2

Regaining Power

At first Lorraine felt overwhelmingly self conscious. She wondered if everybody was looking at her while she stood in a line crammed with people waiting to buy movie tickets. In front of her was a thirty-something white couple dressed in matching Western shirts and boot-cut jeans. And behind Lorraine stood two giggling Asian teens wearing neon skirts and blouses as if it were summer instead of mid-March. Everyone looked like they were paired with someone else. But she was alone. The mousy brown-haired woman standing in front of Lorraine clutched the hand of the man standing next to her. Heads held close together, they spoke softly to each other and laughed in unison. The smiling lady rotated her body until she came face to face with Lorraine. Immediately, Lorraine's posture grew stiff. The woman gave Lorraine a sympathetic glance then turned around and held onto her man even tighter.

Lorraine was tempted to dash out of the line and walk away. No matter how you sliced it, being alone sucked. Many women claimed that they loved being single and didn't mind going to the movies by themselves, but Lorraine wasn't about to fake that sentiment. The girl craved companionship. And tonight, venturing out alone to see the number-one comedy in America and laughing at the funny parts would make her feel even more self conscious.

Lorraine took a deep breath, counted to ten, and quickly eased out of line, wanting to apologize to someone but sensing no one would care.

Eyes blurry, she pulled up the collar of her linen jacket so that it fit snugly around her neck and braced herself for the strong, cool wind that nipped at her that Sunday evening. She took ten steps before she heard her name being called.

"Hey, Lorraine, where are you going?"

She glanced around and was surprised to find Wendell Holmes standing nearby; he was a fellow architect who worked at her firm.

"Oh, hey, what's up?"

"You look like you're going in the wrong direction."

"Well, I was just, um—"

"You were probably doing what I was doing. I was at home surfing the Web. And I clicked on Moviefone and realized this flick I've wanted to check out was showing. I busted my ass to make it over here in time."

"You're not meeting anybody?"

"No, no, no, no." He laughed with ease. "That's how badly I wanted to see this picture."

Lorraine had always admired Wendell from afar while they were at the office. Every day when he'd pass her at work, Wendell had a kind word to say even though they didn't know each other well. And she appreciated his good looks, too. Wendell always wore a neat, low-cut fade and a trimmed mustache; he dressed in impeccable suits with polished leather shoes. But more important than his outward appearance, she was impressed he admitted that he'd come to the movies alone.

Raw truth.

"Which movie were you coming to see?" she asked him.

"Aw, man, should I say it?"

"The truth is always a good place to start."

"I want to see that romantic comedy that everyone's been yapping about. Cold busted, huh?" His eyes gleamed with kindness. "Yep. I'm a sucker for a well-produced romance with clever nuances and great comedic flair. Plus it never hurts to gain some insight about the mysterious mind of the female species."

Now he *really* had her attention.

"Yeah, I'm man enough to admit y'all confuse a brother at times. They say women are simple, but whoever made that up was lying through all her damn teeth."

"*Her* teeth, huh?" she smirked, loosening up. "As if men are uncomplicated, and simple, and easy to figure out."

"We are! That's what y'all don't get!"

"Wendell Holmes, you need to quit. Tell me one simple thing about a man."

"Hey, if you can remember this one thing, it'll save you a lot of heartache. Ya listening? Okay. Here goes! Men are only interested in facts. Ya heard me right. The who, what, when, where, how. Stick to what's factual; trim off the rest. If you do this when you're talking to your man, he will understand you. You'll understand him, too."

"Hmm, give me an example."

"I love this," he said, rubbing his hands together. "Let's say you want your man to hang a painting on that empty living room wall at your spot. What would you tell him?"

"I guess I'd say, 'Baby, that big ole wall sure looks empty.' "

"Bingo! Guess what? It's the wrong thing to say to your man. Wrong, wrong, so wrong."

"I don't have a—" she started softly, but he didn't hear her.

"Instead, try giving your man a hammer. Put some nails in his hand, point at that cheap painting you got from Marshalls, and tell him, 'Sweetie, will you please hang the picture on the wall? I love how you take care of manly things for me. You do such a good job.' " He made his voice sound feminine. She nearly burst out laughing.

"Oh Jesus," she smirked. "It sounds like I'd be giving instructions to a ten-year-old."

He just looked at her and didn't say anything.

"Wendell, I'll have to remember that, but it sounds so . . . I dunno. It's just *too* simple."

"That's because we aren't complicated. Exactly what I've been trying to explain to ya."

They laughed good-naturedly and Lorraine's feelings of self-consciousness completely faded away.

Wendell thoughtfully stared at her and shoved one hand deeper into his pocket. "Tell you what. While we're out here yapping and trying to stay warm, the clock is steadily ticking. You don't look like you're doing anything important right now. Join me in watching this movie. We'll discuss it afterward over a bite to eat. That is, if you don't have other plans."

She agreed to watch the movie with him. They returned to the theater and promptly got in line. When they reached the box office, Wendell graciously paid for their tickets and led them to empty seats near the front of the crowded theater. During the previews, Wendell took her order and made sure to bring back the precise beverage and snack that she asked for. If it had been Posse, and if he were in a nasty mood, he'd purposely do the opposite. If she wanted tortilla chips with cheddar cheese, he'd get the nachos, but he'd take over and add those nasty-tasting jalapeño peppers because, "I love them peppers, Lo. Now be quiet and eat your snack or else I ain't going to the movie wit you no more."

I'd better enjoy this treatment while it lasts.

Once the movie started and the plot began to unfold, she and Wendell laughed at the same lines. They nodded when a character spoke dialogue that rang with truth, and protested when they didn't agree with the characters' actions. When the ending credits rolled, Wendell just sat there with his eyes fixed in front of him.

"See what I'm talking about?" he asked.

"What are you talking about?"

"Ninety minutes later and I am still no closer to understanding women than I was when I first walked in this joint."

Lorraine felt warm and fuzzy inside, noting his silly comments. When she and Wendell got up to leave, she noticed the white lady whom she saw in line earlier. This time Brown Hair didn't turn up her nose. She openly gaped at Lorraine, glanced at Wendell, frowned heavily, and left in a huff. She wasn't with the man she was hugged up with only a couple of hours before.

"Relationships are hard." Lorraine nodded as she grew sober. "They're very hard." She felt she needed to get real. She may have sat next to Wendell and had fun, but the fact was Wendell was just her co-worker. Tonight was good. Tomorrow was another day. As she thought about how in the next twelve hours she and Wendell would be back on professional terms, she felt down in the dumps.

"Hey, what's the matter? You sure got quiet on me." Wendell walked Lorraine to her car, a white-on-white Buick LaCrosse.

She popped the locks on the vechicle and, instead of getting in, she leaned against the door.

"Oh, I didn't realize I was that quiet. Nothing's wrong. Just tired." She yawned. "You know I've been off all last week. I was on a staycation."

"Were you? Nah, I didn't know."

She felt a flicker of anger. Of course he wouldn't know. It wasn't his job to know. She pulled herself together and offered him a warm smile.

"Um, but I really appreciate your inviting me to see the film. I loved it."

"Hey, Lorraine, you sound like you're not going to chow down with me, but I know you're still hungry. All you ate was that little bag of popcorn. You barely sipped on your cola."

"I know."

"I hate to see people waste food. That's one of my pet peeves."

"Sorry," she whispered.

"Hey, there's something stuck on your lip." Without asking he reached out and flicked off a kernel of popcorn from her face. When he brushed his hand against her skin, she noticed his hands were warm, rugged, and strong. Standing next to Wendell made her feel like she had nothing to worry about.

Lorraine's smartphone started ringing. By habit, she dug in her pocket for the phone and saw her ex's name flash.

"Hey, I gotta get this," she apologized and slid her finger across the smooth screen.

"Hello?"

"Hey, how you doing? What's up? What's happening, lady?"

"I'm just now leaving a movie."

"Oh yeah? Who you with? I better not find out you with some other nigga." She heard voices shouting in the background, men arguing like the fools they were.

"Don't even try it, Posse."

"I'm more serious than a mug. I'll hop a plane in a second."

Even though they weren't together anymore and she'd been rejecting his pleas for weeks, she liked that he kept coming after her. She knew that if she told him not to call but continued accepting his calls, he wouldn't take her seriously. But she couldn't help herself. There were only so many times she could stay home in the apartment, cook for one, and watch Tyler Perry comedies on TBS every Wednesday night. Sure, she loved laughing out loud at the sitcoms for hours, but after that, then what?

"Hey, Posse, this is bad timing and I—"

"So you *are* with another nigga? Who is he? Y'all fucking?"

"Anyway, I will call you back later. Bye!" She hung up in the middle of Posse's angry tirade. Whereas before she'd felt calm and peaceful, now her shoulders stiffened with tension.

What in the hell should I do? I don't want my ex to have any kind of power over me. I need to regain my power.

3

Possibilities

I can't believe Posse still knows how to get under my skin. Lorraine stood stiffly in the movie theater parking lot next to her car. She folded her arms over her breasts.

"Is everything okay?" Wendell asked. He stepped beside Lorraine and placed his hand on her shoulder. "If you ever need to talk, you'll find that I'm a good listener. Don't hesitate to find me, call me, whatever."

"How can I call you . . . ?"

He recited his cell and home numbers to her, which shocked Lorraine. She felt warm and decidedly more focused as she added his info to her phone's address book.

"My offer still stands. It's getting late, but if you're a fan of Mediterranean lasagna and bourbon sweet potatoes, I know a good place. Hey, why don't you follow me? I'm in the tan Sebring."

Wendell headed toward his car without waiting for her response.

The second she couldn't see him anymore, she settled inside her car and dialed Posse.

"You better had called me back. Now, I'm not playing wit you, Lo. Don't let me have to come to H-town and kick a nigga's ass. I will do dat."

"I know you will," she purred and placed the call on speakerphone. She fastened her seat belt snugly around her waist. She reached inside her purse, unzipped a compartment, and located a tube of lip gloss. She flipped open the vanity mirror and made her lips glisten with two quick swipes. Posse was quiet, like he was listening for hints of background noise.

Yep, he still loves me.

"What are you doing, lady?"

"I'm about to go out to dinner."

"To pick up something from a drive-through window, right?"

"No, Posse. Not everyone thinks that the Burger King drive-through constitutes a date."

"*Constitutes?* What's with the big words?"

"Look it up in the dictionary."

"If I knew how to spell *it* I would, but I can spell *date*, though; don't try and change the subject."

"So what, I'm going out. What about it?"

"Where exactly the fuck you going, then? And with who?"

"Where? I don't know yet. Who? A wonderful, cute guy I met—"

"Oh no, hell no. What's the number to Southwest Airlines?"

She laughed at Posse and quickly waved at Wendell, who pulled his vehicle into an empty parking space next to her car. He motioned at her to roll down the window. She hesitated, put Posse on mute, then pressed the button and lowered her window.

"Let's head out to I-59 toward downtown."

She nodded and smiled, then quickly rolled up her window. She touched the MUTE button and instantly heard yelling and screaming.

"Hello? Hello? Lo, you hear me fucking talking to you?"

"No, Posse, actually I'm not hearing you right now." She

expertly slid her fingers across her iPhone and silenced Posse's voice.

Seconds later her phone rang. She laughed and rejected the call. The next five times her phone buzzed, she sent her ex straight to voice mail where men like him belonged. She thought of the many times when she'd called Posse in the past, but he was too busy hanging with his boys to chat. He'd promise to call her back when he was alone, but a ghetto man is never by himself. His low-life friends, needy family members, or sorry stragglers are always hanging around. He and his unemployed associates were constantly scheming, plotting, trying to hustle up the next ten or twenty dollars. A whole lot of time and energy was wasted over chump change. As much as she loved him in spite of his ways, whenever Posse would shut her out, she felt unimportant, like she was in the way, as disposable as garbage. Time after time, he chose his friends and lifestyle over her; she knew he would eventually feel guilty and make it up to her, but the vicious cycle was destined to repeat itself.

Tonight, when she hung up on him, she sensed her female power return to her. Since it was apparent that Posse was chasing her, she relished having the upper hand. But Lorraine knew part of that power was due to the two-hundred-forty-plus miles that existed between her and her ex. He was too far away to be considered a serious threat. Besides, now that Wendell was kind-of, sort-of in the picture, she figured she would be safe, and Posse wouldn't stand a chance, no matter how much of a thug he claimed to be.

Half an hour later, she and Wendell sat across from one another, relaxing in a corner booth at Sambuca restaurant. They nibbled on veggie lasagna and listened to live music performed by an acoustic rock band. Sitting in that restaurant, she realized she had willingly and gloriously been taken to a whole new world by a man who possessed class and style, and seemed considerate of her feelings.

"Ahh, you're shivering." Wendell placed his fork next to his glass of wine and quietly observed her.

"Yeah, unfortunately I got a little overheated in my car on the way over here and was trying to get in the restaurant so fast that I left my jacket on the front seat of my car."

"You're welcome to wear mine."

"You sure?"

"Positive," he said and removed his jacket. He stood up and placed the tweed coat squarely on her shoulders. *You're positively wonderful,* are the words that came to her mind as she adjusted his jacket and pulled it closer to her neck.

Wendell was well over six feet tall and had a little bit of meat on his bones, unlike Posse, who was as thin as a goat. Wendell's jacket was so big on Lorraine it swallowed her up, but the warmth it brought made up for the uncomfortable feeling she had from it being oversized. She felt protected and that comforted her. Five minutes later she started sneezing uncontrollably.

"Someone must be wearing some strong perfume," she complained and sneezed again.

"God bless you," he said with an amused look on his face.

"What's so funny?" she pouted.

"I'm sorry, but your nose wrinkles when you sneeze. It's cute. You're cute, too."

When their evening had ended, Lorraine wasn't thinking about Posse. She thought about the complexities of love and loneliness, lust and life. She wanted so much out of life and one of those things was true love. She felt that good love was filled with possibilities.

She wanted to know how it felt to date a man with integrity, who kept his promises 75 percent of the time, who paid for dates 90 percent of the time, who respected her 100 percent of the time. And most important she wanted to know what it was like to be in the life of a man who never, ever referred to his mother as the b-word.

As soon as Lorraine shut the door of her vehicle, she phoned her sister.

"What's up, Joanna?"

"You sound happy and it's kind of late. What ya been doing?"

"Trying to change my life, that's what." She went on to explain how she did something spontaneous by hanging out with Wendell.

"It felt so good to be connected with a man who seems to be on the same level. Is that wrong? Do I sound like a judgmental snob?" Even though the Eafford sisters were raised middle class, they still had cousins who lived on the drug-infested side of Dallas. Their kin didn't have extra money for items beyond food, rent, and utilities. And none of that side of the family ever stayed in community college beyond their freshman year, but Lorraine and Joanna's mother still insisted that they embrace their struggling cousins. She felt guilty for judging certain aspects of Posse's life and hoped her attitude didn't mean she was a bad person.

"Sis, you have every right to make a rational decision about what type of guy you think best fits your personality, values, and goals. Every woman isn't meant to be with every man. And just because you're trying to move on from the likes of Posse doesn't mean you're judging him. Hate to say it, but he ought to be glad you gave him the time of day in the first place. And you didn't break up because he was broke; it's because, most of the time, he didn't know how to act respectfully. There's a difference."

"I guess," Lorraine responded in a hushed tone. "It's just that at one point I loved what he gave me even if it seemed he was someone who shouldn't have been giving me anything. Now I detest everything he stands for. I hate to seem like I'm going from one extreme to another—Posse versus Wendell. But I have to raise my standards. Nowhere to go but up. Definitely wouldn't make sense to find a man lower than my ex."

"Hmm, sounds like you've been doing some serious thinking, sis. Are you truly ready to let go? No more sexy thugs?"

"I've already let go." She failed to mention that she still took Posse's calls.

"Yeah, right," replied Joanna. She knew her sister well and figured all Lorraine had to do was hear Posse's charming/ disgusting voice and he'd reel her in like a catfish from a lake.

"Girl, don't doubt me. Watch me."

"Why the sudden change? Your panties would get wet just from your looking at Posse's tats on his arms and back."

"Back then, all that *was* sexy." She quietly laughed. "And I just wanted to bring his sexy into my life to see what it felt like."

"Oh yeah," Joanna said. "You are the 'I'll try anything once' type of chick."

"If you say so, but that's why I have my sights set on Mr. Wendell. He definitely has the right packaging."

"Yeah, I feel you. Because with Posse it was 'what you see is what you get.'"

"But what if I'm wrong about Wendell? Like how the people at the Dallas firm looked at me and assumed I was a reserved square who'd never be caught dead with a man like Posse, yet I was crazy about him."

"You're thinking Wendell might be freaky behind closed doors?"

"Not that there's anything wrong with that. I just want a man who's true to himself, yet adheres to high standards. I want him to say 'no' to drugs and not rationalize the positive aspects of pot."

"Nothing wrong with that, sis. Just make sure that these new high standards that you're seeking are really the true you.

Wouldn't want to see you get yourself entangled with a decent guy just for you to decide you prefer the Posse kind of guy."

"Oh no, none of that. I've been cured of my attraction to knuckleheaded hood guys. I swear on Tupac's and Biggie's graves."

4

Unusual Pairings

The next day, Lorraine needed to take care of business at her car dealership before coming to work. She normally started her job at seven thirty, but on this day she arrived two hours late. The architectural firm of EDC was located in midtown and occupied the third and fourth floors of an eight-story office building. The Houston branch was mostly filled with wrinkled, white-haired white guys whose marriages had lasted thirty years. A few African Americans and Hispanics, both male and female, were also sprinkled here and there. The fifty-member firm consisted of principals, architects, marketing and finance folks, designers, engineers, and others.

During her first day back at work, Lorraine felt refreshed and ready to resume her professional duties. She emerged from her car dressed in a navy blue skirt suit with matching pumps and a powder blue ruffled blouse. Minutes later, after riding the elevator to the third floor, she lightly waved her magnetic smart card at the card reader in front of her office door and took an anxious breath before entering. She imagined that her in-box was filled with stacks of snail mail or spiral-bound reports, and that her electronic mail had also piled up while she was gone.

But the moment she stepped into her office, instead of seeing only mountains of work on her desk, she watched Wendell emerge from the other side of the cubicle looking relaxed as he held an armful of black binders.

"Good morning, Wendell. What are you doing in my office?"

"Morning, Lorraine. Um, there've been some changes around here. While you were out last week, I was temporarily relocated to your office while mine gets renovated."

Since she'd been working at the firm, she relished having her own space. Even though she liked Wendell, she didn't expect to find him traipsing around her office.

"Are you serious?"

"I know you're probably wondering why I didn't mention it last night."

"Shhh," she whispered and stole a look behind her. It was unlikely anyone heard Wendell, but she felt awkward. She didn't want anyone to know they'd been together the night before. She was especially concerned because when she worked in Dallas, Posse had started popping up without warning at her job, wearing throwback jerseys and baggy jeans and talking constantly in Ebonics. This time around she wanted to present a more positive image to her corporate family and didn't want everyone at work to know whom she was dating.

"I'm sorry, Lorraine, I know this must be taking you by surprise."

"I'm not totally surprised. A lot of changes have been going on, not just at EDC, but at dozens of companies across the state. Blame it on the economy, right?" She laughed though nothing was funny. "There's nothing new about that. Still, it doesn't mean it's easy to deal with."

"True that."

"But it would have been nice if you could have given me a heads-up, um, before now." She sighed heavily and plopped onto her chair. She grabbed a clump of her hair and twirled it in a circle, thinking about how they'd been together last night, yet Wendell had neglected to warn her about what was happening at work.

"How long did you say you'd be here? And don't they know this room only has minor file cabinet capacity?"

"Hey, I'm starting to feel unwanted."

"No, no, no, don't feel that way. I'm just . . . um, shoot. What difference does it make how a person feels? What's *that*? Ha! It is what it is, right? Deal with it," she said to herself more than to him. "This company doesn't revolve around me, I know that much."

"No, but you're still an important part of EDC and no matter what decisions are made, they impact all of us."

"You know, you really don't have to say things like that, Wendell." She was beginning to feel annoyed. She hated when people went out of their way to placate her.

"What I'm saying may not sound sincere and like something straight out of an HR manual, but I do sympathize with you, Lorraine, you gotta believe me."

She nodded, gave a half shrug.

"Look, I swear on the Bible, I will not crowd you. I'll give you your space. You don't have to worry about me listening to your conversations. It's already tight enough in this little tuna can," he said. "I guess the work will be complete in a couple of weeks, according to the schedule. Think you can put up with me for that long?"

"Wendell, I apologize for how I'm behaving," she said, feeling guilty. "I'm coming off like a self-centered kid and I don't want to do that."

"Speaking of age, how old are you?"

"W-what? We weren't speaking of age, but since you asked . . . I-I can't answer that."

"Oh, don't tell me you're one of those sistas who refuses to disclose their age. You look way too young to be having that kind of attitude."

She laughed, relieved that she was feeling a little more

comfortable now that they had changed the subject. "If you say I look young, I can't argue with the truth. I am, by the way; you just won't know exactly *how* young."

"Don't count on me not knowing. I don't have to ask you to find out things about you. I love a challenge."

"Is that right?" Inside she was beaming. It made her feel good to know he may even want to do some outside investigating to find out info on her. Maybe it meant he was interested. Or perhaps he was making polite conversation and she shouldn't take anything he said seriously. At that point, she wasn't sure how he felt. When a woman isn't positive if a man sincerely wants her, it makes her feel uneasy.

"Well, what if I wanted to know things about you? How would I go about getting that info?"

"Believe me, you're going to find out more about me than you probably ever wanted to know now that we're roommates."

"Hmm, like what?"

"Like, I'm big on coffee. I gotta have something *hot* to perk me up in the morning, especially since . . ." His voice trailed off like he was lost in thought.

"You were saying?" She couldn't believe that so far since she'd been at work, she still hadn't booted up her PC. Wendell had an energy that took up all her time.

"Are you stuck on any other type of caffeine besides cola?" he asked, referring to her drink of choice at the movies.

"Not really, but it's hard for me to pass up doughnuts."

"Hey, now we're talking. I have a bad habit of downing a couple of those glazed ones a few times a week. And if you want to stay on my good side, supply me with some egg and potato breakfast tacos. I know an excellent place where you can pick some up for me—every Friday."

"Hmm, should I be getting a steno pad and taking notes, Mr. Holmes?"

"Yeah, you should." He turned around abruptly and went

to his side of the cube and returned holding a large porcelain mug in his hand.

"See this? Only my lips have touched this bad boy."

Lorraine knew Wendell's cup anywhere. When she'd first come to the firm, he stood out and she'd observed him holding his cup many mornings as he headed down the hall toward their kitchen's coffee machine.

"So you're possessive over a cup?"

"I wouldn't say that."

"Then can you say if you're anal?"

"Not anal, but I am protective over things I consider mine. Does that make me anal?"

"It makes you intriguing, that's for sure."

"I could say the same for you, young lady. Um, how can I put this? Last night, you excused yourself and took a call. Unless that was a family member, which I doubt it was, it can only mean one thing. You're in a relationship. Not my business, but I think I should know these things in case you need to take a personal call."

At this point she felt a little insulted. Now that she was getting to know him better, he appeared cockier than she'd imagined.

"If I get any type of call whatsoever that I don't want you to hear, I'll either not answer, or I'll take the call outside or in the lobby. But why are we talking about this? If I was a man whom you were forced to share an office with, we wouldn't be having this conversation."

He opened his mouth, stunned by her growing gutsiness. And for a rare moment, he didn't have a comeback. Instead he simply nodded, smiled, and disappeared out of the office. Coffee mug in hand. Thoughts to himself.

Since their little conversational exchange, Lorraine struggled to figure Wendell out. She wondered if he was this friendly and outgoing with all the employees, or if he was actually warming up to her. What did it mean when he asked if she had a man? Did he really care? Was his competitive side emerging? Or did he simply not want to intrude upon her personal space and want to know her relationship status up front?

Frankly, she didn't know. She sighed and sat at her desk, booted up her computer, and watched as her e-mails began to load. She waited with bated breath; in times past, as a devilish surprise, Posse used to send her sexy e-mails that made her giggle and turn all shades of red until she asked him to tone it down a little.

So he stopped sending her sexy work e-mails, but he always figured out a way to make a connection with Lorraine.

As a matter of fact, even as recently as several hours before, when she first woke up that morning, she turned on her iPhone and realized Posse had sent her three texts. The first one came in at 12:01 a.m.

U sleep?

Then at 1:10 a.m., Posse wrote:

Missin' U

Then at 2:05AM he texted:

Miss Kissing U

(-}{-)

When she saw the symbol he drew, she knew he was thinking of sex, dreaming of kissing her, and remembering how he used to love stroking her body with his large hands and rubbing her clit till she ordered him through clenched teeth to, "Stick it in me. Now!"

Ha! If there was one thing she missed about Posse, it was the sex. She couldn't understand how any woman who'd been used to having sex could go without, especially if the woman had been in a marital relationship where sex was a given. Lorraine knew of some ladies who'd ended their marriages, gotten divorced, and then decided to be celibate. No sex. For years. No way. She mused that if she ever got married and things didn't work out, she might get a divorce but she'd be divorcing her *husband,* not sex.

As she reflected on the past, her mood went from happy to gloomy. Why do people have to break up, be alone, and remain with sorrowful memories of what used to be? Maybe it's because they never should have hooked up in the first place. Let's face it, some couples just weren't meant to be: Sophisticated Robin Givens and unruly Mike Tyson? Obviously a mismatch! Lil Wayne and Lauren London! The talented actress clearly summoned up the courage needed to lay down with that tatted-up reptile plus bear his child. Didn't a pretty girl like her realize she was too good for a rapper? And Kanye West paired with any woman was an automatic mismatch. But unusual pairings were what gave the world a distinctive and compelling flavor. If Lorraine depended on finding a so-called 100 percent perfect match, she might end up being alone for the rest of her life.

She thought of her ex and how he tried hard to stay connected to her. Although it stoked her ego, her heart advised her that Posse could text her till her cell phone exploded, but she was ready for her new possibilities. If Wendell Holmes was the road to something new, she was ready to begin that journey.

5

Nobody Is That Perfect

During her first day back at work after the vacation, she and Wendell barely crossed each other's paths. He was tied up in a couple of hour-long meetings on and off site, and she was occupied finishing up the details of a PowerPoint presentation. But the following day when Lorraine let herself into the office, she was ready to stay professional. Some of their conversation the day before had left her feeling uneasy and she thought the best approach was one that avoided conflict.

She entered their office and yelled "hello" to Wendell from behind the wall of her cube. But he didn't reply. She dropped her briefcase to the floor with a thud and went over to his desk to greet him. The surface of his workspace held the typical mouse pad, printer, pencil cup holder, stapler, and wire mesh in-box.

He's a neat freak.

It disturbed her that not a single stack of paper sat on his desk.

Too good? Can't be true!

Lorraine promptly abandoned all thoughts of Wendell and concentrated on her work.

Later that afternoon, she received an MS Outlook meeting

invitation titled, "Sandcastle Competition." She instantly wondered what it meant. She'd just returned from lunch with Natalie Kruse, a freckle-faced, African-American second-year
architect who worked on the fourth floor. During their hour
break, they visited a Thai food restaurant in midtown and were
joking around and having a good time. Natalie was one of the
few people she'd met in Houston with whom she could let
down her guard.

Lorraine glanced at her e-mail invitation again, picked up
her office phone, and dialed Natalie.

"Hi there, girl. Your suite mate there? S-w-e-e-t?" Natalie
teased.

"Shhh," Lorraine said with mild annoyance. "I called you
about something entirely different." During lunch Lorraine
had felt disappointed that she hadn't seen Wendell all morning.
She felt on the verge of exploding inside, so she took a risk and
casually questioned Natalie about him. Natalie read between
the lines and by the end of lunch, she pegged the two as a new
couple.

"Be serious, Natalie. I got a meeting invite," she said and
began to explain the description.

"Oh yeah, I worked on the team last year," Natalie responded. "It's a whole lot of fun. We get to brainstorm and
come up with ideas about what type of sandcastle we're going
to build that best represents EDC. We'll get to hang out at
Galveston, work on our project, and interact socially instead of
being concerned about work."

"Well, I guess I'll accept and see what this is all about."

"Sounds good. See you later."

An hour later, ten employees sat around a conference table.
A data projector was set up and a white projection screen hung
from the ceiling. Employees milled about holding bottled water
or sipping from soda cans until the meeting commenced. Lorraine was seated next to Natalie. She felt a jolt of electricity

when Wendell silently slid into a chair on the other side of her. He nodded and smiled and she felt her tongue get stuck to the roof of her mouth. Even though they shared an office, it wasn't like she got to see him a lot. He'd be busy doing his thing, and she'd be doing hers.

Lorraine managed to get ahold of herself. She calmly smiled at Wendell and waved. She felt Natalie give her a slick kick, but she pretended to ignore her.

Soon the meeting facilitator began explaining that for this year, EDC was asking five employees who previously worked on the sandcastle project to rejoin the team.

"And we enlisted the help of five other staff members who've never participated to come onboard so you may partake in this wonderful experience. This organization has been putting on this competition for over twenty years. It's considered one of the world's largest sandcastle competitions. And it's gotten so popular that every first weekend in June when the event takes place, some families bring their kids and make it into a minivacation. So we really need to work hard this year. Maybe we can take home the Golden Bucket prize."

Everyone cheered and started clapping in an effort to show support for the annual competition.

"Can you swim?" Wendell whispered to Lorraine without taking his face off the meeting facilitator.

"Since I was five years old," she whispered back, following his lead.

"I'll bet you look good in . . . the water."

Hearing him flirt with her made her feel great, like she was back on the right track. Yet she didn't want to be a typical female and fall for the bait of a man's sweet words.

How can I raise the standard and react differently yet affirmatively?

Her iPhone began to chime loudly. Everyone twisted in their seats and looked in her direction.

"Oops, sorry. I forgot to put it on vibrate." She picked up her phone. Posse! She rejected the call and laid the phone on the conference table.

Two minutes later her phone rang again and started twirling in a tiny circle from the vibrations.

"Must be important." Wendell smiled.

"He's wearing my last nerve."

"A male bill collector?"

"No!"

"A boyfriend who's thinking about you in the middle of the day and won't give up until he hears the sound of his baby's voice?"

This is my chance to be honest and up front. But how many times has a man been 100-percent transparent with me? Why do women always feel the need to be real, but the man refuses to do the same? Should I change my standard of raw truth and try lying for a change and see where it gets me?

"Just something that can wait, that's all. For all you know, I got two different callers within thirty seconds."

"That could be possible but with your big, smartphone screen, I clearly saw the same name twice. Posse, is it? Is that a man or a hip-hop clothing store?"

She burned inside at Wendell's words. Although she perceived he was only teasing, his bluntness put her on edge. This time when Natalie chuckled and kicked her again, Lorraine discreetly kicked back.

Unbelievably, Lorraine's phone chimed again. The meeting facilitator waved to get everyone's attention.

"Lorraine, we're glad to have you on the team this year. Incidentally, our theme for this competition revolves around the iPhone."

"Ahhh, okay," she replied.

"Can we use your phone as a model?" Wendell joked.

"Look, I'm not the only employee who owns one of these things."

"Yeah, but you're the only one whose phone rings off the hook . . . or should I say off the table?" Wendell quipped as Lorraine's phone twirled in a circle on the conference table from the vibrations and fell over the edge. Wendell reached out his hand and caught the phone before it hit the floor.

"Wendell!"

He smiled and tossed the phone into the air, then caught it in his hand.

"Here ya go." He slid it across the table to her. "You may want to learn how to silence your phone."

When the meeting concluded, Natalie strolled down the hallway and accompanied Lorraine to her office.

"I can't believe how he was acting during the meeting," Lorraine said.

"I can. That's how he behaves when he's feeling a woman."

"Stop playing. That man isn't feeling me."

"He is feeling you, and believe me, he will be feeling on you, too."

"Natalie, you know you're wrong."

"We'll see how wrong I am."

Lorraine reached their office before Wendell did and promptly began sorting through a stack of papers on her desk.

She heard Wendell enter the room but she remained focused on her search.

"How can you stand to work that way?" He pointed at four different paper piles on her desk. In addition, binders were spread across the surface, plus trade magazines, and a half-size set of drawings regarding a hospital interior renovation. Lorraine protectively placed her hand on her papers. "Excuse me, but it would do you good to not make comments about my desk. Believe it or not, I know where everything is."

"Do you, now?"

"Of course I do," she huffed. "A messy desk means you're a very busy person."

"Sure it does." He tossed back his head and laughed. He smirked at Lorraine, then went to sit at his desk.

"Hold up a minute, Wendell. I don't like how you're insinuating that I'm messy. I-I mean, I am a bit untidy, but what's it to you?"

"It's a reflection of me, of EDC."

"Give me a break, Wendell! That is so not true. If you're going to talk to me, please tell me the truth because right now I'm having a hard time believing what you say. I've already been through this a million times—"

"Been through what?"

"Never mind. I shouldn't have said anything. Got a lot on my plate is what I should have told you."

"Being busy isn't a good excuse."

She bristled at his comments and struggled to contain her emotions. "Okay, you know what? I was starting to think you're a pretty decent guy. But lately—no, make that specifically since we've begun to share offices—I sense you've been attacking me. I haven't done anything to deserve this. It's wrong, and it's confusing."

"Is it, now?"

"Will you please stop answering me with a question? I feel like you're not taking me seriously."

"Why should I take you seriously?"

"There you go again. Ooooh!" She took a deep breath and vigorously rubbed the corners of her forehead until the tension lessened. "I don't think this is going to work."

"What? Me being here with you in this little office? An office that's no bigger than two huge walk-in closets?"

"It's not the space and how confining it is, Wendell. To be honest, I don't like how you try to act like you have it all together."

"Never that. You just don't know."

"No, I know that your workspace is unrealistic." She jumped up from her chair and pointed at his desk. "Nothing is out of place. That's weird. Nobody is *that* perfect."

"If you judge a person just because their desk is free of papers and pens and books and sticky notes, you don't understand human nature. If you knew that underneath my dry-cleaned three-piece suit, shined leather shoes, and neat desk is a man who struggles to figure out why he's on the earth each and every day, you wouldn't say what you just said to me. You would know that the outward appearance is just a poor cover-up for everything inside that I'm afraid for people to see."

Lorraine could only watch Wendell, who wore a somber look on his face as he cupped his head in his hands and his eyes widened. "If I am so perfect, why did she treat me the way she did? Why couldn't she get that I was feeling her and I wanted to be with her for real but she didn't believe me . . . thought I was just feeding her some BS? But I wasn't."

"Does 'she' have a name?"

"Does it really matter at this point? Look, I don't mean to get all deep on you, but long story short, nothing is ever as it appears."

Instantly she felt a mixture of sadness and compassion. It was true that most people didn't view co-workers as people with lives outside the workplace. Many days people smiled and said they're doing fine whenever they're greeted, but who knew what type of hell they endured just to make it to work that day?

"Look, Wendell. I'm sorry for even bringing it up. It's a stupid comment. Point is your work area can look however you want it to look. Seriously."

"And you, young lady, have a right to do the same. I

shouldn't have said anything about your desk. I was out of line. You shouldn't have even apologized. One thing I neglected to tell you is I-I can get a bit out of hand at times. I think I've now officially spoiled the perfect image you had of me, huh?" He sighed and went to slump in his chair.

6

Tell It Like It Is

After Lorraine and Wendell had their awkward conversation, for the rest of the week Lorraine felt as if she had to walk on eggshells around him. She desperately wanted to compensate for her insensitivity. On Friday, she decided to stop by a popular breakfast taco stand prior to coming to work.

When Lorraine arrived at their office, she was relieved that he wasn't there. She immediately set the brown paper bag containing several food items on his desk. It didn't take her long to locate his favorite coffee mug. Once she logged into her e-mail account, she decided enough time had passed and she strolled down the hall to the kitchen and fixed Wendell a steaming cup of brew.

She hurried back to the office and waited.

The second Wendell arrived at work and said hello to Lorraine, enticing aromas greeted him.

"Is this what I *think* it is?"

"Mm-hmm," she said in the flirtiest tone she could muster. "Now open up that bag so I can watch you handle your business."

"Oh woman, I swear, if we weren't at work I'd pick you up and swing you around in a circle."

"I can't even see it," she smirked. "But I think that's your way of saying thank you, and you're welcome. I didn't buy my-self any, but I'd love to get a tiny bite of your potato and egg taco."

"Your wish is my command." Smiling, Wendell opened the bag and picked up one homemade tortilla neatly wrapped in soft aluminum paper. The food was still warm and the sharp fragrance of cilantro filled the office.

"Mmm, cheese toppings, too. You did a great job, Lor-raine." He unwrapped a small portion of the food and thrust it at her. As she bit into the taco, he stared at her with such a dreamy expression she began giggling. Bits of scrambled egg flew from her mouth and landed on the carpeted floor. She covered her mouth with her fingers and laughed uncontrol-lably.

"I know what *not* to buy you in the morning," he teased and leaned down to clean bits of egg off the floor. He rose up and grinned. "Glad to finally see a pretty smile on your beau-tiful face."

"Oh Wendell. Please," she said dismissively.

His eyes darkened and narrowed. "So you don't believe me? Should I have said your 'ugly' face?"

"No," she said indignantly. "You shouldn't."

"Then why would you give me a hard time when I'm coming from the heart?"

"Look, I didn't mean—"

"I don't understand why women accuse men of lying all the time. If we give you a genuine compliment, you blow us off or act all coy and stuff like you don't know how to respond to kindness. A simple 'thank you' is usually the best answer."

"Jeez, get a grip. I'm sorry. You're being hypersensitive right now." Feeling embarrassed, she swirled away from him, eager to return to her cube.

"Wait, no," he said looking regretful. "Lorraine, I'll admit it. I am feeling oversensitive these days. I–I guess this means we should have a little talk. There's something you need to know."

Wendell wheeled a guest chair across the floor and patted it so Lorraine could take a seat.

"You're beginning to worry me," she said, folding her arms over her chest.

"Don't worry. It's just that in the short time we've been around each other, I can tell you've never met a man like me. I guess I should say there's more to me than meets the eye."

"And you're telling me this because . . . ?"

"The deal is this, as far as my personal relationships go. Wow, this isn't easy to say, but"—he took a deep breath—"I-I met this chick that I caught feelings for and, needless to say, she affected me to a great extreme. Sometimes a woman can do that to you. You'll be so into her, she blinds you to everything around you."

"Hmm, I heard that. She must've been pretty special, huh?"

"It was like I lost my mind. And the only way I can describe it is this: It was like I built a house that had a whole lot of windows, yet I still couldn't see through them."

Lorraine listened to him open up to her and she wondered if she should do the same. She quickly determined a relationship with a man could never develop if she was unwilling to be vulnerable. Even though she was scared to get hurt, relating to people always involved risk.

"Wendell, you're preaching to the choir. But I can preach, too."

"Preach!"

She unfolded her arms and stood to her feet. She began to pace the floor as she talked.

"You see, I know what it's like to be involved with a man who, by all outward appearances, I shouldn't have even been with. We spoke two different languages, and were way beyond the Mars versus Venus type of thing."

"Explain."

"I was educated. *Am* educated," she corrected. "Highly educated. In contrast, my former lover barely graduated high school. He struggled financially, but had the nerve to state that he made one hundred grand a year on his MySpace profile. Truth was he periodically dabbled in under-the-table jobs to make ends meet. And back in the day, magazine articles advised women to stick with someone who shared the same social class, upbringing, and spiritual beliefs. But now, advice columnists tell you not to restrict yourself to just the same old predictable guy who you think you should have. They tell you if you can't find your Ivy-League white-collar guy with the BMW, give a fair chance to the blue-collar man who has an associate's degree and drives the Ford Focus. You hear what I'm trying to say."

"I hear ya."

"Well, keep listening because there's more. The fact that I was an educated black woman who paid her bills on time, listened to classical music, and ate somewhere besides Chick-fil-A every other day made my little high-school-diploma guy feel he had to throw his weight around, put me in my place, tell me that my earning that degree wasn't about anything. It's just 'a stupid little piece of paper.' Can you believe he said that?"

"I believe that his response to your accomplishments says everything about *him*."

"Huh, my ex's reaction said more than I ever wanted to hear," she replied, happy Wendell understood. "Shoot, I studied hard and worked even harder to obtain that 'stupid little piece of paper.' But he was mad, he acted bad, and the boy can keep being sad because I've decided I will *not* dumb myself down and feel scared to share my accomplishments since it's obvious he's insecure and feels like a nobody because he ruined his life with poor choices. Not my problem. Not my fault."

"Baby girl, sounds like he wished he had what you had, but because he didn't have what it takes to achieve success like you did, the only thing he was fit to do was degrade you!" Wendell said excitedly. "That's what haters do."

"I know, Wendell. But don't get me wrong. Half the time he acted like he was proud of me, the other times he would hate on me and I would try my best to stop all that. I mean, how in the hell can a black man despise an educated, good-looking black woman, yet any of these black men would be sooo proud to flaunt a three-hundred-pound white or Hispanic woman who only has a funky G.E.D. but she's a manager at Kroger? Not that there's anything wrong with being a retail manager, but jeez, my issue is with the *man*. I don't understand how some act as if he's got it made only because he convinced a less successful non-black woman to marry his ass. Do you know how awful that makes me feel? As if a black woman who has her stuff together isn't good enough? I'm getting pissed just thinking about it. Humph! That's why I'm by myself right now."

"I'm not mad at ya." Wendell nodded. "Your story makes me wonder about my own sit-u-ation," he said emphasizing his words in a way that made Lorraine grin. She took a deep measured breath, settled in his guest chair, and waited for him to share his story. She appreciated this side of Wendell, the side that didn't mind getting down and dirty. These days telling it like it is was what she wanted. She felt that black men ought to be strong enough to let their woman shine and know that her accomplishments didn't take anything away from him.

"Wendell, you got a situation?" she teased.

"We all got sit-u-ations, let me tell ya."

"I'm listening. Go ahead."

"She walked like a queen who had a throne; head held very high, so high that I was afraid she wouldn't even notice me the first time I noticed her."

"Ah ha."

"Elegant, wore Elizabeth Taylor perfume that smelled so sweet I could taste her. Vivacious shape with smooth brown skin that was so pretty I wanted to cup her face between my hands."

"You liked that, huh?"

"I *loved* that. Loved how she carried herself: strong, confident, sexy, alluring. She had me from hello."

"She said 'hello'?" Lorraine said teasingly.

"Well, I said it *first*, but she said hello back, and she had me and had me and had me until she didn't have me anymore."

"Hold up. You've lost me."

"See, this woman—"

"Again, does this woman have a name?"

"Faye."

"Faye. Got it."

"Faye had *me*, but as much as I wanted her, I never had *her*. She was a pro at playing the cat-and-mouse game. She let me get close enough to sniff it, but she wouldn't let me touch it."

"Ahh, and you really wanted to touch it, right?"

"I wanted to touch it and renovate it, put my hands all in it like it was that sand out there on Galveston Beach. I wanted to dig in it and mold and reshape it and make it everything I wanted it to be."

"But she wasn't down with that," Lorraine said.

"Hey, are you going to let me tell the story in my own words or what?"

"Sorry, go ahead."

"She wasn't down with that," he said sheepishly.

Lorraine felt like smacking Wendell, but she resisted and let him continue.

"The more Faye put space between us, the more I wanted to fill up that space. And I scared her away, frightened her right out of my life."

"Where is she now?"

"She's wherever women go when they're trying to get away from a man."

"She moved to another city, a different state?"

"She might as well have; that's how far she feels from me."

Lorraine could sense that Wendell's playful description of what

happened was nothing to play with. He seemed deeply de-
spondent. In a way she kind of wished he could be with the
woman Faye, since he wanted her so badly. But just because
you want something so badly that you hurt inside and out, it
doesn't mean that obtaining it would ease your pain.

"Wendell, I hear what you're saying and I can relate, but
maybe, for the both of us, not having these people in our lives
is for the best. Some relationships are toxic and they make you
worse, not better. Would that be true in your case?"

"I'll never know, Lorraine. I never got close enough to
even find out if her love tasted like poison. I just wanted a
small sample."

"Well, I can tell you one thing: you have admitted more
intimate things to me than any man I've ever known. Usually
they just won't go there."

"Won't or can't?"

"Maybe both. Guys can barely understand themselves, so it
is hard for them to adequately explain the emotions they feel
inside. To me it seems like some guys lack emotions. They can
be so cold and cruel and uncaring."

"Baby girl, what you don't realize is behind closed doors,
and late at night, real men break down. They cry when they
think about their struggles. Many times they hit the gym, get
fitted up in boxing gear, and take out their frustration on their
sparring partner. It happens every day. Truth."

"I appreciate that." Lorraine thought about all the days
Posse would tell her that he needed to let off some steam.
Sometimes, he invited her to watch him shoot hoops at the
neighborhood basketball court where the white net had been
stolen, but the orange rim would suffice. The guys aggressively
shoved each other, trying to defend their team. They'd dribble
the ball all the way down the court, leap off their feet, fero-
ciously slam that ball inside the hoop, and scream at the top of
their lungs like they were releasing all their pain.

"Maybe I should have taken time to understand my guy a little more. I could rant and rave and accuse him of never wanting to spend time with me. And he'd argue back, tell me I was 'wigging out' or 'you bugging, Lo.' Eww, I hated when he'd say things like that. I'd tell him to speak English. He'd tell me the same thing. We were talking *to* each other but we couldn't *hear* each other. It's really sad when you think about it."

"And so the story continues," Wendell jumped in. "You meet a new man. Y'all hook up. Everything feels rosy. Time passes. Reality sets in. You have your first argument. It's amusing at first. But then the arguments occur with greater frequency. What used to seem cute now makes you cry. And you wake up one day, balled up in pain and hating his guts, and you wonder how you got there."

"One day leads to the next, and the next, and that's how it happens. That's how everything happens," she replied, amazed at how well Wendell understood the dynamics of relationships.

"Hey," he said, glancing at his watch. "We could chat about this topic till infinity. But I need to get a handle on this day and get something accomplished. My damn taco is probably cold and hard and lost its flavor by now."

"Ah haa, sorry!" She extended her hand and was pleased when he accepted it. They shook hands. "We've had an invigorating conversation. I cannot tell you how good it feels to talk to you, Wendell. I mean that."

The rest of the morning Wendell participated in project team meetings. He added data to spreadsheets and reviewed schematic designs of a new classroom building that was being proposed for Rice University. But his mind was split between work and Lorraine. Faye and work. Faye and Lorraine. He felt like he was about to lose his mind. He needed an outlet. Sex was out of the question. Since he wasn't in a relationship and frowned on casual sex, he had to think of other activities to keep his mind occupied. By late afternoon, he knew what he wanted to do.

Thirty minutes before the day ended, he went to the restroom. Almost as soon as he finished up in the men's room and stepped into the hallway, he spotted Lorraine. She held her car keys in one hand, a briefcase in the other. She struggled to hoist her purse over her shoulder.

Here was his chance.

"You're leaving early?" he asked nervously.

"Yeah, I gotta pick up a package from the post office. Why? What's up?"

He grabbed the back of his head and glanced at the ceiling for a second. "You like the Rockets? They're playing the Lakers tomorrow night."

"Oh hell yeah. I love me some b-ball. You got tickets?"

"Um, yeah. If you don't mind, um, hanging out."

"I'd love to go. Thanks for asking."

"Good deal. It's a date!"

"Is it?" she asked sweetly. It made her smile to see that as confident as Wendell seemed, he could still be vulnerable and unsure. The more she got to know him, the less perfect he appeared. And for once, imperfection felt okay.

7

It Ain't Over Till It's Over

Lorraine gripped the edge of her seat in great anticipation. They'd just arrived and were pulling into a parking space inside the Toyota Center Tundra Garage located downtown. Wendell opened her car door and took her by the hand, which surprised her. He didn't hold on to her for long, though; a throng of basketball-game attendees crushed against them and temporarily separated her from her date.

"Hey, are you all right?" he asked with a worried look on his face as soon as they reconnected.

"Oh, I'm fine. As long as my purse is still on my hip, I'm cool," she joked as they walked through the crowded parking garage. Soon they were at the entrance of the stadium. Lorraine opened her purse so security could check for prohibited items. Wendell handed the ticket person his credit card so she could swipe his magnetic strip and print their tickets. Just being in the wide first-floor hallway gave Lorraine a bolt of energy. Many people wore red Yao Ming and Aaron Brooks jerseys. She noted quite a few folks wearing purple, gold, and white jerseys, too. They found their seats in section 110 and waited for the tip-off.

"Oh my God, I can't believe the energy of the crowd," she said.

"It's always like this when Kobe is in the house."

"Beat L.A. Beat L.A."

"Listen to them chant. This is insane," she laughed. "And fun." He offered to buy her a beer and a small pizza and she let him. It felt so good to be with a man who didn't mind paying for dates. So many times when Posse was broke she reluctantly paid for his tickets, drink, and food for the events they attended. She always made excuses and told herself that one day, when he got himself together, he'd pay her back for her generosity. But after dating for months, he was still chronically unemployed and had a hundred excuses about why he never had any money except when it came to buying forty ounces of beer and a bag of weed.

"Let me know if you need anything else. I don't want you to have to worry about a thing."

"Wendell—"

"Wendell what?"

"Thank you!"

"That's what I hoped you were going to say. We worked hard all week long and I just wanted to have a good time tonight and be with someone who's fun to hang around."

"You know what? You're so right. Sometimes we women can get so focused on our jobs and responsibilities that we— rather, I—make up excuses sometimes when it comes to just chilling out and enjoying myself."

"Well, all that nonsense is about to change, especially when you're with me, baby girl."

"I am so happy to be here with you. So, so happy," she purred to Wendell, feeling grateful to be in the company of a man who exhibited class, self-pride, and dignity.

"All I care about is you enjoying yourself."

"Yeah, I'm cool, but I'll feel even better if the Rockets can catch up."

So far they were losing by eight points. But they had another three quarters to go and anything could happen before then.

Aaron Brooks shot four three-pointers in a row. The crowd immediately perked up and got back into the game. Lorraine loved how warm her body felt when Wendell rubbed her arm each time the home team scored.

"It ain't over till it's over," Lorraine sang, and clapped when Luis Scola scored two points with an easy layup. Lamar Odom got the rebound but lost it when he threw the ball out of bounds.

"It's R-r-r-r-rockets' ball," yelled the announcer.

Ecstatic, Wendell and Lorraine high-fived, continued enjoying the game, and engaged in some people watching.

During the second quarter, the Lakers called a time out. Kobe Bryant limped to the sidelines and people began pumping their fists and cheering.

"Crazy, crazy," Lorraine laughed. "But people got to do what it takes to win, right?"

"Right," Wendell said and winked at her. "You need to do whatever it takes to get what you want." She felt a gush of warmth ooze through her veins.

Feeling happy feels so good, she thought.

Soon the kiss camera began aiming its lens at couples sitting in the audience. People would gaze upward, spot themselves on the big screen, laugh, point, and then kiss one another. Lorraine smirked and shook her head at the big display. But when she saw her and Wendell magnified on the monitor, she opened her mouth in shock.

"Play along," he said smoothly and pulled her face close so that his lips touched hers. He gave her a solid kiss and even closed his eyes. When they were done kissing, someone behind Lorraine tapped her shoulder. She laughed and felt embarrassed. By halftime she didn't know what to think. Would Wendell have kissed her later, perhaps when he dropped her off at her car, which she'd parked outside EDC so they could ride in one vehicle? She never dreamed of kissing him, and when it actually happened, it went by so fast that she couldn't remember how she felt when it happened.

A kiss is a kiss, she thought and promptly attempted to forget about it. Because the way Wendell was acting, like he kissed co-workers every day and it wasn't a biggie, she decided to leave well enough alone.

"Hey, let's go walk around," he told Lorraine and stood up. She followed his lead. They marched side by side out of the arena and entered the main hallway, which flowed with people rushing to beer stands, restrooms, and concessions.

"If you want, we can check out the team store and see if they have any fitted caps on sale."

"I'm with you," Lorraine replied and followed Wendell down the hall until they reached the paraphernalia store.

Lorraine went to the right, while Wendell headed to the left toward the hats. She browsed through the store, observing warm-up jackets, gym shoes, T-shirts, and mascot stuffed animals.

As Lorraine eased toward the other side of the store, she stopped in her tracks. An attractive, above average-height woman stood in front of Wendell gazing directly into his eyes. He feasted his eyes on her as if she was the only person in the entire store. The lady grabbed his arm and snorted with laughter. When Wendell laughed with her, Lorraine abruptly turned around and went in the opposite direction. It felt like a deep hole had been dug in her belly. Suddenly she couldn't care less if the Rockets won or lost. She pretended to be interested in some sweatshirts when she felt someone nudge her from behind.

Wendell waved at her and looked serene.

Wonder how he managed that.

"Ready to go?"

"Go home or back to our seats?"

He scowled but ignored her comment. She instantly felt irritated. They left the store and returned to their section.

"Did you hear me ask you a question or are you just ignoring me?" she asked, unable to keep the fight inside that was ready to burst open.

"I beg your pardon?" he asked as they found their seats.

"Did you find anything interesting while you were in the team shop?"

"Ha." He laughed and blushed. "I guess you could say that."

"But what *are* you saying? That's what I want to know."

Wendell gave her a puzzled look and leaned toward her. "You'll never guess what happened. I-I saw"—he gulped—"Faye Luddington."

"Her?"

He casually shrugged. "I was so surprised to see Faye. She said she actually first noticed me—us—on the kiss cam. She fussed at me like she didn't appreciate me forgetting her so fast and getting a new girlfriend. That's what she said. Can you believe that?"

I don't want to believe that, Lorraine thought.

"How did you respond?"

"Told her I was single, you were just my co-worker—"

"*Just* a co-worker," Lorraine snapped.

"Hey, aren't you about raw truth?"

That stung. "Man, you have a lot of nerve."

"Unless you're screaming for the Rockets I'd advise you not to raise your voice. We are both adults and I think we can manage talking in a reasonable tone. We can do this."

She nodded and calmed down, not appreciating his attitude, but also reluctant to make a scene. "What else happened?"

"Um, she gave me her new number. Told me to call."

"And I guess you'll be calling her?"

"I guess, shoot, I dunno."

"If *you* don't know who does?"

"It's been a while since we've talked. It'll be good to catch up."

"Hmm, funny how she happened to show up at the game tonight," Lorraine said, trying to make light of the situation. "I guess that's what happens when we're always thinking about someone, talking about 'em. Sometimes they appear magically out of nowhere, huh, Wendell?"

"I guess," he said and turned away from her to look up at the big game monitor.

8

She Has Nothing on Me

*As long as man is born with a penis, a woman can never truly
exhale. Why? Men are excellent liars . . . . because even though
they're pros at hiding their true character when you first meet
them, who they truly are will eventually be revealed. Think
Tiger Woods (he's a cheetah and he's lion); Jesse James (the
"Decepticon" who lucked out and married Sandra Bullock);
Mark Sanford the governor of South Carolina, who was fool-
ishly in love with a soul mate who (surprise, surprise) wasn't his
wife; and the list continues.*

These were the words written by Lorraine in a journal that
she kept; periodically she'd be inspired to jot down her thoughts,
especially when she was having a tough day and wanted to try to
understand and work through her emotions. Today was one of
those days. She and Wendell hadn't held a personal conversation since they attended the Rockets game a couple weeks
ago. That bothered her. It pissed her off, actually. She didn't
know what to do about it.

She wiped her mouth with a white floral napkin that she'd
packed in her lunch bag. She'd just finished munching on a
tuna sandwich and some salty potato chips that she brought
from home that morning. She silently sat in her office sipping

on a bottle of water while she figured out what to do with the remaining thirty minutes of her lunch break. That's when she retrieved her journal from her briefcase and wrote wherever her heart took her.

She'd gotten writer's block and couldn't figure out what to write next when Natalie popped her head inside her doorway.

"How are things going with you and your boy?"

"Men will be men."

"Excuse me, but I thought the saying was 'boys will be boys.'"

"Tomato, tomato. Same difference."

"Hey," Natalie said and pulled up a chair to sit close to Lorraine. "Something bad must've happened. Usually you're grinning and acting giggly about the great Houston." "Houston" was the weak code name that Lorraine suggested she and Natalie use to refer to Wendell whenever they discussed him in the workplace.

"Things change."

"That fast?"

"It's like this. We went on a date. We were both having a good time until another woman caught his eye. Natalie, I can't stand acting jealous and possessive so I held in my emotions as best as I could. But I don't want to be caught up in a man who's still caught up in someone he's had a crush on. That's *not* raising the standard."

"Maybe Houston doesn't know how you really feel because you're still accepting phone calls from Dallas."

"Hmm, you think he even notices?"

"Hell yeah. How many times have you taken Dallas's calls in private?"

"Every time."

"See there. No wonder Houston is keeping his options open. You're giving the man mixed signals."

"It's not like we've ever truly discussed our feelings for one another. I think that would be premature. And I am trying to get to know him. Day by day. Conversation by conversation."

"And that's a good idea. I think you're so vulnerable right now with this Dallas situation. Dallas keeps you confused."

"Damn Dallas. Damn J. R."

"You're silly. Damn yourself. If you really wanted to get rid of your ex, you could. All you need to do is change your cell number."

"I already looked into that. It costs thirty bucks."

"Girl, you can't afford to not pay the fee."

"I just don't want to go through all the trouble of getting a number changed that I've had since I was eighteen."

"Excuses, excuses."

Lorraine and Natalie heard someone walking down the hallway and changed the subject to how darned expensive it was to maintain a decent hairstyle and cute nails.

"Do we do this for ourselves or for the opposite sex?"

"I don't know why *you* spend money to look cute. But *I* want to look good for myself and for my guy. Lately I've barely been in the mood to comb my hair."

"Not good, Lorraine. I don't care what you're going through in your love life, you gotta take care of Lorraine for Lorraine. A man shouldn't be your incentive for being the best you can be, inside and outside."

"Girl, you're so right." Lorraine swallowed deeply and felt ashamed. Her mother had tried to instill in her the necessity of being strong and handling her business. She wanted Lorraine to have a great life no matter what.

" 'Rain or shine' is what my mother told me when it comes to men," Lorraine explained to Natalie. "She said that it's in a woman's best interests to keep on keeping on no matter what's going on in her love life, because while you're lying up in bed acting depressed and hurting your body by eating a gallon of chocolate chip ice cream, a man is going about his business and not worrying about you. Mama's right. I have to move on. If Houston is into another woman, I can't be into him."

"It seemed you-all made a great couple. It's a shame, too, because you'd think that a man of Houston's caliber would act a little more mature and decisive."

"I guess we were wrong about him. Being wrong scares me. I'm starting to question my judgment, Nat."

"Don't beat yourself up about one little error. We all make mistakes. Just gotta learn." Natalie glanced at her Timex. "Anyway, I need to leave work now. My apartment complex called. Some pipes burst and they advised me to come get my stuff. I live on the first floor, unfortunately," she added. " And no one else is home to do the dirty work."

"Sorry to hear that. I hope you can retrieve your things before they get all messed up."

"Yeah, I'm waiting on a cab. My hooptie is in the shop. I wish taxi man would hurry up and get here already. I can barely afford the fifty bucks it's going to cost for the long drive home."

"Oh, did you want me to drop you off? I can put in for an hour of emergency vacation and get you there quicker than a cab."

"What? Um, no, it's cool. I don't want to bother you."

"You sure? I want to see where you live anyway."

"No, Lorraine, don't worry about me. I'll be fine. You need to figure out your love life, all right?"

Natalie thanked her for the offer. As soon as she left, Wendell strolled into the office, walking slowly with his jacket slung over his shoulder and grinning.

"Wendell, are you serious? Since when don't you have time for me?" Lorraine heard the crackling voice of a female coming through Wendell's cell phone. He was holding a conversation on speakerphone. Lorraine thought that was sooo rude.

"I don't have time because all my free time is spent with my woman," he told the lady.

"What woman? That stick-figure chick you took to the Rockets game? Please tell me you're pulling my leg."

Lorraine's eyes widened. Wendell held up a finger at her.

"Come on, Faye. You know I'm not pulling your leg. That so-called stick figure is the best woman I know right now. We have a good time together."

"Really?" Faye asked in a shaky voice. "I'm having a hard time figuring out what you saw in her. Shit. She has nothing on me. And you know it, Wendell. I'm Faye fucking Ludding-ton." She laughed like she couldn't believe it herself. "I'm the baddest bitch in the game."

"Not trying to take nothing away from you, but what I have is even better."

"Negro, please. Now I know you're lying. It's cool, though," Faye said, her voice loudly popping through the phone. "I tell you one thing. You are dating beneath you. I could look at the chick and tell she's not your type."

Lorraine rose to her feet and took a giant leap toward Wendell. He waved at her to sit down.

"What could you tell about her?"

"Ha! Her shoes were scruffy looking. Looks like she puts her makeup on in the dark. Her T-shirt was wrinkled like she sleeps in her clothes. And the girl's weave was through."

"Um, correction. That's not a weave. My lady was born with her own hair, unlike some people," Wendell replied. "Everything she has, she was born with." He chuckled.

"You're actually defending that puny bitch over *me*? You must be out of your damn mind."

"Now, Faye, don't be like that," he said, sounding mad instead of amused. "Lorraine is not the b-word in any shape, form, or fashion."

Lorraine leaped to her feet again, her face pleading with Wendell to let her address Faye's derogatory comments.

"Yeah, well, like we discussed in the Toyota Center," Faye

said, "don't forget, I'm on the sandcastle competition for my firm. And I'll be checking out your new woman up close. And if I find out she's not better than me, which I already know she isn't, be prepared to hear me tell you about yourself. And you know I will." Faye's voice grew softer. "It's just hard for me to accept this, because I have a need to be the only woman in your bed, sweetie. You know what I mean?"

"No, I didn't know, Faye. Hmm. Too bad you're taking a sudden interest in a brother. Bad timing. I never wait around for a woman. If she's feeling me she better let me know ASAP because I got a nice, long waiting list, if you know what *I* mean."

"Hmm, I know you ought to place me at the top of your so-called list. For real. Anyway, let me go. I'm sure your little girlfriend is hovering somewhere nearby like a helicopter passing over the ghetto. She looks like the insecure type who constantly spies on her man. Good luck with that one." Faye hung up.

Lorraine pounced on Wendell immediately. "What in the hell was that about?"

"Calm down."

"Calm down my ass. You are lying to a woman I don't even know. And she's lying on me; she couldn't even see my shoes."

"Faye's dramatic like that. Ignore her."

"Ignore her? I don't appreciate you letting her talk about me as if I wasn't in the room. And why'd you tell her all that mess about us? You know how I feel about stuff like that."

"You look so cute when you're mad."

"This isn't about how I look. Why'd you let this happen?"

"You're so adorable, even sensual." He made kissing noises and leaned in.

"Stop avoiding my questions. You act just like—"

"Your ex boy?" Wendell sobered up. "Are you trying to replace him with me? C'mon, Lorraine, now's your time to tell me what's up!"

"Ugh!" She spun around and folded her arms. She felt afraid. Confused. Was Wendell playing games? If so, she wanted no part of it.

"Did you hear me ask you some questions, Ms. Eafford? I'm waiting."

He sat on the edge of her desk and folded his arms.

"I think the burden of answering lies with you. Explain to me why you held a conversation in which I am the topic on your speakerphone. You did it on purpose, didn't you?"

"Yeah."

"I'm *not* a toy."

"I know that."

"Apparently you don't."

"You want the truth? It's like this. You are a cool chick. I enjoy hanging out with you. I can see myself doing it again. We're *going* to do it again. Soon. Tonight."

"Wendell—"

"No, really. Faye and me: Hey, let's face it. She'd walk all over me. But you'd walk right *beside* me. I need that type of woman."

"Wendell, don't play. Please," Lorraine begged. She couldn't believe they were having this conversation. She desired to get closer to him, but not like this. Yes, she felt drawn to him even more. The way he was acting infuriated yet intrigued her. He had more layers than she originally thought.

"Lorraine, I swear I'm not playing. We'll meet tonight. At seven. Let's do this."

Wendell came and stood close to Lorraine, giving her a tender and apologetic look. He enfolded her in his arms, pulling her thin frame against his chest. She resisted him but he held on tighter. Being hugged by Wendell felt soothing, yet disturbing. She gave in and rested her head against his chest.

Right then, she didn't care if anyone saw them. Although she didn't appreciate what had gone down with Wendell and Faye, she momentarily forgot how angry it made her feel. Instead, she relaxed and savored how good it felt to be in this man's arms. Comforting. Warm. Loving.

Wendell said nothing as he embraced Lorraine and relished the feeling of her breasts against him. When he felt the beating of her heart calm down, he released her, told her he'd see her later. He busied himself with work for the rest of the day.

At exactly seven o'clock that evening, Wendell called. He informed her that he'd ordered her chicken pesto pasta, rosemary roasted potatoes, broccoli, and a bottle of white zinfandel from La Madeleine. He'd arranged for her dinner to be delivered to her apartment.

"How'd you know my home address?"

"I know, Lorraine."

He apologized for not being able to make it in time to break bread with her, but said he'd be over after eleven. He promised to call her thirty minutes before coming by. A few minutes before twelve, he arrived at her place. He stepped inside the foyer for a few minutes, then suggested they leave. He got Lorraine situated in a limo that he rented and they took off. Wendell asked the limo driver to start off driving around the Reliant Park area. Then he steered the driver north on Main Street so they could pass the Texas Medical Center, Hermann Park, the Museum District.

"Have you ever been on a midnight drive before?"

"I've never been in a limo before," she said in a hushed tone.

"Good."

They ended up downtown. Lights streaming through the windows of several skyscrapers illuminated the sky. Few could be seen on the streets. After he asked the driver to park, he insisted they get out of the vehicle. Wendell clasped Lorraine's hand in his. They ambled down Dallas Street and passed by the Houston Pavilions, a mixed-use commercial development with tenants such as Lucky Strike, Books-A-Million, and Mc-Cormick & Schmick's, a seafood restaurant Lorraine had always wanted to try, and the House of Blues.

"This is nuts, Wendell," she finally blurted to him. But she had a contented smile on her face. Wendell made her feel so protected and important. For that moment he made her feel like the center of his universe.

"I'm trying to build something, here."

"Like what?"

"Trust."

"Hmm."

They continued to stroll hand in hand down Main Street and stopped in front of a display window of the ten-story Macy's. This historic building was the only free-standing central business district department store located in the Southern United States.

Wendell cleared his throat and squeezed Lorraine's hand. "Tell me something. Which artists would you name as the greatest singers ever?"

"What are you talking about?"

"Building something. Now answer."

"Oh okay." She blushed. "Well, if we're talking about the greatest of the greats, you gotta place Marvin Gaye on the list."

"Can't deny that." Wendell lit up. "His voice was like melted butter."

"Smooth, sexy, haunting, soulful. The world truly misses his talent."

"Thank God for sampling, huh? What other singers are on your list?"

"Hmm, gotta go with Sade; the woman is a genius."

"Oh *hell* no. Her songs last way too long."

"Why do you say that?"

"You can turn on the CD player. Pick a Sade song. Get in your car. Go grocery shopping. Come back home. And that same song will still be playing. It's like *damn*."

"Ha, that doesn't mean she can't sing."

"Does too."

"That's wrong. Soo wrong."

"Not wrong. I know music."

"Okay, Mr. Know-It-All. Who would *you* name?"

"Whitney."

"No way. She's lost her voice. It'll never be the same again."

"She's a legend."

"*Was* a legend. Her glory days are over. Seems like yesterday when I listened to her and tried to sing like her when I was a kid."

"You're still a kid—"

"Hey, watch it, brotha." She laughed and disregarded his teasing. "Seriously, I'm glad we still have evidence of Whitney's great singing recorded on CDs. That's good enough."

"So does she get your vote?"

"*You* get my vote, Wendell."

Wendell looked shocked then pleased. He gently grabbed Lorraine's face between his hands. He reached down and pressed his thick lips against hers. He thrust his tongue into her mouth. They closed their eyes and shared a passionate kiss at one in the morning in downtown Houston, where the only people who may have seen them were a few homeless derelicts and a limo driver.

If all her co-workers happened to drive by at that moment, Lorraine wouldn't have noticed or cared. Right then with Wendell Holmes, she felt on top of the world. And she decided that's exactly where she intended to stay.

9

Take Advantage of the Moment

Wendell and Lorraine spent the next few weeks talking on the phone in the evenings, meeting up for dinner one time at a popular Tex Mex restaurant, and checking out a sneak preview of an Idris Elba flick. Things felt so good between them that all they could both do was relish the moment.

By the time the last Friday in April arrived, everyone at EDC was excited. Wendell worked hard that morning and once four o'clock arrived he took off. He made a right turn and pulled into the parking lot of A&E Graphics on Richmond Avenue where the sandcastle workshop was being held. Before he could emerge from his vehicle, his passenger door opened. Faye slid into the seat and slammed the door. Wendell raised his eyebrows in shock. As usual Faye looked and smelled stunning.

"Is that White Diamonds?" Wendell asked, inhaling.

"You remembered." She smiled. "I take a bottle with me everywhere I go."

"And a new weave?" He eyed her.

"I just got it yesterday. You like it, don't you? Here, give me your hand." Without waiting for him to respond, Faye grabbed Wendell's fingers and placed them on top of her hair.

"How does that feel?"

"Store bought." He massaged her scalp and smiled.

"You're so silly. But it feels good, doesn't it?"

"I-I, um—"

"Go ahead, Wendell. I want to feel your hands in my hair. It turns me on."

"Does it?" At first Wendell didn't know what to believe. But his body answered for him. The more he played with Faye's hair, the more he felt himself getting an erection. He didn't know if he should take advantage of the moment and grope this woman all over while he had the chance, something he'd wanted to do in times past. Or should he stick to the matter at hand and attend the stupid workshop?

"Do you like what I have on?" Her eyes gleamed with desire. Faye wore a yellow silk halter dress with a plunging necklace that emphasized her cleavage. The dress stopped at her thighs. She crossed her legs and glanced down at them. There they were: some of the most luscious thighs Wendell had ever seen, only inches away from his fingers.

Faye's body was in the best shape of any woman he'd ever known. Maybe it was because she regularly engaged in kickboxing and cardiovascular training at the twenty-four-hour gym. She took pride in and worshipped her body like it was her god. Faye was so eye catching she could easily rival any *Maxim* cover girl and had the curves and legs to prove it.

"You haven't told me if you like what you see, Wendell." Her soft, delicate voice was barely audible.

"You look amazing, Faye. Always have." He couldn't believe she was sitting next to him in his ride. He'd always dreamed of being close to her, so for this to happen in such an unexpected way threw him.

Faye twisted around in her seat, crossed one leg over the other, and whispered, "I'm not wearing any underwear, Wendell."

His eyes bugged as he moaned.

"I love hearing you moan like that. I want to hear you do it again, but louder."

"Faye," he gasped, hitting his hands on the steering wheel. "I think we're going to be late. You aren't even dressed to go to the workshop."

"That's because I'm not going to the workshop. I'm going to your place. C'mon, let's go. Can't you smell how bad I want you, Wendell? Can you taste it? I can taste you."

"Dammit, Faye," he muttered to himself. He'd promised to meet Lorraine at the workshop so he could go over the objective of their team project. He knew she was running late and would be expecting to see him. But Faye looked so hot. She had all his attention. She aroused him till it hurt. And he'd been told to never let a good hard-on go to waste.

"So," she said, licking her lips. "See what I'm doing to my lips?"

He nodded.

"I want to do that to your dick." She paused. "Every man has a name for his penis. What's yours?"

"Joe-Joe," he uttered.

"I'm going to stick Joe-Joe deep in my mouth. I'm going to lick Joe-Joe with my tongue like he's a chocolate ice-cream cone sprinkled with nuts. And then I'm going to suck your asshole from top to bottom. You ever been sucked there before?"

Hearing Faye describe what she wanted to do to him made Wendell grow harder by the second. A little tent popped up in his slacks. He felt dizzy and weak. His mouth sprang open in his attempt to respond. Faye quickly leaped on him and thrust her tongue into his mouth. He let her take him deep inside her mouth where it was hot, wet, and slippery.

Faye reached down and grabbed his pants and rubbed him over and over until he exploded in orgasm.

His cheeks flushed with red. "I'll have to go home and change."

"Now *that's* change that I can believe in. Let's go."

"What about your car?"

"Wendell, are you even serious?" She leaned back, buckled her seat belt, and waited for him to start the ignition. Within seconds they were speeding away from the A&E building. Wendell heard the horn of a car honking but he ignored it and prayed that if things got messy between him and Lorraine, they could be cleaned up and worked out eventually.

He couldn't get home fast enough. Even after they got out of the car, Wendell looked to his left, his right, and behind him.

"Oh, you think she followed you?"

"Huh, what are you talking about?"

"Stick-figure chick, that's who, but enough about her. I'm the one who's coming home with you to come inside of you when we make some serious love in your bed."

Wendell wanted to say so much; he had a million questions but he decided to keep his mouth closed. He opened the door of his condo and let Faye inside. She immediately walked past the living room, dining room, and kitchen, and went straight to his bedroom even though this was her first time ever setting foot inside his place.

"How'd you know where—?"

"You've seen one bedroom, you've seen them all."

She turned on the overhead light and observed his neatly made king-size bed.

"That's perfect, Wendell."

He ignored her while he walked past her to the master bathroom. He closed the door, unzipped his slacks, and stepped out of his soaked drawers.

"Hey." She knocked. "I'm coming in." She opened the door and stood gaping at his hard-on while he stood holding his penis in his hand.

"Do you mind?" he croaked. But he couldn't protest for long. Faye's nakedness was a sight to behold. She stood with her hands on her hips looking sexy and confident. Her long hair grazed her shoulders, her breasts resembled plump melons, and most important, she had a Brazilian bikini wax.

"I want you to eat my pussy, but I want us to take a shower first so I can get it good and clean for you. C'mon, turn on the water and make it as hot as possible. Do you have any shower gel?"

Wendell stood speechless as he watched Faye step into his stall.

"What are you waiting on? I can't wait to fuck you. Hurry up so we can get started."

He shook his head, tried hard not to laugh, and twisted the knob until a blast of steaming hot water shot out. All thoughts of Lorraine completely vanished.

Faye giggled and embraced Wendell from behind, lightly kissing his shoulders. She grabbed his penis and stroked it over and over again.

"Hi, how are you doing Joe-Joe? When we're done showering I'm going to introduce you to Luscious . . ."

I can't believe Faye is here with me, naked in my shower. Faye is the baddest bitch in the game.

Later that evening, Wendell pulled up across the street from Lorraine's apartment and put the Sebring in idle. He saw her waiting on the other side of the street. He honked his horn and waved.

She crossed the street and watched as Wendell jumped out of the car to open her door.

Lorraine slid into her seat, folded her arms, and glared once he settled in again.

"Well?"

"Well, what?"

"You still haven't given me a good excuse as to why you missed the workshop. I waited and waited on you. When I tried to contact you, all the calls went to voice mail."

"I told you, something came up. I turned off my phone and let it charge for a couple of hours."

"I'm sorry, Wendell, but from what I know, you do not need to turn off a cell phone just to let it charge."

"You don't believe me?" he exclaimed, trying to look of-fended.

"I don't know what to believe anymore," she huffed and blew out a frustrated breath. "I just think that if you need to tell me something, now's your time to do it. Does that sound familiar?"

Inside Wendell was dying, torn, and plagued with guilt. How was it that he went from zero women to two hot chicks in less than a few weeks? He couldn't believe he was in this sit-uation and had to figure out how to handle it.

"Raw truth, Wendell."

"Are you sure you know what you're asking?"

"If I'm going to get hurt, it may as well happen sooner than later."

"I don't want it to happen at all. It's *not* going to happen. And that settles it. All you need to know is that I'm here with you right now. We're about to go on a fantastic date. I'm still trying to build something with you. I am. And that's the truth."

"Are you serious, Wendell? I hate being toyed with."

"Either take it or leave it, because that's all I can tell you. You gotta trust me."

"Hmm, I still don't believe that you think that men are simple and easy to understand. It's just not true." She wrinkled her nose then sneezed.

"Gesundheit!"

"Thanks. Must be something in the air."

"Love?"

"Don't even try it."

He laughed cheerily and forced himself to relax. As he drove off from her apartment, he tried to hold a conversation with Lorraine. But his thoughts were heavy with the good time he'd just shared with Faye. Was Faye a keeper or a part-time lover? Was it worth it to juggle the two women for a little while longer, or should he release Faye if he felt like he'd gotten her out of his system? If he *did* have enough guts to tell the raw truth—that he actually admired and wanted to hang out with both females—would he still get what he wanted in the end? Truth was good but also risky. For now, he decided to keep his thoughts to himself. Especially since Lorraine was still pissed at him for standing her up.

They ended up downtown again. But this time Wendell had a concrete plan. He parked near Discovery Green. They walked past the fountain where dozens of children splashed and ran through the water as it blasted through the spouts. A menagerie of trees, flower beds, and gardens filled the green park and exposed Lorraine to one of the most natural settings she'd ever visited.

"It's good to see a little bit of a smile on your face," he exclaimed. "But I don't know how long that's going to last."

"Why do you say that?" she asked defensively.

"Because of that." He pointed at a hot air balloon that was tied to a wooden post right in the center of the park.

"You expect *me* to go on *that*?"

"Yep, I do. I want to take you places you've never been before; we're going to do things we've never done."

"Oh, Wendell, I don't know," she replied with uncertainty.

"Come on. 'Disco Green' is the place to be when you want to have good, clean fun. And that's what we're about to have, dammit. I need this. Bad."

Twenty minutes later Lorraine and Wendell found themselves three hundred fifty feet in the air, floating around downtown Houston from inside a huge white hot air balloon decorated in aqua and red stripes.

"Damn, I can't believe how far out we can see. There's the freaking Williams Tower." Lorraine laughed and pointed.

"And if you look over here, you can see the Gulf of Mexico."

"This is insane, Wendell. You're insane." She loved the feeling of the wind hitting her cheeks. Riding made her feel as if she was transported from all her worries.

"I hope you mean that in a good way."

"Humph, I hope so, too."

Following their sky-high excursion, Wendell took Lorraine to Scott Gertner's Skybar and Grille, where they enjoyed the best views of downtown she had ever seen. Lorraine had a good time relaxing on an open terrace while listening to jazz and sipping on mojitos. When Lorraine asked Wendell to join her for a dance, he felt he was in the clear.

"So you're not mad anymore? You forgive me, my lady?"

"Your what?"

"I think it's okay to start calling you that, don't you?"

"I don't know. I think you need to quit while you're behind." She smirked to let him know she was teasing.

"I think you enjoy giving me a hard time, Lo."

"Ugh, please don't call me that. I've done a great job trying to forget about my ex. He hasn't contacted me in a minute and that's the way I like it."

Wendell gave her a sober look. "Are you really trying to move on?"

"I am. If only I could know you're doing the same."

"If you knew that, then what?"

"Then I'd be okay with you calling me your lady. But until then, Lorraine will do, thank you very much."

10

How Much More Can I Be Humiliated?

Faye couldn't believe it. She was accustomed to men chasing her in hot pursuit while she looked over her shoulder and laughed. Being desired by men was like pressing a needle in her vein and injecting herself with heroin. Nothing felt better than making men lose their minds. But Wendell Holmes was different. She'd assumed after they'd had sex that night he'd be blowing up her cell, begging her to return for a repeat. Or maybe he'd do what others had done and insist she move in. Wendell did neither. That intrigued Faye. It was as if he had used her, and not vice versa.

Tonight she was at home, fuming mad. Earlier she'd placed some oversized dark sunglasses over her eyes, rented a fancy sedan, and driven past Wendell's condo a couple of times. But his place appeared to be completely dark. The drapes were drawn. It meant he wasn't home. Or if he was, he was having sex. With Stick Figure. Faye shook her head vigorously, not wanting to believe that Wendell would choose someone so dreadful and desperate looking over *her*. Jeez, what was the world coming to? She blamed her string of bad luck on jerks like Tiger Woods, men lucky enough to have beautiful, intelligent, cultured women at their side—women so stunning they made men look like kings—but instead the undercover sluts preferred to get it on with trashy pole dancers who got their start sucking on bananas. She hated men like that.

In her heart, Faye knew that Stick Figure didn't quite fit the "ho bag" description, but in her mind, if a man picked *any* woman over her, the girl was an automatic low-life wannabe tramp player hater who could never truly compete with her. Yet in a way, Stick Figure was competition because if she wasn't, wouldn't Wendell be with Faye?

"This is not even happening," she said through clenched teeth, almost wanting to scream. "How much more can I be humiliated? I don't do humiliation!"

Faye wailed as she stared at her reflection in the full-length mirror. She resembled a young Donna Summer: huge, pretty doe eyes, thin nose, and thick, pouty lips. Faye's bone-straight hair was so long it reached her behind. She clamped her hair in a ponytail just to avoid sitting on it. She'd purchased eighteen-inch hair extensions because she knew most men were shallow enough to be swayed by lengthy hair. And she needed men to love her. Every man. That's also why she wore new clothes daily, preferring to buy dresses and skirt sets fresh from the mall rather than dry clean the clothes she already owned. She had a strong need to always stand out in a crowd and would do anything to achieve that.

But now she didn't know what to do. She couldn't believe that although she'd gotten weak and called Wendell three times, *three*, he hadn't called her back. She didn't leave a message. She wasn't the type of woman to leave a message. But the fact that Wendell had caller ID should have been motivation enough for him to return her call. See if she was okay. Phone her to let her know he'd been missing her bad and wanted to kick it with her.

"I always get what I want. And I want Wendell."

Wendell stood in the doorway of Lorraine's apartment. They'd just returned from their date. He briefly came into the apartment to use the restroom and chitchat. But now he was ready to head out.

"Listen, young man. I had an incredible, unforgettable time. But it still doesn't excuse you for leaving me in the lurch at that workshop. I felt so lost."

"Sorry about that. But the other team members were there. I knew Lance was coming and asked him to help you out if needed. Did you see him?"

"Lance is such a boring gossip, plus he can't hold a candle to you."

"Aww, baby," Wendell said. She tugged at his heart. He just wanted to wrap Lorraine in his arms and hold her. He felt bad for what he'd done, but sometimes before a man can fully let another woman in, he must get a different woman out of his system. He hadn't planned on being with Faye. It had just happened. And it had been important for him to carry out his fantasy with her so he could move on and be with the chick he really wanted to be with.

"Lorraine, that will never happen again. Fingers crossed," he said and winked. "I am not trying to hurt you. God knows you've been through enough. You deserve to have the exact type of guy you want. Decent, honest, considerate, loving, protective, classy. I can be that. I swear. I *am* that."

"Wendell, I want to believe you, but sometimes I just don't know."

"Don't you have a good time with me? Haven't I proven to be way different from guys you've dated in the past?"

"Yes, and yes. For one thing, I appreciate that you haven't tried to push up on me. You've been a gentleman. My mother would love a guy like you."

He stiffened but recovered. "I want us to wait and take our time."

"Well, since you've been celibate for so long, I guess waiting a little while longer won't hurt."

"Um, yeah. So, I gotta skedaddle. See ya later. At work?"

"Come here," she said in a sexy, commanding voice. She raised her head and planted her lips on his. They enjoyed a long, wet, and warm French kiss that made her dizzy with passion.

"Mmm, I love your lips so much. But we need to stop or else we'll end up in bed. That's not what I want to do. I'm trying to do something different, ya know?"

"I know," he croaked. Right then he thought that being with Faye wasn't so bad. If Lorraine had such high standards that she'd be forcing him to hold off from having sex with her, he didn't feel so bad about getting some on the side. After all, he wasn't married to the girl; he desired her, no doubt, but a man had needs. And if the time came when she fully wanted to give herself to him, he knew he could drop Faye like a skillet of hot chicken grease.

Hey, I'm not even with Faye anymore. That was a onetime thing.

"One more thing," Wendell said. "Guess who's coming to the Toyota Center this Saturday?"

"Tell me," Lorraine squealed.

"Maxwell and Jill Scott."

"Oh my God. I heard the promo on the radio the other day. Are we going?"

"You and me. This Saturday. Buy yourself a pretty dress." He opened his wallet and handed her a crisp hundred-dollar bill that felt smooth to the touch. "Choose something hot that shows off your legs."

"Aww, you're sooo awesome. Thanks so much." Lorraine was so astounded by Wendell's generosity all she could do was blush and lean forward to give him another quick kiss. Wendell waved, turned around, got in his car, and sped off.

"This is working out better than I thought," she said a half hour later while talking to Joanna on the phone. "You know how you wonder if you can ever meet the right type of guy who fits the bill? Well, I'm a witness, it can happen."

"What did Mr. Wonderful do this time?"

Lorraine filled her in on all the details of the most recent events.

"Who knows how long this will last, but for right now, girl, I am loving how he's being extra attentive, caring, and considerate."

"Hmm, sounds like he's good at compensating for his previous blunder," Joanna reasoned. "But still be careful, sis."

"Hey, I know what I'm doing." Lorraine flinched, slightly irritated. "Wendell's the real deal. Nothing like you know who."

"Compared to Posse, an eighth grader will appear to have class and style. Don't compare every man to Posse, though. You'd be doing yourself an injustice."

"I think I'm getting my just due now, though; that's what makes me so happy." Lorraine thoughtfully bit her bottom lip. Although she was happy that her ex had stopped pestering her with his annoying phone calls, sometimes she'd be sprawled in bed at night, clutching her pillow. She'd close her eyes and imagine which woman he was with and she'd wonder what made him stop calling even though she'd asked him to. Her pride made her want to believe he still longed for her. And she'd softly sing Brian McKnight's lyrics, "Do I ever cross your mind, any time?"

"I will say this," Lorraine allowed. "The fact that a man who claimed to love me can move on just like that makes me wonder if he was telling the truth in the first place."

"Girl, please," Joanna said. "Just because a man says he loves you doesn't make his words automatically true. The only person who can never tell a lie is God himself. The rest of us are subject to error."

"I know all that," Lorraine snapped. Knowing the truth didn't mean it always felt good or comfortable. That's what raw truth did: exposed the sides of life that weren't always pretty.

"The best thing to do is get over it. Let him move on so you can, too."

"If he has moved on, it couldn't have happened at a better time," she said to herself, hanging up from talking to Joanna. "Now that I've finally connected with a decent, sincere man, who has time for ex-boyfriend drama?"

That Saturday morning, Wendell woke up and felt himself being kissed all over his forehead, cheeks, and lips. The fragrance of White Diamonds reeked on his pillows.

"Turn over," Faye commanded as she rubbed her fingertips across his erect nipples.

Wendell, not one to argue with a horny female, flipped over so that his stomach rested on the red satin sheets. Faye carefully straddled him and sat on his back like he was a pony. She rocked back and forth trying to develop some friction as she rubbed her body all over his.

I can't believe I've been with this woman for twelve hours, making nasty love all night long.

Faye smiled as she leaned over to plant wet kisses against every part of his neck.

"You like that? How about that? Mmm, I've missed this and I refuse to give it up. I want my Joe-Joe every day, every night."

When Wendell didn't answer she knew just what to do. She flipped him over until he was flat on his back. She grinned and was overjoyed to see this gorgeous, sexy creature totally under her control. Power turned her on. And the stronger the man, the sexier and more powerful she felt, especially if the man let her have her way without a fight.

"You are *too* adorable, Wen. Just perfect." She laughed and lowered her mouth to Joe-Joe. "Hey there," she said, softly grabbing his penis. She thrust him inside her mouth and closed her eyes. Faye was willing to pleasure this man to the point of gagging. She was no fool. Men loved blow jobs. And if a man could find a woman who was willing to get him off without protesting, that woman was a keeper.

Faye sucked Joe-Joe every hour on the hour all that day. When she finally let Wendell take a breather so he could drag himself to the restroom, he snuck his cell phone into the bathroom and locked the door.

Please forgive me for what I'm about to do.

He powered on his phone, which had been off ever since Faye had popped over to his place last night wearing a gorgeous lavender negligee underneath a maxi dress. His eyes loved what they saw and he knew he couldn't say no. He let her in. They went straight to his bedroom and got undressed. All thoughts of Lorraine disappeared from his mind and he wouldn't allow his heart to focus on her at all. Until now.

As he suspected, she'd left him two voice mails and one text. A classic question:

Where r u?

He texted her back.

Something's come up. Can't go 2 concert. Sooo sorry.
Will make it up 2 u. XXOO.

He sighed. Turned his phone off, relieved himself in the restroom, took off his bathrobe, and stepped in the tub to take a shower.

"Come get it while it's hot," he yelled after unlocking the bathroom door.

Lorraine's hands trembled as she read the text.

What in the hell is he talking about? We've been planning this date all week. I'm wearing the damn dress he paid for. So what's really going on? What came up?

Lorraine tried to calm herself, but it's hard for a woman's mind to stay rational when fear twists at her heart so much she can barely breathe or think.

Be careful.

Her sister's warning resounded in her head.

Lorraine slumped on the edge of the sofa and kicked off the high heels she'd been wearing. She glanced at her watch.

The concert would begin in ninety minutes. But Wendell had told her to be ready early. He'd proposed eating seafood and having drinks at McCormick and Schmick's prior to the concert. Lorraine had been elated and pumped up for this date the entire week. She'd felt pleased that their relationship was progressing and appreciated how Wendell tried hard to make up for disappointing her.

But now?

She heard her doorbell ring and leaped up to her feet.

Thank God. We're still going. Whatever issue he had obviously has been resolved.

She grinned as she flung open her front door. She set her hands on her hips and frowned.

"What brings you here, Posse? And how'd you find out where I live?" At first she barely recognized her ex. He wore a short-sleeved striped polo shirt with white linen slacks and oxford sneakers that were so white they looked brand-new. But though the clothes were different, his eyes looked the same. Light brown and dancing with danger.

"'Sup, my lady? I'm jonesing for some 'Rain.'"

"Rain? I thought I was Lo."

"You told me not to call you dat no more. So I'm switching it up for my gal. Hey, you gonna let me in or we gonna chop it up with the door wide open? C'mon, be hospital."

She couldn't help but grin. "It's hospitable, silly."

"I knew dat. Just trying to make ya laugh."

"It's scary that it didn't take much to make me laugh."

"What's dat supposed to mean?"

"Never mind."

Posse took it upon himself to breeze past Lorraine and enter her apartment. He held a plastic Kroger bag in one hand, and clutched a beat-up yellow toothbrush in the other. She inhaled and smelled men's deodorant and shampoo. Sighing, she slammed the door and followed him inside to the living room.

"I see you brought your overnight bag."

"Yep, yep."

Lorraine felt annoyed that he had the nerve to flaunt his toiletries as if he just knew she'd let him spend the night.

"You took a chance and drove all the way to Houston in your beat-up Corolla?"

"How you know I still drive that?"

"I know you, Posse. So why would you drive down without even calling? Huh?"

"Told you why. I'm missing my gal. My lady. My sweet thing."

"Posse, don't give me that. It doesn't even sound right."

"Raw truth, baby."

"If it's so true why didn't you check for me before now?"

"I had to come up with my master plan. Give you some space. Back away long enough for you to miss me. Then show up when you not expectin' me so you can see with your own eyes dat I'm missing you, too."

"Yeah right."

"Man, why you gotta be so hard, huh? Don't I even get a hug? I ain't seen your rusty ass in a minute."

She tried not to blush as she forced herself to appear emotionless. Getting over a former lover wasn't as easy as "get over it" sounded.

Posse spread his arms and broke out in a charming yet vulnerable grin. Looking anxious, he took a deep breath, walked up to Lorraine, and wrapped her in his arms. A tiny gasp escaped from her mouth. She pressed her nose against his neck and inhaled his familiar musky scent. Rough neck masculine. Bad boy strong.

"Ooooh damn, see this what I'm talking 'bout." He patted her on the ass and squeezed. "Your little curves done filled out. You looking hot in this fancy dress. I'll bet you got on a pink thong, huh?"

"Mmm." She grunted again as he squeezed her tighter.

"I'll be damned. You don't got a date, do you?"

"No," she replied in a barely audible voice. She decided to untangle herself from his embrace.

"Good. Now you do. You going out. Tonight. With me. Let's roll."

"Are you kidding me? You just pop over here unannounced and think I'm going to hang out with you on a so-called date? I don't think so."

"Baby girl, just chill," Posse said in his raspy voice. "You need to be ready to roll just like dat. Stop being a tight ass and acting all scary like something bad might happen. Remember back in the day? We can do 'us' like we used to do. And don't front. I know you used to love chilling with your boy."

"That was then, Posse."

He winced at her bluntness. "Don't say dat, Lo. C'mon now, please."

When her pet name rolled off her ex's lips, her heart softened. And his new look didn't escape her. She knew all that was for her. She also saw the pain of love swimming in his eyes. The fear. Uncertainty. To see a man like Posse show that he had a heart underneath his tough exterior endeared him to her. Either she was a fool, or she was human, too. And the fact that he was here in her apartment meant he hadn't totally forgotten about her. Maybe he still loved her. But was it too late for that kind of love? The kind of love that gave her an adrenaline rush yet made her feel so unsure about the future?

11

Some Kind of Fool

Surreal. Lorraine couldn't believe she was hanging out with Posse. Before she'd agreed to go out with him, he asked if he could wash up and brush his teeth. She said okay but made him throw away his disgusting, old, yellow toothbrush. She located a blue toothbrush that had been previously removed from its plastic container and gave him some privacy so he could freshen up.

Once he emerged from her restroom, she remarked, "Why brush your teeth if you're going to put the gold grill back on? If you want to hang with me, you're going to have to remove the grills. They look so hideous."

"They look so what?"

"Ugly, dude. You look so much better with your own teeth."

"Okay okay okay."

He insisted on driving her car and refused to tell her where they were going until they arrived downtown. He made a right turn and drove up the ramp of the Toyota Center Tundra Garage. She began to hyperventilate when he located a parking spot on the third level, the same floor that Wendell had parked on when they first attended the Rockets game.

Posse jumped out of the car, fled to the passenger side, and opened her door.

"These fools act like they can't come through Dallas. So at the last minute, I got two tickets to the Houston concert and prayed the good Lord would answer your boy's prayers. Let me listen to ole Maxy Max and Ms. Philly Girl singing while you stand by my side."

I never knew men like Posse prayed. Like my mother told me, it's obvious God is no respecter of persons.

They exited the car and headed toward the stadium entrance. With each step she felt more of a rush of excitement gush through her veins. Lorraine convinced herself that taking a chance with Posse, if only for this event, would cause no harm. Besides, Wendell was a no-show again. He was becoming unreliable. And how would it have looked if she'd sat at home waiting on the phone to ring and stressing over Wendell's whereabouts?

Although she never imagined being with Posse again in a million years, she appreciated him doting over her. He pulled out their tickets, located their seats, and once she got settled he winked and told her "BRB."

True to his word, he soon returned, his face bright with exhilaration.

"Hey, I got you some popcorn and a margarita with my own dough, you dig?"

She laughed. Nodded. Tried to relax and settle in her seat so she could watch Maxwell croon while the women swooned.

Oh well. I didn't get to go to the concert with Wendell, but at least I got to go. Irony.

"You liking the concert, Lo? I mean Rain?"

"Yes, Wen——. Yes, Posse."

"What?"

"Um, I started to say, *when* I go to concerts, I always have fun," she mumbled.

"Huh?"

"Nothing."

When Posse absentmindedly reached out and grabbed her hand, she tried to imagine that the warm skin that was grasping her fingers belonged to Wendell.

Screw him. She removed her hand from his.

"Hey, Posse. Question for you," she said suddenly as he stood close to her looking relaxed. "In your opinion, which artists could be counted as some of the greatest singers of all time?"

"Easy. Drake. Pac. Kanye."

"They're rappers, dude. Name singers," she said, frustrated.

"Real singers? Like on an Aretha Franklin level or something? Um, I'll get back with you on dat one."

During intermission, Lorraine felt an urge to exercise her legs. She excused herself and exited the auditorium to go stand in a long line that snaked outside the ladies' room.

"Hey, Lorraine!" Lance, one of the computer application developers at her firm, waved at her. "What's up, young lady? You're enjoying yourself?"

"It's all right," she said wistfully.

"Well, too bad you left the sandcastle workshop early that day. You missed it."

"Missed what?" she asked in monotone.

"You know Tim Daither? One of the principals?"

"Of course," she replied. *What does he think I am, stupid?*

"Well, you know that they hired me to maintain the Web site, right?"

"Yeah."

"So I go up there to attend the workshop, and girl, check this out. Daither's wife came up to the workshop getting all loud like she was a black woman or something."

"Oooh, Lance, you know you're wrong," she replied, mildly amused.

"Tell the truth and shame the devil, girl. Anyway, Miss Thang was storming all over the building, going from room to room, snooping and giving the evil eye to every cute woman who came up in that joint. She caught herself trying to roll her eyes at me, too. She ain't got a thing to worry about. Humph."

"That sounds crazy. Why wouldn't she just go to EDC?"

"Girl, she got banned from coming up to her hubby's job, hello."

"Shame." She started to laugh but didn't want to give Lance the satisfaction. "Okay, so why is she hanging out at the workshop looking for women?"

" 'Cause that sixty-year-old rascal who swears he's a younger Burt Reynolds is trying to get his groove on sister-girl style. This pasty-looking fella who sings that same old tired song every Monday about how much he loves his dear wife is banging a woman who's not his wife. Someone who works at our firm. And his wife wasn't having it. She looked so funny racing all over A&E. Lucky for her whoever Daither is sleeping with never showed up, but that didn't stop his poor wife from going around asking all kinds of questions."

"Oh okay, sounds like one big mess," Lorraine said in a bored tone. "Anyway, good seeing you. I'll talk to you later."

Toward the end of the concert, Posse grabbed Lorraine's hand so tight she winced from the pain.

"Ouch, do you mind?"

"Lo, your body is here, but I know you. You not having a good time. Maybe coming to H-town was a bad move. I must be some kind of fool." His voice was full of emotion, which made Lorraine feel worse.

"Posse, it's not you. I just have a lot on my mind. Y-you've actually been perfect tonight."

"But not perfect enough for a chick like you. I can never meet your standards, huh?"

"Standards? What are they?" She laughed though nothing was funny. "They're almost a joke."

"No, don't say that. You gotta right to know what you want in a man. I just wish *I* coulda been dat man. . . ."

"Posse, not now."

"When? Next week? Next month? Or never?" He had a rare frightened look in his eyes. Lorraine knew the guy had been through a lot of hardship in his life. Poverty. Racial discrimination. It wasn't as if he was given the proper guidance so he could make the best choices. And he definitely had no say regarding the zip code he was born in. So what, he was from the hood. He knew pain, suffering, and despair as a daily way of life. But didn't he still have a heart? Didn't ghetto boys need love, too?

"Posse," she replied gently. "Given the circumstances, this isn't the best time for me to make that kind of decision. But I will say that in spite of what's happened between us, you will always hold a special place in my heart."

"Hallmark card? Or raw truth?"

"A little of both." She winked.

He winked back and his worried look was replaced by a somber one.

"You're good peeps," Lorraine told him in an attempt to cheer Posse up. He nodded but didn't say anything.

As the concert concluded and people spilled out into the aisles to leave the auditorium, Posse made sure to grab Lorraine's hand. He carefully weaved his bulky fingers between her soft ones. She let him. She barely cared anymore. She needed love, but love was so damn confusing. Emotions were so deceiving. How could she maintain a level head when so much was going on around her lately?

"You know what?" Posse asked as he leaned in close so Lorraine could hear.

"What?"

"Jill Scott. Maxwell. They at the top of the list. Throw Luther Vandross in there, too. RIP."

Lorraine beamed at her ex and felt better at that moment than she had all day.

Moments later she and Posse entered the wide hallway that led to the Toyota Center's exit doors. She glanced a few feet in front of her and locked eyes with Wendell. He glanced at her, then at the guy wearing a conservative shirt, slacks, and shoes. But the fitted cap covering the top of his braids and the tattoos scattered across his bare arms told Wendell what he wanted to know. His eyes penetrated Lorraine's and screamed, "How could you?"

Her eyes hollered back, "What the hell are you doing here?"

Posse was too busy scanning the crowd to notice the heated body language between Lorraine and Wendell. And when Posse spotted six guys wearing wife beaters and sagging pants, he instantly released her hand.

"BRB. Don't go nowhere."

Wendell swallowed deeply and thought fast. He grabbed Lorraine firmly by the arm and escorted her down the hallway. She had to practically run to keep up with him. She yelled questions at him. The venue's hallway was filled with the clamor of voices. It was pointless to reply. He didn't answer. He didn't stop. He just needed to get away.

12

Access Granted

Lorraine stood barefoot, staring blankly out the window of their room they'd just checked into at the Crowne Plaza Hotel downtown. Her sandals lay sprawled on the tan carpet next to the front door. The room was complete with the typical king-size bed, chair, desk, and drawers. She may have been fully clothed, but the dour expression on her face made her feel naked and violated.

Wendell pulled his shirt off over his head so that his chiseled set of abs was front and center. He calmly waited for Lorraine to turn and feast her eyes on his body. He wanted her hands on him, too. But the woman didn't move. She slouched and silently contemplated the night's events.

Needing to break the ice, Wendell told her, "Lorraine, I-I'm so very sorry."

"No. You're. Not."

"Okay, my apology may sound inadequate, but will you let me prove to you through my actions how I feel?"

"Wendell, the only reason you want to apologize is because godly intervention allowed me to catch your black ass at the concert. It's not like you picked up the phone and tried to call me before now. You know how I know that? Because, as usual, when you don't want to be bothered, you turn your damn phone off."

"I wasn't in an area where you'd be able to hear me."

"Bull, Wendell. Total bullshit. Do you know how pissed off this makes me?"

"I know you're mad because you don't usually go off like this. But babe, please." He caressed her shoulder. "That's why I'm trying to make it up to—" He kissed her softly on the cheek.

"I can't even believe I let you convince me to come to this stupid hotel. Do you think I'm going to be impressed just because you have the money to bring me here? You actually think I'm ready to give you some just because you want to stick your dick inside of me?" She examined him narrowly.

"Look, I said I'm sorry. Can we squash this? I don't even know why we're arguing—"

"Please don't act as if you don't know what I'm talking about or why I'm so mad I could strangle you. You're wrong, Wendell. Totally wrong. And I will not let you treat me this way. Just because you come in a nice package and wear a decent suit and tie doesn't mean you can behave any way you want as if a woman has no other choice but to accept it. You're even worse than my ex."

"At least someone like him can get second and third chances."

"*What?* So you're putting the fault on *me* for how *you've* been acting lately? Listen, Wendell. I do not deserve this back-and-forth, wishy-washy treatment. I hate it. It's rude. You're not considerate at all. You're an ass."

"Now hold on, you're going too far."

"And I can go farther, too, Wendell, because you've pushed me to my limits this time."

"You're going to have to give me a pass, Lorraine. I came to the concert, late as hell, but at least I showed up."

FROM ONE LOVER TO ANOTHER

"Shut up. You came to the concert without me. Big difference."

"But—"

"No buts. I hate excuses. Why is it that men always get de-
fensive when they know they've fucked up? What the hell is
that? Be a real man and admit when you're wrong."

"I *am* a real man. Much more of a man than that thug you
took to the concert! Did you have to buy the tickets and pay
for your own food?"

Tears sprang in her eyes. She reeled back in shock.

Before she could respond, she started sneezing uncontrol-
lably. She started trembling and looked in his eyes.

"You took Faye, didn't you?" she said in a shaky voice.

"W-what?"

She sneezed again. "Don't lie to me, dammit. I am allergic
to White Diamonds. And whoever wears fucking White Diamonds is the reason why you stood me up. Wendell, how
could you? You played yourself. I'm out of here."

She clenched her teeth and prepared to race out of the
hotel room. But Wendell clutched her by the arm.

"Let me go."

"I'm not done talking."

"There's nothing to talk about. You're a liar."

"And so are you!"

"What did you call me?"

"You're just as hypocritical as I am, Lorraine. Do you think
I'm so into you that I don't notice other things going on?
Lance told me some stuff."

"He didn't tell you anything because he doesn't know anything."

"Hello? Are you listening, Lorraine? He told me how he
overheard you talking to Natalie about how much you've
missed having sex with your ex."

"What? That bastard. He heard wrong," she snapped.

"And he printed out this, which is not something you can lie about." Wendell went to his pad folio and withdrew several sheets of letter-size paper.

"How can you explain this, Ms. Eafford?"

A few days ago, Lorraine had created e-mails from her work account. Messages that she'd typed, but saved in her drafts folder because she couldn't decide if she actually wanted to send them.

Hi Posse, Have you checked out the rates for Southwest Airlines from Dallas to Houston? They're real cheap. I could use another mini-vacation. We could hang out.

And . . .

Just woke up. You were in my dream. Damn, I wish you could still hold me through the night. I felt so protected with you next to me. But I guess it's too late to admit these feelings now, huh? I know I probably keep you confused. I keep my damn self confused, too. LOL.

"Why is he snooping in my e-mails?"

"He's the fucking IT administrator. He's granted access to all that shit. And he's who I talk to when I really want access to the true Lorraine. That's the only way I can get the raw truth about you."

"You son of a bitch. You know what? This isn't working for me. I'm out."

"Bye, Lorraine!"

She gasped, then quickly located her purse and grabbed her shoes. She opened the door and fled from the room. Throat thick with pain she moaned, her head filled with confusion. She tried to pray and wished right then that her dear mother, whose prayers she usually rejected, was thinking of her. Lorraine half-ran down the hall until she reached the elevator. It took so long for the elevator to stop at her floor that she headed farther down the hall, opened the door to the interior stairwell, and decided to race down seven flights of stairs.

As soon as her bare feet got her down one level, she let out a muffled scream. Her face was soon drenched with a stream of heated tears she'd been holding in for months. A guttural moan escaped her lips, her vision soon blurred by burdens she could no longer carry.

"I can't believe I'm crying . . . over a man." She wept and clumsily held her face in her hand; the heat of humiliation poured over her like raindrops.

Men who rarely cried were born to make women cry. And what reason could God give for creating men who seemingly did whatever they wanted to do without suffering punishment? Men who routinely cheated, lied, and hid their true nature from their wives or girlfriends and thought nothing of it. "This is how we're wired," they explained as if that belief makes wrong behavior acceptable. Was God a chauvinist? Didn't he care about women's feelings?

Lorraine's heart throbbed with pain every time she entertained these thoughts. It made her feel that expecting a good and honest relationship was unrealistic. Based on the rate of divorces and couples breaking up in general, why should she even want a man?

By the time she finishing crying, she felt exhausted. She located her cell phone and dialed.

"Lo?"

"Hi!" she said breathlessly.

"Why you breathing so hard?"

"Tired." She nodded. "So tired."

"Where the hell you been? I told your hard-headed ass not to leave. I was gone only fifteen. Came back and your ass got ghost."

"I know. It's complicated. Can you please come get me?"

"Now?"

"Um, yes. You have my car and I have no other way to get home."

"Damn, Lo. I-I was watching the game. LeBron's shooting the lights out these fools."

"W-what?"

"Okay okay okay. Where you at?"

"I'm still downtown. Pick me up outside the Toyota Center."

"You was there all dat time? You couldn't have called before now?"

"It's complicated."

With darkness surrounding her, Lorraine walked three miles back to the Toyota Center and waited for Posse. In all that time, Wendell never called her. Posse spotted her on the corner and pulled up. She slid onto her seat and gave him a grateful smile and a warm kiss on his lips. "I can't believe I'm saying this, but tonight . . . finally . . . it seems like you've become my perfect man. My knight."

"Oh yeah? Lo, you got a nigga rollin'." He blushed. "That's what I like to hear."

Posse drove them back to Lorraine's apartment. When they arrived in front of her apartment unit, the living room windows were illuminated.

"I thought I turned off the lights before we left," she murmured as she waited for Posse to open the passenger door.

Posse used her keys to let them in. She placed one foot inside her apartment and stopped. Six unfamiliar guys wearing hoodies and baggy blue jeans were sprawled together on her sofa and love seat. Lit cigarettes hung from their mouths. Some drank beer, others smoked weed, and the television volume was turned up as loud as possible as they watched an NBA game.

"What the fuck is going on? Who are these people?"

"Lo, calm down. These my H-town partners. That's Weazy." He pointed. "There's Little Mike, his daddy Big Mike, G-Low, Din-Din, and Simeon. Remember, I ran into them at the concert—"

"Why the hell are they in my place drinking up all my beer? And you know I hate the smell of pot. This is bullshit."

"Calm down, my lady."

"I'm not your lady. We don't live together, Posse. Everybody listen up. You're going to have to leave . . . right now."

"What's got her panties all in a bunch? These hos be bugging," she heard one snaggle-toothed guy mutter. "Better put your lady in check."

"Huh? I don't think so. This is *my* place. I don't know you and I don't want to know you. You're going to have to get the hell out of here." She spun around and faced Posse, bristling with anger. "I pegged you all wrong. You're full of shit. And you'll never change."

"Your snobby ass will never change either."

13

Good Attracts Good

On Monday when Lorraine arrived at work, his desk was cleaner than ever. Nothing that belonged to Wendell could be found in the office. She picked up the phone and dialed Natalie. "Can you please come see me ASAP?"

The two ladies huddled together whispering. "Have you seen Houston today?" Lorraine asked.

"No, not at all. Y'all lovebirds must've really had a huge fight."

"Tell me about it. In a way I guess it's for the best. I barely wanted to show up today. I don't want to face this guy. He's a liar."

"Maybe he felt ashamed of himself. They usually do after a while."

Lorraine laughed. "Girl, you sound just like my sister."

"I guess I am in a way." She smiled.

"Thanks, Nat. Anyway," she said cautiously and made sure the office door was shut tight. "Can you believe that idiot Lance was monitoring my e-mails and had the nerve to print them out and pass them around like they're a birthday-party invite? I could file a complaint and get his silly butt fired. What manager does stuff like that?"

"Idiot managers. Don't worry about Lance. Just be careful with the paper trail."

"Ha. There won't be any more paper trails. I'm so through with men I don't know what to do."

"Yeah, but Houston may have moved out of the office, but you gotta face him at the sandcastle meeting today," she whispered.

"No, I'm not. I'm pulling out."

"What? It's too late to get anyone else."

"I honestly don't give a fuck. Do you think I can work side by side with that guy after all he's put me through? Stupid!"

"Yeah, he *is* stupid to chase a piece of ass over you."

"I'm talking about myself. I never should have gotten involved with him. It's too close for comfort when things go wrong."

"But you didn't know how it would end up."

"True, but still . . . I really don't want to ever see his face again. And it's not like I can go out there and find me another high-paying job real quick. The architecture industry is already suffering."

"Don't be so extreme. You and Houston will be fine; just give it some time."

Lorraine's iPhone buzzed.

"Oh God, I wish he'd just leave me the hell alone." She let Natalie glance at the call screen.

"Two-one-four area code? Must be Dallas, huh?" She giggled. "Girl, that man loves you to death, I don't care how bad he talked to you the other night."

"Verbal abuse isn't love, Nat. You know that."

"I think Dallas just doesn't know how to properly express himself. But anybody can see the love is there, even though he sounds very rough around the edges."

"Yeah, well, whatever."

Later that afternoon, Natalie stopped by Lorraine's office, pointing at the wall clock.

"I'm here to escort you to the meeting." She laughed.

"This isn't funny." She gave Natalie a worried look. "I told you I'm not going to that meeting. I don't want to be anywhere he is."

"Lorraine Eafford, do not give your power to another human being. Don't let him scare you. You've worked hard on this project and deserve to come to the last meeting before the competition. You brought energy and creativity to the team. We need you, girl."

"Oh, Nat. Only for you would I change my mind."

The two ladies spoke quietly as they entered the conference room. She breathed a sigh of relief when she didn't see Wendell in the meeting. The team facilitator passed out the agenda and information regarding their assignment for the actual competition, which would be held next weekend on Galveston's East Beach.

"Get there early so we can set up the tent. Some of you have been assigned to transport the materials, the carving tools, our team T-shirts; others will bring the ice chest, the food, and plenty of beer. See you next weekend. We start carving at ten sharp."

"Hey, girl. Thanks for convincing me to regain my power." Lorraine laughed as they left the meeting. "I would have been hidden away in my office for nothing. Knowing Wendell, he's not even thinking about me. He hasn't called. No text. No nothing."

"Sounds like you're still feeling this guy," Natalie replied.

"Love is complicated," Lorraine admitted. "Like my mother likes to say, 'You can cook a man's breakfast with electricity, but you can also cook the man.' And at this point I can choke him with the same hands I'd use to hold him in my arms. It's frustrating."

Natalie felt her phone vibrate. She looked at the caller ID. "And family is frustrating, too. Damn. Something's come up and I need to get home, but my car is in the shop and the person who I carpooled with is at an off-site meeting."

"Hey, you need me to drive you home?" Lorraine asked. "I'll put in for emergency vacation time. I don't feel like being at the office anymore. Let me run to the ladies' room and I'll meet you downstairs in the parking lot."

"Oh wow, I don't want you to go out of your way for me."

"It's my pleasure. You've been there for me . . ." she said softly and couldn't finish her sentence because of the knot that swelled up in her throat. "See you in a bit."

Lorraine rushed to the ladies' room and was happy that the first stall was available.

She sat on the toilet and told herself to e-mail her boss about leaving early as soon as she got back to her office.

Just when she was about to flush, she heard voices.

"Shhh." A female voice giggled. "I don't want anyone to hear us."

"Then that means I probably won't do a good job."

"Daither, you're a nut."

"I'm about to nut all over you."

Lorraine froze. She couldn't believe Tim Daither was inside the women's restroom. Anyone could just walk in there. Why would a man be so foolish and take such a dangerous risk?

I guess big-mouth Lance was finally right about a rumor.

She heard a stall door open and close. The sound of the lock twisted. More giggles. Moans and sighs.

Lorraine wanted to leave. But she couldn't. Her ears were wide open. Listening to the sounds of betrayal.

"Mmm, mmm, that feels so good."

"Hop on me," Daither gasped.

Lorraine could imagine his pasty white face turning red.

She held her hand against her mouth as she tried to figure out which co-worker was stupid enough to have sex with the married boss.

"Faye. Oh shit. Keep going. Don't stop."

"Yes, big Daddy. You like it like this? Ohhhh. Tim baby. Who? Who? Who's the baddest bitch in the game? Say my name."

"Apparently, Daither's messing around on his wife even though Faye isn't exactly an EDC employee. I hate when gossipers can't even get the gossip totally right."

"Girl, this is so twisted. Do you think Wendell knows?" Natalie asked. They were headed to her apartment and she was trying to get over the shock of the news about Daither.

"Who cares?" Lorraine snapped. "That's what Wendell gets. I don't feel sorry for him."

"But you've got to tell him."

"Ha! I'll let Lance have the honors, for what it's worth. He's the one who knows everybody's business."

"Yeah, but it would seem since you still care for Wendell that you could give him that heads-up."

"Why should I protect him? He didn't protect me! He made a fool out of me." She thought long and hard. With every passing second her heart grew harder. "Men like Wendell reap everything they've sown. Why be greedy? Why not just pick one of us instead of stringing me along and making me think he's so into me?"

"Because sometimes it's hard to pick just one, Lorraine." Natalie gave her co-worker a knowing look and turned her attention back to the road.

As they neared Natalie's community, she told Lorraine which streets to turn down. The farther out they drove, the more the environment changed. Old abandoned houses with missing bricks lined the boulevard. Big brown Dumpsters lay on their sides with garbage spilling out to meet the street. Women so skinny they barely weighed eighty pounds walked up and down the street carrying nothing but a dazed look on their face. They wore tight blouses and short skirts but no purses were in their hands.

"This is your neighborhood?"

"Yeah. Unbelievable, huh?"

Natalie instructed Lorraine to make a left turn into a huge apartment complex with a guard house stationed at the entrance gate, but no guard was there. They drove through the open gate past units that had windows boarded up with plywood.

"Do people actually live here?"

"Yes," Natalie said in a loud tone. "I can't afford to rent a luxury apartment. Have you seen my paycheck lately? So I stay with my mom, my sister, and her two kids. Our place is nice, though, very clean and well-organized. More important, I'm surrounded by the love of my family. You can't judge everything by how it appears on the outside."

Lorraine drove her car into an empty parking space next to a rusted sedan that sat on bricks because it had no tires.

"Wow! Well, um, thanks, Natalie," she said sincerely, giving her a tight hug. "I mean that. You've taught me so much . . . so much."

Lorraine drove home and immediately went to her bedroom, removed her clothes, and slid underneath the covers. She lay in bed pondering the state of her life and why certain issues were such a struggle. Lorraine realized she may have questioned God, but she still needed Him.

"I'm a good woman. I'm a good friend. Good attracts good. Please send good to my life, dear Lord. And if there's anything I'm doing wrong to block my blessings from coming to me, show me. Help me. I need help."

Thankfully she drifted into a blissful sleep. But her two-hour nap got interrupted by the sound of her iPhone alerting her of a text.

I can admit I haven't been honest. Although I was trying 2 build something w/u, it was premature. My mind was on someone else. My bad. Bad timing. Hope u understand. Hope u forgive me 2."

Lorraine erased all of Wendell's messages and removed his info from her address book.

"Good attracts good," she whispered to herself and turned over to go back to sleep.

14

Change for the Better

The next Friday morning, an endless blue sky stretched across the sandy beaches of Galveston Island. Seagulls soared over miles and miles that made up the Gulf of Mexico. As far as Lorraine's eyes could see, people of all colors, shapes, and ages gathered on every inch of East Beach. She smiled as she knelt on the blanket, hoping to keep from getting messy. It didn't matter. Sand was everywhere. She wielded the carving knife, being careful to smooth out the rough edges of the sculpture created by EDC. Named "The Fountain of Youth," the exhibit consisted of three children playing around a water fountain.

Competition was stiff. One firm built roller coaster tracks with cars; another designed a skyscraper with windows, a roof with a bar on top, and an outside elevator. Another firm laid out a beer-guzzling drunk who had passed out on the street clutching a huge container of the frothy liquid.

"This has been an unbelievable experience," Natalie squealed. "My hands are filthy but I love it."

"Humph. Everything I eat tastes like glass and dirt. Not loving it," Lorraine teased. She felt good inside and looked great outside. She wore light makeup and sported a new medium-length layered hairstyle that she'd requested for the summer.

She wore their firm's bright orange T-shirt and a tight pair of denim shorts with decorative beading.

"Well, I think my work is done. I'm tired. I stink. I'm thirsty," Lorraine complained.

"I'm game for getting a bite to eat."

"I'm right behind ya." They ventured a few yards over and stood under the shade provided by the company tent. The ladies picked up prepacked lunches and beers and sat down in some lawn seats so they could check out the happenings and take a break.

"Don't look right now, but guess who just showed up?"

Lorraine stiffened. "Oh no."

"Be cool. And yes, she's with him wearing big old sun shades like she's some type of movie star. I can't stand people who put on airs."

"Why is she with him? She's on a competing firm."

"Obviously not."

"I'm sorry, but it is so rude and insensitive for Houston to bring that lady here. He knew I'd be here."

"Girl, it just goes to show you that some guys only care about what they care about."

"I've lost my appetite."

"Like hell you did." Natalie glared at Wendell, who took a seat a few feet away from them. "This brisket sandwich is to die for. Take a bite. Now!"

"Yes, ma'am."

"Hello, ladies." Wendell nodded. He came and stood next to them with a nervous smile on his face.

Natalie said hello. Lorraine kept eating.

"Wendell, we've almost finished the sculpture. Why did you even show up if you were going to be late?"

"I had some business to handle before driving down." He coughed and cleared his throat.

"What's up, bitches?" Faye smiled and stood next to Wendell.

"Did she say what I think she said?" Lorraine asked. She hated when people she barely knew acted familiar with her.

"She's just kidding," Wendell explained. "Faye is friendly like that."

"So I've heard," Lorraine murmured.

"Eww, I see some folks that I want to chat with," Faye said excitedly. "Hook up with you later, love?" She gave Wendell a quick peck on the cheek and hobbled off toward a group of women.

Wendell gave a stunned look but quickly recovered when he caught Lorraine staring at him.

"You picked her," Lorraine finally spoke. "And for what it's worth, I hope you're very happy together. I mean that."

A couple hours later as the crowds dwindled, Lorraine was relaxing by the company tent when she noticed boisterous activity toward the end of the beach. She spotted Wendell rushing toward that direction and tapped Natalie. "Let's see what's going on."

They edged closer to the scene and heard loud voices.

"Please tell me the truth. I already know everything anyway," yelled Daither's wife.

"I don't know what you're talking about, lady," Faye screamed back.

Daither's wife reached out and tried to smack Faye across the cheek. But a tall, gorgeous brunette blocked her from hitting the bikini-clad Faye.

"I wouldn't do that if I were you," the woman said quietly. She placed her arm around Faye's waist and comforted her. "I told you about spreading yourself thin like this, now you're going to have to get yourself under control or else I'm out."

Wendell's quick footsteps slowed down until he was standing still. He watched the tall woman kiss Faye on the lips. "What the hell is going on?" he asked.

Lorraine sighed and asked Natalie to excuse her. She went

and faced Wendell. "If you need someone to talk to, I'm here to listen. No judging, just supporting."

"I feel like such a fool."

"You can't help that you were attracted to her. And you had the right to find out if she's the best woman for you."

"Now that I know she's not, I feel like I let a good one get away."

"Wendell—"

"No, Lorraine. You really are the best woman I've known. I can't blame you for getting sick of my shit."

"Well, thanks for admitting it, although I am doing fine right now. It's no biggie."

"You're the best, Lorraine," he said with regret. "And another thing. I can't believe I'm admitting this, but you were right: Men are complicated. We are. Half the time, we don't really know what we want. And our egos lead us the other half of the time. If I were a woman I'd be confused, too."

"If you were a woman you'd probably have a better chance of hooking up with your girl," she said and pointed at Faye and her girlfriend, who were walking away together.

"Oh, that's cold. I never thought . . ."

"You can't always judge people by how they appear on the outside."

Lorraine smiled at Wendell and decided to keep her mouth closed about Faye's other sluttish ways with Tim Daither.

Let him find out on his own.

"Ms. Eafford, if it's okay, I want to make things up to you."

"You really don't have to do that."

"No, I have to do something to prove to you I'm not the asshole you thought I was. I'm a decent guy who temporarily lost his good judgment. It happens. There's no good excuse but I owe you."

"But I don't want anything from you, Wendell."

"Can I have one small thing, though? Can we just start all over . . . ?"

"As friends," they both said at the same time. They laughed and hugged.

Two months later

Lorraine couldn't believe her eyes. She and Wendell had just finished having dinner at McCormick & Schmick's in the Houston Pavilions. She'd thoroughly enjoyed their conversation and couldn't get enough of her delicious entrée of Oysters Rockefeller. As they were about to leave, Lorraine knew she'd drunk way too much wine. She could no longer hold it in and needed to relieve herself. Just when she was about to enter the small corridor leading to the restrooms, she saw a man with short-cut hair wearing a pin-striped suit.

She sucked in her breath when she heard his voice.

Posse?

"Hey, Lorraine Eafford. How you doing?"

She took in all of Posse; the way his jaw was free of facial hair, she could see his entire set of teeth: the gold teeth were gone. He looked almost normal.

"I'm shocked to see you here in Houston. You haven't moved here, have you?"

"Nope," he laughed. "We drove down here just to eat at this spot. My girl, she loves some steak and I wanted to make her feel special." Posse looked longingly at Lorraine. She resisted the familiar longing tug that used to make her weak. Part of her was happy that he seemed to be doing well. The other part of her was a bit jealous that he'd take the woman he now loved to a nice restaurant all the way in Houston.

"This woman you took out, she must really be something special."

"She is," he responded with a grin. "She's the best thing that ever happened to me."

"Now Posse," Lorraine responded, unable to help herself.

"You mean to tell me you were faking it when we were together?"

"Oh, you got jokes." They laughed. It felt good. She felt at peace. Lorraine knew it was okay to finally let go. Her past had been healed. Her ex had moved on and seemed to have matured and more important, he had stopped begging her to be in his life. He no longer dominated her thoughts. If she really loved him like she thought she did, she had to be willing to wish the best for him and not interfere with childish envy.

"Well, it was good seeing you, Posse. I mean that," she said. She grabbed her belly and rubbed it. She really needed to get going before something embarrassing happened.

Just then a short, bony woman exited from the ladies' room and pushed past her.

"Before you go, this here is the best woman who ever happened to me. Mama, I'm sure you remember Lorraine?"

He kissed Lorraine's hand and let it go. She was shocked. He really had changed for the better. That realization caused her to feel conflicted inside. Maybe if she'd been patient, she would have been around to benefit from his eventual transformation.

"Hi, Lorraine. Son, isn't this the same woman you were just talking about like a dog while we ate?"

Lorraine frowned. Posse glanced at the floor then at her.

"Well, isn't she?"

"No, Mama. That was Loretta, not Lorraine."

Lorraine made a move toward the ladies' room.

"Say what?" he said loudly, drawing unwanted attention. "You think you all dat? You just gone walk away from me without saying good-bye, dawg?"

She stopped in her tracks and slowly turned around.

"I knew it was too good to be true, Posse. You haven't changed at all. You're such a loser and I wish I'd never met you."

"What the fuck? You trying to clown on me, bitch?"

"Posse, I'm not your bitch. I'm his," she said as Wendell walked in the corridor and came and stood next to her, placing his arm around her.

"And another thing," she said. "Remember when you came over to my apartment and brushed your teeth with that nice blue toothbrush I got you? Well, I scrubbed the toilet seat with it the day before. So now you're literally full of shit."

"W-what?" He looked sick and spat on the carpet.

Smiling with confidence, Lorraine turned around and let Wendell escort her from the restaurant. When they got to the parking lot, she looked up into his eyes.

"Thanks for dinner. It was great."

"Glad you enjoyed yourself."

"Yep. And I guess I'll head on home since I really have to use the potty." She pointed at her belly.

"Right," he laughed. "So . . . can we do this again real soon? As friends, of course?"

"Um, no."

"No?"

"I'm afraid not. No doubt you've done a good job at trying to make amends. I love that about you."

"But?"

"You're a good man, Wendell. A class act, and although I know you're not the type to call your momma, or even me, the b-word, you still can't be with me." Lorraine smiled and gave him a confident look. "So sorry."

She shrugged and walked away, with her thoughts already on the possibility of a new lover.

If you enjoyed *Crush,* don't miss

Suspicions

by Sasha Campbell

Coming in May 2011 from Dafina Books

Turn the page for an excerpt from *Suspicions.* . . .

TIFFANY

"*Guuuurrrrrrl*, I met this dude from Jamaica last weekend. Trust and believe me when I tell you, he was a straight-up Mandingo!"

"Peaches, sit still before I burn your ear!" Damn! How was I supposed to style her hair if she kept moving? Besides, I don't know what made her think I wanted to listen to her talking about getting some from a dude she barely knew.

"Oops, my bad!" Peaches chuckled. "It's just not often that I find a man with some good dick."

"Ooh! I know that's right," cackled some toothpick with a jacked-up weave, sitting in the chair beside her. "I ain't had a man with anything worth talking about in a long time. They either can't get it up or when they do, it ain't worth my time."

While everyone on the salon floor started talking about men's private parts, I simply pursed my lips and kept on flat-ironing Peaches's hair. I don't know why my clients always think I want to hear about their sex lives.

"Shhhh-shhhh! I don't know if y'all know this or not, but . . . Tiffany don't know nothing about getting laid."

I grabbed a comb and pointed it at Debra, ready to cuss her behind every which way, but decided not to waste my breath. She's the newest stylist at Situations and, unfortunately, my booth happened to be right next to hers, which meant she had eavesdropped on one too many of my conversations. In fact, it was a bad habit I was determined to break. "Debra, nobody asked you to be spreading my personal business," I mumbled. What she needed to be worried about was that no-good baby daddy of hers.

Debra gave an innocent look, then had the nerve to wave her hand like she was dismissing me. "I don't know why you getting mad. You should be proud to let everyone know you're not getting none."

"Not getting none?" Peaches's head snapped in my direction, her bubble eyes big as saucers. "What's up with that?"

Now all eyes were on me. Damn, why she all up in my business? "I'm just not out there trying to give it up to everybody." I wasn't yelling, but I had definitely raised my voice.

Debra started laughing. "Everybody? Hell, you haven't given it to anybody."

I gave her a nasty look. With God as my witness, before long she and I were going to have it out. "Some of us were raised to hold on to our virginity for the right man while others weren't." I don't know why I was even trying to explain to a bunch of chicks who wouldn't understand that some of us didn't believe in giving it up to every Tom, Dick, and Harry they come across.

"Okay . . . lemme get this straight. You saying *you're* a virgin?" Peaches asked for clarification and swung her seat all the way around so she could look at me dead in my mouth. Thanks to Debra, they were all trying to get in my business.

"Did I stutter? I'm saving myself for the right man," I replied with a mean glare. "Now turn around." I was done discussing my personal life. Unfortunately, Peaches wasn't finished yet.

"Hold up, Tif. What about that cutie pie who picked you up the last time I was here?"

I glanced around to see if anyone else was listening. The last thing I wanted was one of these trifling females in the salon to try and push up on my man. "What about him?" I said with attitude.

"I *know* you gotta be getting some of that," she said like she'd caught me in a lie. *"Sheee-it,* I would."

"Puhleeze," Debra cackled. "Tiffany ain't gave him shit!"

"You lying?" Peaches's mouth was hanging open, then all of a sudden she and Debra looked at each other and burst out laughing. "Dayuumn, Tiffany. I ain't mad atcha!" I was seconds away from telling Peaches to get the hell out my chair because I didn't give a damn if she believed me or not, but she was one of my best clients and times were hard.

The skinny chick sitting in Debra's chair threw her hands up in surrender. "Hell naw! I heard it all."

The conversation wasn't anything new to me. My girls had always thought it strange that I was twenty-seven and still a virgin. All of them couldn't wait to fall in love and have sex, while I had the willpower they didn't have to say no. I won't say it had always been easy, but it was either wait or deal with Ruby Dee. My mother was one woman you didn't want to mess with. If she said keep your legs closed then you better do it. Her fist was the only chastity belt I had ever needed.

I glanced around the floor, then took a deep breath before I said, "Why is it if a woman says she's a virgin, she has to be lying?"

"Damn, Tiffany, it's not like it's a bad thing. It's just, well . . . almost unheard of," Debra said defensively.

When Peaches finally stopped laughing, she said, "Also, there is this thing called *being horny.* Hell, I lost my virginity when I was fourteen."

And that's why she had four kids. I reached for a brush. "So what? Everybody ain't like you. My mother taught me that what I have is precious and I need to make a man earn the privilege after he makes me his wife." I probably sounded like I thought I was all that, but so what. Women needed to have more respect for themselves.

Debra sucked her buckteeth like a horse. "I know that's right, girl! Make those niggas beg for it." That wasn't at all what I meant, but I doubted Debra would know the difference.

That anorexic-looking chick with the jacked-up weave had the nerve to give her two cents. "You a better woman than me, because there ain't no way in hell I would marry a man before I knew what he was working with. I think about all those women back in the day who couldn't have sex until after they got married, only to find out that not only couldn't her husband fuck, but his dick wasn't even circumcised."

"Ugh!" Peaches was laughing so hard, she practically fell from my chair. "I couldn't even imagine. Call me a ho if you wanna, but to me it's just like sampling a piece of meat in the deli. I need to know what I'm getting before I spend my money!" She flinched. "Ouch!"

"That's what you get for moving. I told you to sit still," I replied and tried to keep a straight face. That's what she got for being all up in my business.

Now everybody wanted to get in the conversation. They were shouting back and forth across the room with the chicks sitting in the waiting area. I half listened as I worked on my client's head. I've heard this topic time and time before, and I'll admit there have been times when I wondered what it would be like being married to Kimbel and what if he doesn't satisfy me. But on the other hand, as my best friend told me, you can't miss what you've never had.

Ms. Conrad lifted the hooded dryer from her head. I should have known her nosy behind was listening. "I'ma tell y'all, I was married to my husband for twenty years before he decided he wanted his freedom. Charles was the only man I had ever been with so I had no idea what I was missing. But leaving me was the best thing he could have ever done for me. I now got a man in my life who makes my toes curl."

"Shit, I know that's right. This dude I was with last night had my toes curled and me calling out his name!" screamed some tall chick sitting in the lobby.

Ms. Conrad glared at her. "That's the problem with all you young folks. You're too busy trying to get yours. Relationships are supposed to be about a lot more than just sex."

Debra waved a hot comb in the air as she spoke. "True, but sex is important. If the sex is bad, then so is the relationship." She shook her head. "Tiffany, I don't see how you can do it."

Toothpick chick gave me a curious grin. "So, is your fiancé a virgin, too?"

Damn, they're nosy. "Nope, but he knows I am and he respects that." I wasn't about to tell them Kimbel spent half his time trying to convince me to give it up. Part of me felt the only reason he proposed so soon was because he knew that marrying me was the only way he was going to get some. But Kimbel was rich and he could have any woman he wanted, yet he picked me, a little girl from the projects who grew up in a single-parent home. I truly believed he wouldn't have asked me to be his wife if he didn't love me.

"How long y'all been together?" Toothpick asked.

"Six months. He proposed on Valentine's Day." I held out my hand so she could see the three-carat solitaire surrounded by emeralds that I wore proudly on my finger.

She barely looked before she frowned. "And you think your man's been faithful all this time?" As soon as I nodded, she started laughing. "Honey, puhleeze! Just 'cause you're not fucking doesn't mean he ain't. He's a man and a man's got needs that someone else is more than willing to fulfill."

I hated bitches like her. I shook my head. "I trust my man."

"I trust mine, too . . . as far as I can see him. Because the second you turn your back there's some hoochie trying to ride his dick. My baby is fine; therefore, I keep his ass on a short leash."

Debra started yanking weave out her head. "That's because Ricky ain't no good. Ursula, shut up."

She rolled her eyes. "Whatever, you know what I'm saying is true."

Ms. Conrad came to my defense. "All of you need to quit. There is nothing wrong with this young lady saving herself for the right man."

Peaches turned on the chair again. "Yeah, but how do you know he's the right man until you find out what he's working with and, better yet, if he can work it?"

"I know that right!" Toothpick high-fived Peaches and ignored the pissed-off look on my face.

"Just because we don't have sex doesn't mean we don't do other things." I don't know why I felt like I needed to prove something to these ghetto chicks up in here.

Peaches glanced over her shoulder and gave me a strange look. "Things like what? And I hope you're not talking about oral sex. Because last I checked, that was considered sex as well."

"No, it isn't," Debra said and tossed a sponge roller at her.

"Yes, it is. There was a news report on *Dateline NBC* a while back about all these high-school kids giving each other head because it's supposed to be cool. Kids think it's okay to have oral sex."

While they debated the issue, I tuned them out and thought about what they said. I would never admit it to any of them, but there were many times when I was tempted to give in to the moment and let Kimbel have exactly what he wanted. But every time I was that close to spreading my legs, I heard my mother's nagging voice in my ear, saying, "Why buy the cow if the milk is free?" But I'm not going to lie. These heifers in the salon had me thinking. It had been six months since we started dating, which meant Kimbel hadn't had any in half a year. I was confident he wasn't getting any. Some might call me arrogant. Others might call me stupid, but I trusted my man. However, the last thing I wanted was for him to get tired of waiting, then go out and get him some from one of those trifling chicks in the streets. Now don't get it twisted. I wasn't about to give up my virginity before saying, "I do." Nevertheless, my mama ain't raised no fool. I was just going to have to prove to my man that what I have would definitely be worth the wait.